THE MADDENING
LORD MONTWOOD

By Vivienne Lorret

The Rakes of Fallow Hall Series
The Elusive Lord Everhart
The Devilish Mr. Danvers
The Maddening Lord Montwood

The Wallflower Wedding Series
Tempting Mr. Weatherstone (novella)
Daring Miss Danvers
Winning Miss Wakefield
Finding Miss McFarland

THE MADDENING LORD MONTWOOD

The Rakes of Fallow Hall Series

VIVIENNE LORRET

AVONIMPULSE
An Imprint of HarperCollinsPublishers

Excerpt from *Chasing Jillian* copyright © 2015 by Julie Revell Benjamin.
Excerpt from *Easy Target* copyright © 2015 by Kay Thomas.
Excerpt from *Dirty Thoughts* copyright © 2015 by Megan Erickson.
Excerpt from *Last First Kiss* copyright © 2015 by Lia Riley.

EPub Edition JULY 2015 ISBN: 9780062380548

Print Edition ISBN: 9780062380531

AM 10 9 8 7 6 5

To everyone reading this page, thank you.
You've brought me joy simply by giving this book a chance.
Wishing you countless smiles, a sigh-worthy love,
and a happily-ever-after of your own.

~Viv

St. James
Winter 1822

Lucan Montwood wanted to get drunk. Dead drunk.

This gaming hell was the perfect place to start. Shadows from sconces writhed along the dark red walls in the same manner that rage roiled within him. It blazed inside of him like the brazier in the corner that kept the room uncomfortably warm. Exhaling into his glass, the charred, oaky essence of whiskey teased his nostrils. The tip of his tongue contracted, waiting for the familiar flavor. But it was no use.

No amount of liquor could erase the events of this day.

He lowered the glass down to the polished table.

"Come, come, Montwood. You're too slow." Rafe Danvers clinked their glasses before tipping his own back. He whistled low in appreciation and rubbed a hand through his unruly dark hair. Then, reaching for the bottle, he poured another three fingers. "Everhart and I have an entire night planned for you. This is only the first stop."

Lucan's friends sought to distract him. The three of them sat at a corner table. Across from him, Viscount Everhart absently scratched the bridge of his nose where he sported a sunburn. Having just returned from his latest expedition, even his short crop of hair was bleached ash blond by the sun. "Quite right. We plan to lose our shirts at hazard, and then we're off to one of Lady Ramsey's infamous parties for endless hours of debauchery."

"I could not ask for better friends." Lucan held up his glass in a salute to his fellow *fallen angels*. At least, that was what Lady Ramsey called them, often stating that they were too handsome to be anything other than angels, but far too wicked to be allowed in heaven. In Lucan's case, Lady Ramsey likely didn't know how right she was. As for Everhart and Danvers, they battled their own demons. And their strength had helped Lucan through his darkest days.

Twelve years ago, after his mother's death, they'd offered similar methods of nurturing. Whiskey, gambling, and women. What else could a man require?

"*Justice*," said the voice that raged inside him.

Earlier today, he thought the justice he craved had arrived. The man who'd beaten and abused both him and his mother, before ultimately killing her, had been arrested, although not for her murder. Instead, the crown had charged the Marquess of Camdonbury—Lucan's father—with treason.

It was a small victory for Lucan, but he'd intended to celebrate nonetheless. For treason, the marquess could not cry "privilege of the peerage." For treason, he would hang.

Yet when the magistrate interrogated Camdonbury for unlawfully coining ten thousand pounds, something absurd happened. The magistrate had released him. By all witness accounts, Camdonbury claimed to have evidence against his steward, Hugh Thorne. Apparently, Lucan's father had issued a persuasive argument, because shortly thereafter, Thorne had been arrested for treason.

"Thorne has worked at Camdonbury Place for thirty years. The man is loyal to a fault," Lucan said, more to himself than to his friends. He knew Thorne too well to believe the rumors. "It isn't true."

In fact, he'd been the only one who had watched over the marchioness when Lucan had gone away to school. For that alone, Thorne had earned his unswerving allegiance.

If Thorne was found guilty, he would hang by week's end. And the Marquess of Camdonbury would claim another victim.

"Thorne is a good man. I remember how he visited you at school after..." Everhart's words trailed off into the black void that always surrounded the death of Lucan's mother.

In all these years, Lucan hadn't spoken of her or how she'd suffered. Because he still carried the guilt of not being able to save her.

At the thought, Lucan drained his glass. The liquor burned all the way down, adding fuel to the injustice churning in his stomach.

Danvers poured another round. "To Thorne."

It was a somber toast, but effective. They tossed back the whiskey in one swallow, and Danvers filled the glasses once more.

Lucan studied the way the golden light from the sconces skimmed across the whiskey's surface, his mind elsewhere.

Earlier, he'd gone to the magistrate, professing Thorne's innocence. He'd even spoken out against his own father, the same way he'd done after his mother's death. But as before, he was escorted out onto the street.

Apparently, Camdonbury had anticipated Lucan's actions. He'd warned the magistrate about the probability of this allegation ahead of time, claiming that his *wayward son* would find a way to rebel against being *cut off* from the family.

Lucan issued a humorless laugh. "I would like to know how a disreputable marquess can utter the words 'cut off' and suddenly the *ton* takes notice as if this was the gossip *du jour.*"

A short while ago, Lucan had been refused admittance to White's after having severed all ties with the Camdonbury title. He'd been snubbed in Hyde Park. Then he'd been barred from entering the townhouse where he'd lived for years. Obviously, his landlord didn't realize Lucan had been paying his own debts for most of his life without any familial assistance.

"This is not a matter to take lightly," Everhart said, interlacing his fingers as he rested his forearms on the table. "Yours is not merely a threat to bind your accounts. Your father knows how you earn your living at the tables. By cutting you off, he's removed your standing and even your credibility."

Lucan pondered this for a moment. Everhart was the son of a duke and knew how the pressures of societal scrutiny could cripple a man's way of life.

"Then I shall endeavor to be more charming than ever," Lucan said with a practiced grin. Yet inside, his mind turned. His father was too cunning for today's events to be mere happenstance. It seemed almost as if he'd planned this carefully.

In one fell swoop, Camdonbury had absolved himself of any culpability of the charges against him and also made himself a martyr by having a younger son who would choose a steward over his own family. No one would question Camdonbury's actions or blame him.

Lucan knew his father had wanted to cut him off years ago for casting a shadow of doubt on Mother's death. He'd only needed an excuse.

Now Lucan was separated from the Camdonbury title but also from the way he made his living as a gambler. Oh, he was sure that he could still find ways to gamble. Gaming hells weren't too particular, after all. Without credibility, however, he could sit across the table from someone who sought to cheat him and not have the ability to call him out. Even worse, he could *be* the accused, which made his finances and future precarious. He would have to choose his opponents carefully.

Danvers clapped his empty glass down. "Or you could simply remove yourself from town and continue your ventures elsewhere. I've been contemplating that very thing for a while now."

Since Danvers's parents had received the cut direct, he'd spent little time in society, if one discounted gaming hells and highborn widows.

"It is something to consider," Lucan said, even while knowing that he could not remove himself from town. Not completely. He had obligations, especially now.

If Hugh Thorne were to hang by week's end, then who would watch over his daughter?

Admittedly, Frances Thorne was only a year younger than Lucan and quite capable. He suspected that in the years since her mother's death, she'd been watching over her father more than the other way around.

She was no longer the same young girl who'd visited her father at Camdonbury Place and had stolen surreptitious glances at Lucan when their paths crossed. Despite his most honorable of intentions, Lucan had stolen a few as well and flirted on occasion. Yet he'd always maintained his distance. Of course, he told himself that the reason was because she was the daughter of the family steward. One did not dally with the servants or their families, after all. However, he often wondered if there was another reason, but instinct told him not to pursue the answer.

Nonetheless, he did keep an eye out for her. The Thorne family cook was a chatty woman who was easily persuaded into conversation with the milkman. Coincidentally, that same milkman earned a few coins for his trouble when he relayed the same conversation to Lucan's cook. Or *former cook*, rather, as of today. Along with his former home and former bed.

Lucan furrowed his brow. It was selfish to think about where he would live from this day forward, when Hugh Thorne had much larger worries.

"You require another distraction," Everhart said to Lucan in such an austere tone that few would dare contradict him. "Let's adjourn to the inner sanctum of the hazard room."

"Aye. It's time for some sport," Danvers agreed, leading the way.

Lucan agreed as well, though for different reasons. He wanted to forget the look on Hugh Thorne's face.

The man had been in a complete state of shock when the Bow Street Runners had escorted him in shackles to the magistrate's office that afternoon. Standing outside on the pavement, Miss Thorne had been pale with worry, twisting a lace handkerchief in her grasp. He'd never seen her look fragile until that moment. The impulse to go to her and offer comfort had been impossible to deny. He'd even bumped shoulders with someone as he was escorted through the door.

When he stood before Frances, however, her gaze had turned hard. She'd speared him with palpable hatred, no doubt seeing him as much at fault as his father. Without a word, she expressed a vow to hate Lucan until the end of his days. In answer, he silently vowed to make amends. Such was the sum of their unspoken communication before they parted ways.

It wasn't until later that Lucan wondered why she'd been there alone. From what he knew, Roger Quinlin had been courting her for the past two years. As a suitor, it would have been Quinlin's responsibility to comfort Miss Thorne and to see if anything could be done for her father.

Yet now as Lucan entered the green-and-gold room in the center of the gaming hell, who should Lucan see but Roger Quinlin. Amidst the raucous clamor of gentlemen crowded around the long, oval felted table, the man in question shouted at his dice. Quinlin was wild-eyed, with a hank of mud brown hair drooping over his forehead, and one hand gripping the upraised lip of the table. Lucan had seen the look of desperation on enough men to recognize it in an instant.

He wasn't the only one who noticed either. Danvers turned his head and spoke low. "What are the odds that he bet his last shilling?"

"I've seen sharks in the Indian Ocean that looked less hungry," Everhart replied, doubtless remarking on the frenzy of men who'd wagered against the caster. The scent of blood was ripe in the air.

Both Danvers and Everhart moved a step forward.

Lucan remained apart, scrutinizing the tableau before him. At the moment, he was more concerned for Miss Thorne. Was Quinlin here to win enough money in order to marry her? It would be a noble gesture, though the notion unsettled Lucan somewhat. At five and twenty, Miss Thorne should marry, of course. However, in Lucan's opinion, Quinlin wasn't right for her. Obviously, the frantic man standing across the room possessed little control over his impulses. A man like that could hardly make a worthwhile husband.

Lucan knew from his own life that dark deeds were born from a lack of control.

"Pardon me, my lord," a footman said, stepping into view. He bowed and presented a card on a gold-plated salver. "Your presence is requested in our private study."

Cautious, Lucan lifted the card. *Viscount Whitelock*. "And he requested Lucan Montwood?" Lucan asked. Since they had never spoken, nor did they keep the same company, he had to be certain.

When the footman bowed once more, Lucan discreetly left the hazard room. They walked down a narrow corridor lined with doors, leading to private rooms known for their high-stakes games. One had to have a special invitation to participate.

At the end of the hall, the footman opened a door. Silk paper embossed in gold lined the walls of the small room. The glossy surface reflected the firelight in such a way that it was almost as if he were stepping directly into the fire.

Standing near the mantel and apparently oblivious to the roaring heat, Whitelock turned. With the light behind him, shadows grew long over the angular lines of his aristocratic face. He kept his attention on the footman until the door closed with a succinct *click*. Then his dark gaze shifted to Lucan.

"I will not insult you by pretending an interest in becoming acquainted," Whitelock said. "After your episode in the magistrate's office, you can easily discern why I would choose to meet in private."

Lucan shook his head. "Not entirely. The *reason* for this meeting eludes me. However, I understand that a man with your spotless reputation cannot afford the taint of association with someone like me."

Whitelock's mouth curved in a smug grin. "I assure you, it is more so a matter of *preference* and not a matter of what I can *afford.*"

True enough. After a prudent marriage, the man was richer than Midas. But Lucan was in no humor to continue the mystery of Whitelock's request or to grant patience this evening. "My friends are waiting for me. They will wonder where I have gone—"

"Quite right. There isn't much time, especially for Hugh Thorne." Whitelock paused long enough to gain Lucan's undivided attention. "Which brings me to my purpose. If you truly believe in Thorne's innocence, then perhaps there is a way I could assist you in gaining his freedom."

Lucan was not easily surprised. After the life he'd led, he was always prepared for the worst, but not this. Still, an ingrained sense of doubt prevailed. He'd been taught to figure out the trick of any game he ever played. "If that is true, then why not go directly to Thorne with your assistance?"

"I don't know Thorne," Whitelock said, matter-of-fact.

"You don't know me either."

"A mutual acquaintance alerted me to your plight. Instinct tells me that you would not allow an innocent to fall to his death." The viscount straightened the seam of his glove in a bored fashion, as if a man's life weren't hanging in the balance. "The question is…do you believe in his innocence?"

"Without a doubt." Thorne's innocence was the only thing Lucan was certain of at the moment. He still wasn't sure how to read Whitelock. The man shifted in and out of appearing either arrogantly benevolent or arrogantly manipulative. From what Lucan knew through rumor, most people were inclined to believe the former.

"Then our agreement will be a simple one. The evidence that Camdonbury provided to the magistrate will be"— Whitelock pursed his lips—"*misplaced*. Therefore, without any more than an accusation from Camdonbury, a man who'd been charged with the same crime, it is unlikely that Thorne will be sentenced to hang. Although, the crown still takes theft of currency seriously. Therefore, he will be sent to debtors' prison for the sum of the coining offense, which I understand is ten thousand pounds."

Lucan nodded. He'd learned as much at the magistrate's office.

"Assuming that your current financial state is not entirely flush," Whitelock continued, "I am offering to loan you the sum, to pay on Thorne's behalf."

A loan of ten thousand pounds? Lucan suspected he had finally learned the rub. "To be repaid in how much time?"

Whitelock's grin returned. "Such an amount is not easy to come by, even when one *has* familial connections. I suppose a gambler with your particular skill would need—*hmm*—three years."

Three years? Lucan refused to react to the insult. He'd earned and lost ten thousand pounds on a single hand before. He certainly wouldn't require *three years*.

"And if I fall short?" Lucan asked. Even though he knew he wouldn't fail, it was important to have their agreement laid out in concise terms.

"Then the evidence against Hugh Thorne will resurface," Whitelock remarked, seemingly forgetting one important fact: Thorne could not be tried again for the same crime. Then, as if reading Lucan's mind, he added, "If you are thinking of *ne bis in idem*, allow me to assure you that I'm certain the magistrate's charges against Thorne could be cleverly worded, and in the event of the reappearance of the evidence, he will be charged with treason, found guilty, and then hanged."

The viscount's craftiness sent a rush of unease through Lucan. "How will you accomplish *misplacing* whatever documents Camdonbury supplied?"

"That is not your concern. All I need from you is your answer."

Time was of the essence. Likely, Whitelock knew that Lucan had no other choice. If he accepted, then he would acquire a great deal of debt. If he didn't, then he would have Thorne's death on his own conscience, knowing for the rest of his life that he could have prevented it.

"When I pay you the ten thousand pounds, you'll give me all the evidence?"

"Of course. Doubtless, you know of my reputation. I have no enemies."

Lucan knew there was no other way. He held out his hand, confident in his gambling ability enough to procure the sum. "Then I accept."

Whitelock's grip was surprisingly firm for an older man. Before he let go, that unnerving smile reappeared. In the same instant, the fire hissed over a log and flared, casting sinister shadows over the viscount's face.

Then, he reached into his breast pocket, withdrew a thick packet, and handed it to Lucan. When it changed hands, the edges of the banknotes flashed. Obviously, Whitelock had been confident as well. Lucan would be careful not to underestimate this man.

"One more thing," Whitelock said with a snap of his fingers. "My card, if you please. Since I would rather not make waves with my political connections, no one can know of our meeting. In fact, if anyone discovers our association or learns of our agreement—anyone at all—then you will soon find yourself in Thorne's place."

Lucan obliged and handed back Whitelock's card. He understood the need for secrecy, yet the threat was harsher than need be. "I will not speak of it. But might I ask why you would not wish it to be known that you saved an innocent man from the gallows."

"I am generous, but I cannot abide beggars. I prefer the benefits of choosing my own charities. Besides, I find that a kindness given is always repaid tenfold." Whitelock crossed the room to the door and rapped twice. "I imagine you are clever enough to find an excuse for your absence when you return to your friends."

Lucan nodded. "Then we will meet once more in three years."

"Precisely. I will contact you."

A single knock came from the other side before the footman appeared. He escorted Whitelock down a dark corridor, leaving Lucan alone, staring down at the ten thousand pounds in his grasp.

If all went according to plan, Thorne would not hang after all. A rush of relief swept through him. It wouldn't take Lucan any time to earn the money and absolve the debt. Yet there was something about Whitelock that unnerved him. As he walked back to the hazard room, Lucan couldn't help but wonder if he'd struck a bargain with an incredibly generous man...or with a devil in disguise.

Chapter One

June 1824
Two years, six months later…

Frances Thorne blinked twice at the booklet in her grasp.

"I told you it was scandalous," Kaye said, crowding closer for a better view.

Together, they walked to the second floor box window of Mrs. Hunter's Agency and Servant Registry. Outside, the London street bustled with the raucous clamor of carriages, handcarts, horses, and all the people one would expect on such a fine June day. Frances, however, paid little attention.

She adjusted her brass-rimmed spectacles. The afternoon light illuminated the palm-sized booklet of men's fashions from Paris. Turning another page, she lingered on the sketch of a man dressed in boots, breeches, shirt, cravat, waistcoat, and…nothing else. No frock coat or tailcoat, just a fitted striped waistcoat.

While the page on the left side of the booklet displayed a frontal sketch, the right displayed the…*backside*. And what a fine sketch it was.

Frances let out a slow breath. Fanning herself with the booklet, she blamed the warm weather for the rush of heat to her cheeks and neck. "And you say that you found this at your uncle's shop?"

"It was on his worktable this morning," Kaye said, angling her face toward the cooling breeze of the makeshift fan. Kaye lived with an aunt and uncle above his tailor shop, and Frances knew she occasionally borrowed sketches, though never an entire booklet. And never one with such detail to the—*ahem*—backside.

Frances stopped fanning and studied the sketch once more. Solely out of appreciation for the artist's skill, of course. Never mind the fact that she was the last person who would be considered a dilettante. "You don't suppose there was an actual gentleman *fitted* with these clothes, do you?"

"I'd like to think there was." Kaye snickered and tucked a corn silk lock of hair behind her ear, her blue eyes dancing. "In fact, I'd like to think that he might walk through the door of Mrs. Hunter's one day, take one look at me, and—"

"And not be a lecher like nearly *all* the other men we deal with?"

"Yes, well"—Kaye sighed—"at five and twenty, I'm beginning to wonder if I wouldn't mind a lecher so much, as long as he was *my* lecher."

At seven and twenty, Frances knew precisely what her best friend meant. Frances, however, was still holding out hope to find the one person who could restore her faith in men. Which would not be an easy task, considering that her own father dashed those hopes on a daily basis.

"Do you suppose your very own lecher is out there, right this instant?" Frances closed the booklet and looked down at the street below.

A black landau with a matching pair of high-steppers in the harness stopped in front of the shop. Even before the door opened and the occupants stepped forth, she knew it was Lady Binghamton. Her ladyship often brought her maidservants here to have them instructed on how best to escape rogues and roués. *Artful Defense* was a service that Frances had provided for the past two and a half years, since she'd first begun work here.

For Mrs. Hunter, these lessons were an amenity offered by the agency to loyal patrons at no charge, and therefore with no additional wages for staff. For Frances, this instruction—in addition to her clerking duties—provided a way to honor her mother's memory. Her mother had been passionate about Frances's knowing how to protect herself, even to her very last days.

Mother had told her of a dear friend—a girl who'd trusted the wrong man. The girl's naivety had been ripped from her most cruelly. Elise Thorne's most fervent wish was for Frances never to suffer like that girl had.

That had been the reason why Frances had begun to offer lessons in defense, adding her own adaptations to what her mother had already taught her.

"I wonder who her ladyship has brought this time," Kaye mused, nudging Frances with her elbow. "Soon she'll be running her own abbey, and all her maids will be dressed in habits. It makes me wonder about the late Lord Binghamton."

"We dare not." Frances already imagined that his lordship had likely not been the best of men. Especially since his widow of more than forty years believed all men to be cads of the first order. And if a lady with much more experience in life was so jaded, then what hope did Frances have of not becoming just like her?

"True. Perhaps even a lecher of my own wouldn't be for the best."

A heavy gray cloud passed in front of the sun, offering a glimpse of their reflections in the glass. Their teasing expressions had gone. Now, they stood with heads bent and hands clasped like mourners at a funeral.

"Girls!" Mrs. Hunter called from below, ringing the brass bell that was always within her reach. "Put on your best faces. Lady Binghamton is here. Make sure you tell her how much we appreciate her patronage, but don't mention a single word about *Tuttle's Registry* down the street. Not. A. Word."

"Yes, Mrs. Hunter," Frances and Kaye said in unison, which brought a grin to both of them. Mrs. Hunter had been quite prickly since the other agency had opened a month ago.

Kaye drew in a breath and lifted her eyes to the low, sloped ceiling. "Is my best face on straight? I do hate when I put it on crookedly."

"Then you'd better tuck your smirk in your pocket." Frances laughed, earning a slight pinch from Kaye before she turned and headed downstairs.

It wasn't until her friend disappeared that Frances realized she was still holding the scandalous booklet. She couldn't possibly greet Lady Binghamton or Mrs. Hunter with *this* on her person. Looking around for a place to hide it, she went to the window where the sash was pulled up just enough to leave a finger-sized gap. *Or a booklet-sized gap.*

Standing there, her gaze drifted down to the street again. Lady Binghamton was stepping onto the pavement, her charge hovering close to her side. They were of the same build, both slender and petite. The younger woman's face, however, was hidden by a long-brimmed straw bonnet, like a horse wearing blinders. This was, perhaps, why she did not see the boy bounding toward her until it was too late. Jostled by the lad, the young woman spun directly into her ladyship's path. Lady Binghamton's black embroidered shawl went awry, slipping from her shoulders and heading straight for the gutter.

And down into the gutter it would have gone too, if not for the sudden, gallant rescue by a gentleman in a gray tailcoat and top hat.

The gentleman had appeared out of nowhere. With an elegant sweep of his arm, he snatched the shawl from certain destruction. Her ladyship turned, her hand to her mouth. The man bowed at the waist, presenting the wayward silk like a knight in shining armor asking for his lady to wear his colors.

Frances held her breath, watching the scene unfold with avid interest. Was it possible that the ideal man truly might exist?

Just then, a breeze blew, disturbing the tails of his coat. The ends parted, one draping across his back and exposing his *perfectly* formed backside.

Frances craned her neck. The same breeze also dislodged his hat, forcing him to bend further, extending a rather muscular leg behind him. She swallowed. A pulse fluttered at the side of her throat. The midday sun seemed suddenly alive in her very own stomach, heating her to impossible degrees.

He must be very handsome, she thought, because even Lady Binghamton smiled at him.

Donning his hat, the gentleman straightened. The tails of his coat—*unfortunately*—fell back into place. Then, he proffered his arm and gestured to the door of Mrs. Hunter's.

He's offering to escort them inside this very shop! Frances quickly realized that she was standing one floor too far away. Without delay or checking to see if her best face was on—because, in truth, she only had the one—she made haste down the stairs.

"Come, come, Miss Thorne," Mrs. Hunter said with a hurried wave of her hand. "Stand beside Miss North. There. Oh, your cheeks are flushed. We do not want to appear sickly to Lady Binghamton."

"I'm certain it was merely the sun in the window upstairs. I'll be sure to open the sash at the back of the shop to make the room more comfortable for her ladyship." Frances glanced to the door, her breath coming up short, her lungs tightening in anticipation.

"What is that in your hand?" Mrs. Hunter tugged on the booklet. Kaye issued a mew of distress.

Oh dear! Frances had forgotten to leave the booklet behind. Thinking fast, she tugged back and slipped the booklet up her sleeve in a flash. "Merely a fan. Nothing more."

Beneath a curly silvery wig, Mrs. Hunter's painted eyebrows puckered. The plump flesh of her cheeks drew together like a snag in a stocking as she pursed her lips. "You are paid to be on your best behavior *always*, Miss Thorne."

"I have not forgotten, Mrs. Hunter."

Thankfully, Frances was saved any further reprimand when the door opened.

Lady Binghamton entered, followed by the young woman with the long-brimmed bonnet. The gentleman stood in the shadow beneath a scalloped-shaped awning and held the door. It took all of Frances's training on societal politesse not to give him her attention. Instead, she offered a demure curtsy to her ladyship and bid her good afternoon.

"Mrs. Hunter," Lady Binghamton began, her tone firm and clipped, her mouth set in a grim, permanent frown. "I have a request for your services. The matter is of some urgency."

"You honor us greatly with your patronage, my lady." Mrs. Hunter bowed her head, because, apparently, a single curtsy was not enough. "I have tea prepared in my office if your ladyship would care for refreshment."

Mrs. Hunter's office was a large oaken desk at the opposite side of the room. From her perch, she typically kept close watch on every dealing that Frances and Kaye had with the servants who came in seeking work, and also the ladies and gentlemen who sought to hire them.

Displaying an excessive amount of deference, Mrs. Hunter drew Lady Binghamton and her charge across the room. In the seconds that passed, Frances worried that the gentleman would close the door and leave. That he would simply go on with whatever errand had brought him to this street. Yet to her surprise, he lingered. In fact, he stepped inside.

Frances dared a look. Then, an instant, unwelcome jolt of recognition trampled through her.

Lord Lucan Montwood. He was the farthest thing from a gallant knight of old she could imagine. No wonder he lurked in the shadows. He belonged there. Not only was he a renowned gambler and rake, but he came from an unscrupulous family. His father, the Marquess of Camdonbury, had accused her very own father—their former steward—of treason. In the two and a half years since, she'd suspected more than once that the marquess had been guilty of the coining offense.

Now, her father wore a thief's *T* branded into the flesh of his thumb for the rest of his life. The punishment for such a crime was usually death by hanging. Yet by some miracle, the evidence against her father had disappeared. He'd been released from gaol but never once spoke about it.

Her breath came out in a rush of disappointment. Against her will, she curtsied, but only because Mrs. Hunter kept scrutinizing her behavior of late.

"Miss Thorne." Lucan Montwood flashed a smile, revealing a dimple on one side of his mouth. She imagined a serpent must look the same before giving a taste of his venom.

"My lord," she said through gritted teeth. After introducing Kaye, who then turned to help Mrs. Hunter with the tea, Frances expected him to leave at once. Yet he did not.

Lucan doffed his hat and tucked it beneath his arm. Not a strand of his dark hair was out of place. And beneath a thick brow, his amber gaze held a peculiar light, there in the shadows. The color of his eyes had always fascinated her. In her youth, before her mother's death and before his family had betrayed her father, she would visit her father at Camdonbury Place. Yet all the while, she'd hoped to cross paths with Lucan. Even though they were only a year apart in age, he'd always seemed so worldly to her. And with those eyes, he'd looked at her as if he knew *worldly things*. The types of things that her mother had warned her against.

Her infatuation had been a girlish one, born of naiveté. Soon enough, she'd learned that men like Lucan were born deceivers. And Frances had had her fill of deception.

"What a serendipitous meeting," he said. "Had I not been nearby, I'd not have had the opportunity to renew our acquaintance."

Since he knew of her vehement dislike of him, she chose to ignore his goading. "Her ladyship was quite fortunate that you happened along. Although, I am surprised that you chose to rescue a perfectly *innocent* shawl instead of sending it to the gallows, as you and your family are wont to do."

He stared at her for a moment—long enough for her to adjust her spectacles—as a slow, daring grin revealed that dimple of his once more. Truly, a man so diabolical should not have such an appealing dimple. She loathed that dimple and the man who wore it.

"If I'd known that I had an audience, I'd have sent a wink to the"—he pointed upward with one long, gloved finger—"second-floor window? You must have rushed down the stairs. That would explain the high color of your cheeks when I first walked in. Ah! And there it is again."

Drat it all. Normally, she was clever about hiding her thoughts. On the outside, she made sure to keep a proper, respectable appearance, hiding her adamant curiosity of the opposite sex. Leave it to a serpent to conjure a way of seeing beneath. "The light is dim where we stand. You are only revealing your own arrogance for what you wish to be true. I merely caught a glimpse of your…*manipulation* of her ladyship's shawl."

"Your judgment of me is harsh indeed. I suppose it is true that the wasp gives no warning before she stings," he drawled, inclining his head. Then he leaned forward ever so slightly and lowered his voice to a whisper. "But what a sweet pain it is, Miss Thorne."

Wasp, indeed. Yet instead of feeling justified or even contrite, Frances felt the thrumming of her pulse and the heat of midday burning inside of her. The scent that swirled around her as he drew back left her befuddled. She would expect that a rake known for gambling would smell like whiskey, smoke, and whatever else one might find in a gaming hell. Instead, he smelled of freshly ironed sheets and what she could only describe as *midnight*—a dark, earthy fragrance sweetened by the dew on the grass.

Before she gathered her wits enough to offer one more sting, he slipped away, the door clicking shut behind him.

Then, not ten feet away, Mrs. Hunter rang her insufferable bell. "Miss Thorne."

Frances jumped at the sound. Her legs were unaccountably unsteady, as if her bones had turned to ribbons that might curl beneath her. She was far too old to be prone to such behavior, she thought, and lifted a hand to the brooch that held her fichu in place. It served to remind Frances why she was here, and why her work was so important.

Then she turned, her best face fixed in place. "How may I be of service, Mrs. Hunter?"

Her employer smiled approvingly. "Lady Binghamton would like to utilize your services. Her niece, Miss Farmingdale, has need of your instruction in *Artful Defense.*"

The young lady in question had removed her bonnet, revealing a comely face framed by a wealth of deep auburn curls.

"My niece," her ladyship began, "has led a cloistered life for her education. Now, that she is under my charge, I have decided to employ her as my companion. Though I doubt she will ever be far my side, I require assurance that her person will remain unchanged throughout the duration of her life."

At the word *unchanged*, Miss Farmingdale's chin jerked up, and she stiffened. From across the room, her peridot green gaze speared Frances with a look that seemed to rail at the injustice of such a fate. Standing to the girl's back, neither Mrs. Hunter nor her ladyship saw it, but both Kaye and Frances did. They exchanged a swift sideways glance of commiseration.

Frances nodded her understanding, which Mrs. Hunter took as acquiescence. "Very good. Miss North, escort her ladyship and Miss Farmingdale upstairs. Miss Thorne, a word, if you please."

Once they were alone downstairs, Mrs. Hunter stepped close. "I needn't remind you that your position here depends very much on pleasing patrons like Lady Binghamton, need I?"

As before, Frances said, "No, Mrs. Hunter. I understand."

"After the debacle with Lord Whitelock, it is a wonder that I am still in business." She exhaled audibly and brought her hands up to primp the curls of her wig. "We are fortunate that he is such a kind and agreeable gentleman."

"Yes, ma'am." It was true. Stomping on Lord Whitelock's foot, while Frances was in the process of instructing one of his very own maids, was unforgivable. She still couldn't quite figure out how it had happened. Yet accident or not, she was fortunate that he was the one who had insisted on Frances's keeping her position here. If not for him, then she would have lost not only her job but her rooms as well. Between her and her father, she was the only one earning a wage.

In the years since her mother had passed away and her father had been branded, their lives had fallen into gloom and chaos. They would be out on the street if she lost her situation.

"We provide this service of yours without gain. It would be better for the agency if you spent more time remarking on the suitable servants we have listed in our registry than in giving instruction to the ones who are not," Mrs. Hunter reminded unnecessarily. "As it is, with all that I've said and with the new agency down the street, I cannot afford one more mistake, Miss Thorne."

A sense of dread filled Frances, reminding her of the booklet up her sleeve. The edges of the paper rasped against her skin, making her itch, but she dared not scratch.

Not one more mistake.

After his brief encounter with Miss Thorne, Lucan found himself oddly distracted. And hungry. His stomach felt empty, as if he hadn't eaten for days. Somehow, he doubted mere food would satisfy his appetite. *Miss Thorne, however…*

He shook his head before he finished the thought, and aimed to concentrate on food instead of another, more delectable alternative.

Leaving the servant registry office, he strode directly to the corner bakery. Yet his thoughts remained on Frances. He'd always thought her a rather intriguing woman, hiding a mystery behind those spectacles. Her eyes were sumptuous and smoky, a color somewhere between a velvety brown and a plush gray. With lashes so long they nearly touched her lenses. Her dark brown hair was the color of the burnished bronze lamp on his bedside table. And her plump lips hid a slight overbite. She'd never smiled at him. Even when she was younger, she'd shyly kept that part of her a secret. So each time he'd caught a glimpse of her teeth, he felt a low growl deep in the pit of his stomach, like a beast awakening after a long slumber and in need of sustenance.

He was grateful for her waspish sting, because he preferred to keep that beast slumbering.

Inside the bakery, he filled his lungs with the tantalizing aroma of rising yeast and sugar. His gaze honed in on the platter of glazed buns beneath a glass dome. His mouth watered.

Tempting fate, he made his purchase before returning to the pavement.

In all his eight and twenty years, Lucan had never tasted a bun. Now, he lifted it up and drew in another breath. This pastry smelled exactly like the ones that the cook at Camdonbury Place had often baked. They had been his father's favorite. In fact, they might still be, but after being *cut off* two and a half years ago, Lucan did not know for certain.

Yet he did not mind. He preferred the severed ties rather than the cruelty he'd experienced in his youth. His father was a brutal man, quick with a backhanded fist. It'd had come when Lucan least expected it.

"Win the trick, and a glazed bun will be your prize," his father had said, slurring the words through his drunken lips.

Lucan remembered looking down at the cards, not yet old enough to know the game, let alone the trick of it. Asking a question that day had earned a beating, no bun, and no supper either. Then, locked in the nursery, he'd cried for himself, wondering why his elder brother—the *heir*—had never been punished. In fact, Vincent had stood by laughing all the while.

Later on, after Father drank himself into a stupor, Mother had stolen away to comfort him. *"Poor little spare,"* she'd often crooned during these nights, rocking him gently. *"Why was the sweetest boy born second?"*

The next time he'd stood in the Great Hall, Lucan had known better than to ask a question but had earned a backhand for not figuring out the trick all the same.

It had been worse when he'd won, however. Because then his mother had borne the brunt of *his* punishment. *"Why are you clapping, whore?"* his father had bellowed as his fist hit the side of her head with a sickening thud.

To this day, Lucan remembered that hollow sound, the sharp, interrupted cry that had followed, and the *crack-thump* of his mother's head hitting the hard stone floor.

He'd hated feeling powerless. Hated feeling hungry. And hated the sight of those glazed buns. In fact, he'd vowed long ago never to eat one.

Gradually, he'd found other methods to gain his supper. He'd learned to charm the cook and the maids, and by the time he'd left for school, he'd developed a talent for it. He'd used his prison wisely, mastering all sorts of tricks and games. He'd even discovered that playing the miniature nursery piano had helped with his dexterity, eventually making him a master of sleight of hand. It was during this time that he'd first begun to realize that he could pour out everything he felt through music—fear, frustration, hatred…

Yet while he was away at school, there had been no one to save his mother from his father's daily requirement of violence.

"*She fell down the stairs and hit her head, son,*" Hugh Thorne had said during a special visit to Lucan in his fourth year of school. "*She never woke up.*" But they'd both known the truth.

More than anything, Lucan had wanted to save her. He'd devised so many plans for her to stay with families who'd lived closer to him, but each time, she'd declined, stating that her place was by his father's side and that she would be ashamed if anyone knew.

In the end, that choice had killed her.

Abruptly, his thoughts shifted to the present. A feeling of resolve washed over him now, helping him resist taking a bite of the glazed bun he held. Each time he resisted, he felt in control. Not at all like his father.

Out of the corner of his eye, Lucan spotted a familiar tuft of wheat-colored hair in the crowd and was reminded of his purpose. Leaving his spot in front of the bakery, he rounded the bend and then dashed across the street between a cart and a phaeton before slipping into the narrow alleyway to wait.

It wasn't long before the boy appeared. That dried wheat hair stuck out straight from his head. There wasn't much to the lad—he was all arms and legs, with a long neck supporting a round face, most of which was spattered with freckles. Resting a hand against the wall to catch his breath, the boy wiped beads of sweat from his brow.

"It…ain't…fair," the boy said, panting after each word. "You could at least *pretend* not to see me."

Lucan resisted the urge to smile. "It is your job not to be seen, Arthur. I've been trying to teach you that since you first tried to pick my pocket, nearly two years ago now."

At the time, to make matters worse, when caught, the lad had opened his mouth and unleashed a torrent of prior crimes. Yet the sheer panic in the boy's eyes had kindled Lucan's sympathy.

He'd seen too much of himself in those eyes. Therefore, to calm Arthur, Lucan had used a few sleight-of-hand tricks as a distraction. Soon, he'd gained an avid follower. The little scamp was a wily one too. No matter where Lucan was, Arthur would find him and beg to learn more. Lucan had agreed, but only if the lad promised to stop picking pockets. To aid Arthur in that endeavor, Lucan had found him a job as an errand runner at White's.

"Even though I've been away these past months, that is no reason for you to forget all that I taught you." Lucan had been in Lincolnshire, plotting to marry off his closest friends.

"I've been busy, I have," Arthur said, taking in a few gulps of air.

As an orphan, his was a typical tale of a street urchin. The only difference was that he had an older sister. Henny Momper had been attending the Winchester Asylum in the hopes of learning a proper servant trade. Unfortunately, when their parents died, she left the school to watch over Arthur.

Then a year ago, Arthur and Henny were taken off the streets and began working for Lord Whitelock. Since the viscount was known for his generosity, in addition to taking in the less fortunate and providing them employment, this normally wouldn't have gained Lucan's interest. However, since he owed Whitelock ten thousand pounds, it had.

"Ran all the way from Lord Marsen's, I did." Arthur's gaze lingered on the pastry in Lucan's hand. "I heard Lord Whitelock tell the driver that his meeting would take a while and to find himself a cup of tea in the meantime."

Marsen. Lucan had lost a monkey to him last night. It could have been worse—a thousand pounds instead of only half the sum. The pity was, he'd actually assumed that Marsen was a good sort. Of course, that was only until the jack of hearts had made a sloppy appearance from Marsen's cuff.

Lucan's odd friendship with Arthur had taken a turn when the lad began to work for Whitelock. While it might not be scrupulous, Lucan started using an unsuspecting Arthur as an informant.

He hadn't set out to, but one day, Arthur had been chatting on as he usually did and mentioned Whitelock's meeting with a gambler—a man to whom Lucan had lost at the tables the night before. Then the following week, Arthur had reported a meeting with a different gentleman. That story was similar, as well—it had been with another man to whom Lucan had lost a substantial sum of money.

Of course, the fact that Lucan had run into a two-year losing streak at the tables, defeated by the very men who had met with Whitelock, could all be happenstance.

But Lucan didn't believe in coincidence. In fact, he suspected—for reasons unknown—that Whitelock wanted to make sure he *couldn't* pay back the debt of honor. And if Lucan didn't come up with ten thousand pounds in the next few months, Hugh Thorne would go back to gaol and soon face the hangman's noose.

Was it any wonder why Lucan had had to resort to a wager amongst his own friends? Ten thousand pounds to the last bachelor standing in a year's time. And now, with Everhart and Danvers happily settled, in a few short months, Lucan would finally win and remove this debt for good.

Lucan handed over the bun, watching the boy's eyes grow as round as his head. It always helped to have a spy who was employed by the one you were spying on. "And here I was, about to let this go to waste. It's good thing you came along when you did. I would offer a cup of tea, but clearly I wasn't thinking of entertaining." He gestured to the brick walls of the narrow alleyway and the damp cobblestones at their feet.

"There's always tea tomorrow," Arthur said around a mouthful. Then, after taking a moment to swallow audibly, he wiped the glaze from his lips and stood ramrod straight as if he were imparting news from the royal palace. "My sister is now the housekeeper of Lord Whitelock's hunting box in Wales."

From chambermaid to the viscountess's companion and now head housekeeper? Usually, servants worked their whole lives to reach such prestige. Not to mention, usually only educated, highborn women—most likely a dependent relation—became companions. Yet Henny Momper had managed the implausible in a year's time. If it weren't for Whitelock's unblemished reputation, people might start to make assumptions.

For the boy's sake, however, Lucan bit down on his suspicions. "I offer my congratulations. What a boon for your sister and, I imagine, for you as well." Whitelock's reputed benevolence was one of the reasons that Lucan had accepted the debt on Thorne's behalf. It made no sense that Whitelock would make it impossible to pay it back.

Yet circumstances suggested otherwise.

Arthur puffed out his chest. "Before Henny left at the end of last month, she said that after a while she'd make sure to set me up as a groom in the stables there."

"Good on you." Lucan ruffled his hair, glad for the boy. At the same time, however, he would miss him. He'd grown fond of the former pickpocket.

"His lordship is still looking for a new companion for Lady Whitelock. He'll go to Mrs. Hunter's tomorrow."

This surprised Lucan. Whitelock was returning to Mrs. Hunter's so soon? That would make the second time this week. Moreover, if his purpose was to find a new companion for his wife, a servant registry was hardly the standard method.

Yet, the fact that he kept returning to that particular servant registry tolled a warning through Lucan. He'd learned years ago not to discount this instinct.

With the Hugh Thorne's life hanging in the balance once more and with Whitelock's sudden interest in the agency where Frances Thorne worked, Lucan almost wished that he did believe in coincidence. But this was starting to feel like a game—one of which he didn't know the trick. Not yet.

Now, he needed to figure out how Frances Thorne factored in to Whitelock's new interests. Which meant that Lucan needed to stay close to her, even at the risk of awakening the hunger inside of him.

CHAPTER TWO

"Frannie?"

Frances pretended not to hear her father's voice and continued down the stairs from their third-floor apartment in the ramshackle boarding house. She was in no mood to speak with him. This morning, when it had come time to pay their landlady, Mrs. Pruitt, there had been no money left in crockery hidden in the floorboards beneath Frances's pallet. He'd done this before. Most likely, it had ended up in an alehouse. He tended to imbibe too much when he was anxious. The only problem was, he never came to her with his worries. He only came to her with his excuses. She should have known better and found a more secure hiding spot. But deep down she wanted him to find the strength to be a real father once more.

Now, Mrs. Pruitt was waiting by the front door—*barring it, really*—with her stubby hand open. Without any further delay, Frances took nearly the last of her wages and placed the shillings in the older woman's palm. Not saying a word, the landlady scrutinized each coin. And to each coin, Frances silently bid a final, painful good-bye—one that she felt in the pit of her stomach. Those shillings should have gone to their grocery account. When satisfied, Mrs. Pruitt sniffed and leveled a hard look at Frances before moving to the side.

Opening the door, Frances looked over her shoulder at her father who'd made his way down to the landing. She was already running behind schedule because of the pointless search for the rent money. "I don't have time this morning, Da."

She couldn't afford one more mistake or else Mrs. Hunter would let her go.

Once outside, she could hear her father's shuffled footsteps behind her. In the more affluent parts of town—where they used to live—there wouldn't be much traffic on the street at this time of morning. Yet here, early risers gained the advantage. Therefore, it came as no surprise that the pavement was just as crowded as the street. As was her usual method, she kept close to the buildings and walked at a steady clip. Beneath the awnings and overhangs, she was less likely to have the contents of a chamber pot dumped on her head.

"Frannie, you're walking too fast," her father complained, catching up to her. He added a short wheeze at the end until she relented and slowed her stride. Gradually, he matched her pace. "There's a good girl. Now, hear me out."

She already knew he was going to pour out a list of excuses for why he took the money—excuses that would hold as much weight as a handful of air. "This wasn't the first time."

"You know how hard it's been." Beneath his glove, he rubbed the place over his branded thumb. "I can't find work."

"I have *found* work for you." She'd put her professional reputation at risk by calling in favors from the housekeepers and lady's maids for whom she'd helped find situations. Yet each time, her father disappointed her.

"I am too old to be a footman—carting trays, buckets, and portmanteaus up and down the stairs."

"That was a last resort, Da." And he well knew it. She let out an exasperated sigh. "The clerk's position at the solicitor's office was perfect for you. Mr. Youngblood did me a great favor by even offering his consideration. Yet you did not last a month."

Hugh Thorne opened his mouth, uttered a monosyllabic sound, and then closed it again. Removing his hat revealed a short crop of graying hair, which had receded to form a soft U shape above his forehead. He tried again. "I wasn't ready for that job at the time, but I am now. If you could find it in your heart, Frannie... You know how much I love you. I never wanted to be a disappointment as a father. If your mother were alive today, I would be a different man. I'm sure of it. One more chance. That's all I need."

She closed her eyes. *One more chance.* Yet she didn't have another chance. And asking for another favor from the names on her dwindling list just wasn't something she was willing to risk. Not today. Not when they could both be out on the street tomorrow.

During Miss Farmingdale's instruction yesterday, the scandalous booklet had fallen out of Frances's sleeve, opening directly to the *backside* page. If Miss Farmingdale had been determined to remain *unchanged* all the days of her life, she would have gasped or even swooned. Fortunately for Frances, when Miss Farmingdale lifted the slender pages from the floor, her brows had gone up, followed by the corners of her mouth. She'd passed the booklet back to Frances surreptitiously, but it could have turned out drastically differently.

"I'm sorry, Da. There isn't anyone I can call on today." When she opened her eyes and saw his dejected expression, his brown eyes as sorrowful as a basset hound that had been cast out in the rain, she softened the blow. Like always. "Perhaps next week I'll learn of something new."

"Next week, then." He nodded and slowly donned his hat once more, before offering a small smile. "I'll look around and perhaps find something today. Don't you worry, Frannie."

She swallowed down a rise of churning guilt. "I'll see you later, Da."

Frances watched him turn back and cross the street in the direction of the shipyards. A feeling of dread swirled with the guilt, making her glad she hadn't eaten. Then again, without food at home and little money, she couldn't have eaten regardless. And with that thought, she felt a sense of purpose drive away the unpleasant bitterness.

When she rounded the corner, she was surprised to see Viscount Whitelock standing by the door to Mrs. Hunter's. She readily dipped into a curtsy. "Good morning, Lord Whitelock."

"Miss Thorne, a pleasure as always," he said, the rich cadence of his voice suggesting a life that wanted for nothing. A long life, well spent. In truth, he was the same age as her father. And—according to what he'd told her when they'd first met—might very well have *been* her father, if her mother had chosen differently.

Coincidentally, she'd first encountered the viscount by her mother's grave. He'd been leaving a spray of forget-me-nots on top of her headstone. When he'd turned to leave, he'd stopped suddenly and stared, wide-eyed, at Frances. It took a moment for him to recover. Then, after an informal introduction, he explained that at one time, both her father and he had vied for her mother's hand.

As the accomplished granddaughter of an earl with a modest dowry, Elise easily could have married a peer. Yet she'd chosen love instead. For that, Frances could find no fault in her decision, no matter how many times in recent years she might have wished for fewer worries.

Lord Whitelock wore the years of his life differently than did her father. The lines of his face were taut and angular, even at his jaw. In contrast, Hugh Thorne was a little softer, with the hint of jowls beginning to form. While Viscount Whitelock was still handsome enough to garner a glance or two from the lady's maids running errands this morning, her father was more of the cuddly sort.

"I wonder if I could ask a favor of you," the viscount said with an open gesture toward the door of Mrs. Hunter's.

Frances's thoughts veered to Mrs. Hunter's desire to sell more of their paid services. Since meeting him a few months ago, Viscount Whitelock had become a frequent patron. Could it be that he needed to hire a new servant? Turning the key in the lock, she suppressed the urge to blurt out that very question but opted for the more professional response instead. "How may I be of service, my lord?"

Frances opened the door to allow him inside, but instead, he held the door for her. She didn't dare argue with a viscount.

Familiar with Miss Thorne's schedule, Lucan knew she was an early riser. He, on the other hand, was not. He winced as shards of sunlight sliced over the rooftops and onto the pavement. Nevertheless, he trudged toward Mrs. Hunter's that morning, waiting to see if Whitelock made an appearance.

Across the street on the west side of the bakery, Lucan kept to the shadows, his hat low on his brow. That was when he spotted Whitelock's carriage one street over. After leaving his driver, the viscount appeared to be taking a slow stroll in the direction of the registry.

Soon enough, Arthur scampered up beside Lucan. The lad started chatting away, and normally, Lucan would listen to every word. Today, however, he found himself distracted by the sight of Miss Thorne, rounding the corner. While her serviceable, common, work-a-day lavender dress in no way hinted at her noble bloodlines, the subtle elegance of her carriage and the graceful lines of her shoulders and throat revealed a mark of innate quality to anyone who paid close attention. Most of all, it was quite clear that she did not belong here, working for a pittance and finding servants to work in the *ton's* townhouses. No, she should be hiring servants to fill her own house instead. But she'd had no one looking out for her, not Quinlin, not her father, only Lucan, albeit without any direct interference.

In all the years of his acquaintance with Miss Thorne, Lucan had maintained a respectable distance, making an effort to keep his flirtatious teasing to a minimum. So why—after scarcely encountering her these last two years—was he suddenly unable to stay away?

The reasonable explanation was that he needed to discover why Whitelock was returning here so often of late. Yet Lucan wasn't entirely certain his motivation was solely driven by Whitelock. It might have something to do with the way Miss Thorne had adjusted her spectacles yesterday...

His thoughts drifted as he pondered this unforeseen distraction. However, the moment he saw Miss Thorne enter the empty shop with Whitelock and no chaperone, he became fully alert. He did not like the idea of her being alone with Whitelock. Flipping Arthur a coin for tea and a glazed bun, Lucan sent him on his way. The lad should not witness what he was about to do.

Using the skills he'd acquired at school during years of sneaking in and out of the dormitory, not to mention a few bedrooms in the years that followed, Lucan crept between the back of Mrs. Hunter's shop and the neighboring one and then deftly scaled the brick. The aging façade gave him ample toeholds, but not all of them were secure. Yet in the end, he slipped in through a tiny upper-floor window.

He crept to the open doorway at the top of the stairs in time to hear Whitelock say, "*You set a fine example, Miss Thorne. I can see that you adhere to your own counsel by never allowing the merest suggestion of impropriety.*"

A breath of relief rushed out of Lucan. *That's my girl*, he thought, feeling a wealth of pride an instant before taking note of his own words. *My girl?* Now where had that come from?

It was peculiar, to say the least. Yet for now, he shrugged it off and renewed his focus on the conversation below stairs.

Inside, the shop was dark, with slashes of light slipping through narrow wooden slats and spreading across the hardwood floor. Frances walked to the box window to open the shutters and let in the light.

After Viscount Whitelock's compliment about her *fine example*, she allowed herself a small smile at the perceptible praise in his tone. It was always nice to be appreciated, especially after the debacle of stomping on his foot. "Thank you, my lord."

He removed his hat. At his age, a full head of neatly trimmed salt-and-pepper hair was quite the asset and complemented his regal bone structure. But more than that, he possessed an aura of kindness. She'd never known a lord and master to take such a keen interest in ensuring that the women in his employ were tutored on the art of defense. In fact, in her dealings with the servant trade, she'd found the opposite was true. In some instances, the one person a maid needed to fear the most *was* the master of the house.

"It may seem rather greedy of me, but I have come here today to request more of your time." He took a step into the room but remained standing on the outer rim of light that spilled onto the floor. "The excitement of these lessons has stormed through my townhouse like a carnival at Covent Garden. I'm certain it will only be a matter of time before the maids at one or more of my country estates will desire to be included as well."

"Such news is an honor to learn, my lord. My greatest hope is that I will be here at Mrs. Hunter's for a long while to come." As soon as the words were out, she wished she hadn't allowed herself to continue past *my lord*.

The lines surrounding his shrewd gaze drew together. "Is there a reason why you shouldn't be? I do hope it has nothing to do with our brief encounter."

"No, my lord," she said immediately, feeling the heat of embarrassment in her cheeks. "Although, I would like to apologize again, and I hope your foot was not too injured."

"As you see, I've no need of a cane as of yet, and I refuse to hear another word of your apology," he said with firm sincerity. "Now, I will hazard a guess that the similar agency that opened down the street might have something to do with the uncertain nature of your situation."

Glad that Mrs. Hunter was not here, Frances offered a tentative nod.

"Ah. Well, then that brings me to the other reason I came to see you this morning." He paused long enough to spark her interest. "Since my beloved wife is bound to her rooms, her greatest pleasure is having someone read to her. I enjoy doting on her, and if I could, I would be with her all day, but alas... I cannot. Many people depend on me."

Lucan held back a wry laugh. Whitelock was a humble man, to be sure, but one who wanted *everyone* to know his sacrifices. The man was skilled in his delivery. Charming, even. He almost made a person want to believe that his heart was pure, and he had nothing to gain by helping others. Lucan had been taken in, after all. At least, at first.

Listening closely, however, he was finding this paragon difficult to believe. Whitelock was up to something, and Lucan didn't like the nature of the suspicions tossing back and forth in his head. To him, it sounded like a veiled attempt at an assignation with Miss Thorne. But surely even Whitelock wouldn't make such an offer. Thus far, there had been no rumors about him in a scandalous vein. And yet…

The low timbre of Whitelock's voice made the hair on the back of Lucan's neck stand on end. Without thinking, he took a step forward. His foot landed on a loose board, which creaked beneath him.

"I could compile a list of suitable candidates for your lordship to interview," Frances said.

"I knew you could, Miss Thorne," the viscount said with a smile that didn't quite reach his eyes, but with his next words, the reason became clear. "The problem is, I will only be in town for a short duration. In fact, I leave within the week for the estate I mentioned. With all that's to be done in the meantime, I'm not certain I could give interviews. The more I think on it, however, I believe that *you* would be the perfect candidate."

She didn't know what to say. On one hand, she didn't want to lose her job at Mrs. Hunter's. She enjoyed the additional service that she provided, even if it didn't bring in any coin.

Yet on the other hand, Lord Whitelock had made her a generous offer by excluding all other potential applicants in favor of her. "I'm honored, my lord, but I—"

Frances broke off when she heard a noise from above. She glanced toward the narrow staircase, absently wondering if she'd left one of the windows open yesterday. Then thinking back, she knew she'd closed them because she'd had to stuff the scandalous booklet between the back window and sill when Mrs. Hunter had come to hurry her along.

The sound was likely just a mouse.

Drawing her attention again, Viscount Whitelock removed a slender case from his inner breast pocket. The gold glinted in the sunlight. "I'm merely extending a courtesy to one whose mother was a dear, dear friend of mine." He stepped forward and offered her a calling card.

Grateful beyond words, Frances took it. He could have no idea how his offer had removed a great burden from her shoulders, although she hoped she would never need use it.

"Present this at my door, day or night, Miss Thorne. I will always have a place for you."

"Thank you, my lord."

Inclining his head, he donned his hat and left her alone in the office. Frances smiled to herself, gratified at having been right about her impression of the viscount. Had she known there were such gentlemen in the world, she might not have become so jaded. She wished there were more men like him.

"I am honored, my lord, but I—"

Lucan had almost been able to feel Miss Thorne's gaze on him through the floor. Beneath the fine lawn of his shirt, his skin prickled. He'd held his breath and felt his heart thrum inside his chest. Slowly, he'd eased off the floorboard and took a backward step toward the window. Just in case she came up the stairs, he'd wanted a quick escape. Yet he hadn't wanted to leave until Whitelock was gone and she was safe.

Then, the viscount said something that earned Lucan's surprise. *"I'm merely extending a courtesy to one whose mother was a dear, dear friend of mine."*

Whitelock had never mentioned the acquaintance. If that were true, then why hadn't Whitelock come forward himself in Thorne's defense years ago?

It was past time that Lucan had some real answers. And now that he knew Thorne and Whitelock were connected by Thorne's late wife, Lucan knew exactly where to get them.

When Whitelock and Miss Thorne's conversation concluded, Lucan turned toward the open window. That was when he spotted a palm-sized booklet on the floor. Bending down, he picked it up, wondering where it had come from. There were no tables nearby, and the chairs were on the other side of the room. The room was neat and tidy, therefore not likely to have errant papers littering the floor.

Then suddenly, he noticed a small corner of torn paper stuck to the window casing. *That* was where the booklet had been? Apparently, he'd disturbed it upon entering. He would take care to return it when he left.

But why would anyone keep a booklet stuffed in between the sash and the casing? Studying the object more closely, however, presented another question. Had Miss Thorne been the one who'd hidden this book of sketches?

After his meeting with Arthur yesterday, Lucan had felt an uncanny need to come back to the street that evening to keep an eye on Miss Thorne. Because of that, he knew she'd been the last one to leave and close up the shop. Thumbing through the book, he wondered if Miss Thorne had an interest in the tailoring of men's fashions. Or perhaps her interest was of a more primitive nature.

She was seven and twenty, after all. Not the age of a debutante but of a full-grown woman. A woman, likely, with needs and desires. A woman whose spectacles and smoky eyes guarded all sorts of mysteries.

Hearing her on the stairs now, he slipped back through the window. It wasn't until he was on the ground that he realized he still held that booklet. Tucking it into his pocket, he grinned up at the window. He would simply return it during their next encounter.

He was already looking forward to it.

She didn't want Mrs. Hunter to catch her staring at the calling card, so Frances hastily tucked it into the pocket she'd sewn into her calico dress. Giving it pat, she lifted her gray apron from the hook. She put it on, the letter *H* embroidered above her left breast, and tied the ribbons in the back.

Frances took pride in her daily uniform. While some with an aristocratic bloodline might be tempted to dress above their current station, she was not one to put on airs. She accepted her altered circumstances and strove to perform her job to the best of her ability. After all, she held a position of great importance and enjoyed her labors, especially helping young women become more educated in ways to shield themselves from deceitful men.

Men such as that would likely be better served by a day's labor than idleness and gambling, amongst other more scandalous pursuits. Her near betrothal to Roger Quinlin had taught her as much. Of course, she'd only found out about his true nature once her own circumstances had changed.

Lucan Montwood was another man who would be better served with some form of occupation. She thought of him as she took the stairs. What did a man of no fortune, no property, and no trade do all day? Likely, he spent hours gambling and the rest of the flirting or engaging in similar…activities. Her pulse quickened at the thought.

Their encounter had left her unsettled yesterday afternoon. She couldn't help but wonder why he'd lingered. It couldn't have been for her sake. Moreover, he hadn't appeared to have business with Mrs. Hunter or an engagement with Lady Binghamton, other than holding the door. So, then, why?

By the time she reached the top of the stairs, she could think of no reason and summarily decided to cast him from her mind. She quickly scanned the room and found the two straight-backed chairs and small wine table exactly where she'd left them. The front window was closed. Her assortment of props for her instruction were hanging neatly in a row against the back wall. And the back window was…*open*.

Oh dear. How could that be? She recalled closing it herself after taking one final peek at the booklet. *The booklet!* Alarmed, she rushed to the window. Lifting up the sash, she searched the sill and the floor but found nothing. Then, she peered outside toward the alley below. Still nothing. With the building across the way close enough to reach out and touch, she searched the slanted roof, wondering if it had blown away in the wind.

How could she have been so careless?

Frances closed the window, pressed her forehead against the glass, and drew in a breath. Peculiarly, the seductive aroma of freshly ironed sheets and midnight air filled her nostrils.

She started. Spinning away from the window, she half expected to see Lucan Montwood standing behind her. But he wasn't there. The room was still vacant. Even so, she didn't feel alone. Obviously, the lingering effects of their meeting were proving difficult to forget. Perhaps it would simply take a more concerted effort. Thankfully, she wasn't likely to encounter him for a very long time. What reason could they possibly have to meet?

By tomorrow morning, her thoughts would be completely free of Lucan Montwood.

Chapter Three

Leaving Mrs. Hunter's agency, Lucan went in search of answers. Hours later, he found a drunken Hugh Thorne in a gaming hell. Once they were a safe distance outside, he glanced back to make sure no one had followed them. None yet, at least. Just in case, however, he raised his hand for a hack.

"Betting your last farthing is one thing, but begging for a line of credit for one hundred pounds? *That* was a fool's move, Thorne," Lucan growled under his breath. He'd lost count of how many times he'd saved this man's life in the past two and a half years. So many, in fact, that he was beginning to question if this would turn into his life's pursuit. Aunt Theodosia would certainly have a laugh over that. His mother's elder sister was forever telling him that he'd missed his calling as a saint. But what saint had murder in his heart?

Thorne walked to the hack with the shuffled step and slumped shoulders of a broken man, shaking his head all the way. "I was sure I had something this time."

Closing the door once they were seated, Lucan tried to rein in his temper. "Gambling is not a profession. I know that better than most."

"They make winning look so simple." Thorne stared down at his hands as if they were flush with cards. All the right ones.

"Losing is even easier." Lucan wasn't getting through to him. "What about that last job I arranged for you? Langley needed a clerk for his shipments. You were the perfect man. I don't understand why you left in the middle of the day and never came back."

This wasn't the first time, either. Lucan had arranged several jobs for Thorne, calling in all sorts of favors. Not to mention, he knew that Miss Thorne had supplied several opportunities as well. Now, his list was all too lean.

"Did I?" Thorne frowned, the deep-set lines around his mouth resembling something of a horseshoe. But one with all the luck running out. "I'm certain that couldn't be the case. I only would have left when the job was finished."

"And there was a five-pound note missing from the till."

Thorne reared back against the squabs, eyes wide. "I don't know what you're suggesting, sir, but I can assure you that I am not a thief. I managed your father's accounts for years without incident, until…"

And that was where their conversations concluded each time Lucan asked why Thorne had left a job.

When Langley had confronted Lucan about the missing money in the till the following day, to save face, Lucan had worked a little sleight of hand trickery and produced a five-pound note that, by all appearances, had been crumpled and stuck beneath the lid. Langley had known better, of course, but had accepted the money as remuneration.

It also wasn't the first time Lucan had paid from his own pockets to cover Thorne's debts. Not to mention the ten thousand pounds he owed Whitelock by the end of this year. Thinking of the debt brought Lucan back to wondering why Whitelock had approached him with the original offer. Why not approach Thorne if they were friends?

Asking Thorne straight out, however, was not an option. Thorne did not know about the bargain Lucan had made with Whitelock, nor would he. As far as Thorne knew, and nearly everyone other than the magistrate, there had been no fine. Whitelock has used his connections to maintain absolute secrecy. Yet even if the stipulations of the agreement weren't secret, Lucan still wouldn't want anyone else to know what he'd done. He wasn't the type of man who wanted attention or praise for freeing an innocent man from the gallows. Any gentleman with a sense of compassion would have assisted in whatever way he could.

"I would like to help you, Thorne, but I am running out of options. Do you have any friends you can rely upon? Perhaps an old school chum you haven't spoken to in a while?" he asked, hoping Thorne might admit to an association with Whitelock.

Thorne returned to wallowing and turned a dejected gaze toward the window. On a sigh, he said, "None."

"A peer of the realm who might owe you a favor?"

Thorne shook his head.

Impatient to uncover the connection, Lucan pressed on, abandoning subtlety. "A man with your education—a grandson of country gentleman, no less—likely attended university with one or two nobles. Come to think of it, I believe Viscount Whitelock is near your age."

Thorne's expression went from self-pity to stone cold in an instant. "*Never* mention that blackguard's name to me again."

Blackguard? An icy chill slithered over Lucan's skin, collecting at his fingertips. Thorne was the first person he'd ever heard speak out against Whitelock. Lucan's suspicions heightened, yet he knew better than to assault Thorne with a barrage of questions. It was important to make Thorne feel comfortable if he was to gain any information. Glancing out the window, Lucan settled back in his seat, giving the appearance of ease. "Then you know him."

"We attended university together," Thorne said through clenched teeth.

"Surely, you could call on him…as a friend."

"We were not friends. We were rivals," Thorne spat. His hand shot out in an angry swipe over the knees of his trousers, as if to remove unseen filth. "He tried to take my Elise from me, wooing her with all manner of deceptions. Then, he became obsessed with her, never letting her out of his sight. She thought we were all chums, the three of us. It wasn't until he forbade her from spending time with me or stepping out with her friends that she started to see through him. And one afternoon, after he'd followed her to the museum, she'd told him that she didn't want his friendship anymore." Thorne stopped, his hands curling into a fists.

Lucan found it hard to keep the appearance of ease when alarm sprinted through him. He was tired of not knowing the whole of Whitelock's character. More and more, Lucan was beginning to wonder if he'd made a deal with a more calculated villain than even his own father, but one with all the appearance of goodness.

"And then that blackguard convinced her to ride with him through the park, so that he could apologize. Only that wasn't what he had on his mind. Instead he—" Thorne broke off and shook his head, as if to wipe the memory away. He cleared his throat. "He *frightened* her. Later that summer, she married me. Three years after that, she blessed me with Frannie—the perfect portrait of her mother. Every time I look at her, I can see Elise, and it's like I haven't lost her at all."

Lucan felt as if a loadstone pressed against his chest. His lungs seized in the familiar sense of dread that had claimed him in his childhood. Whitelock had been visiting Mrs. Hunter's agency more and more. Could it be that when he'd first seen Frances, his old obsession with her mother had returned?

"*Present this at my door, day or night, Miss Thorne. I will always have a place for you,*" Whitelock had said earlier. Now, Lucan wondered if there was a double meaning behind it.

Chapter Four

Early the following morning before work, Frances fought her way through the crowd gathered at the Covent Garden market. With only a few coins, she hoped to have enough for a fish. It had been a long while since she'd eaten fish, or meat for that matter. Her usual fare consisted of boiled potatoes or turnips with wild onions. Yet she often managed to save enough for her father to buy a meat pie from the corner shop. If he was going to find work, he needed the strength, after all.

In their old lodgings, they'd been charged for room and board, with one meal a day included. However, they'd had to move several times over in the past two years when the rent money went missing. After that, all Frances could afford on her wages was a room *without* board. Under Mrs. Pruitt's supervision, she was allowed the use of one pot and the stove in the kitchen for three pennies a week extra.

Today, Frances wanted a piece of fish, a potato, a handful of carrots…and some peas would be lovely. A basket on the edge of a stall table was brimming with peas, bright green and all snug in their pods. Frances liked to eat them raw, popping them between her teeth like a confection.

Gripping her basket, she held up her free hand and called, "Peas for a ha'penny?"

"Whot, whot," the stall owner said, his ruddy face pinched and sour as if she'd squirted a lemon in his eye. "Tuppence for the peas."

If she gave tuppence just for the peas, she wouldn't have enough left for the fish. She held up her coin, determined. "Just two farthing's worth of peas, then."

He grumbled and looked over the crowd. She knew that the more he haggled with her, the fewer sales he would have. In the end, he snatched her coin and tossed a goodly number of peas into her basket.

"Thank you, sir," she said, pleased by his sudden change of heart.

Leaving that stall, she went through the market and had the same luck with the carrots and two large potatoes. Now, she had a penny left. She hoped it would be enough for a fine fish. Yet the stall-keeper refused to barter. He wanted tuppence or her absence. Repeatedly, he waved her aside in favor of calling others forward.

Frances held her ground. "What about that smaller one, there on the other side?" She didn't need the largest fish.

The scowl the man gave her looked as if she'd insulted his person. "Nay. Ye 'ave the price. Pay it or be—" He stopped suddenly, squinting as he looked over her shoulder. Then, grumbling, he said, "A penny it is."

Before he could snatch the coin from her hand, however, she looked over her shoulder.

There, standing in the shadow of the awning not two steps away, was none other than Lucan Montwood. By all appearances he looked to be out for stroll. He lounged against the wooden post with his black John Bull tilted to the side and a shilling pinched between his thumb and forefinger.

She suddenly wondered at the good fortune she'd experienced this morning. "Have you been following me?"

Did he think he was doing her a favor? If so, why? The only thing he'd managed to do so far was to disturb her sleep. Last night, she kept falling into the same dream—one where she stood near the second-floor window of the agency. Only in the dream, she hadn't been alone. Instead, she'd found herself in Lucan Montwood's passionate embrace, his skillful hands playing over her flesh, his hungry mouth claiming hers and robbing her of breath.

She'd awoken gasping for air, her head fuzzy and half-expecting to find Lucan Montwood lying beside her on her pallet. And each time she'd attempted sleep again, she ended up in the same dream.

So much for casting him out of her thoughts. Worse, she shouldn't give a passing thought to a gambler. They were the worst sort of men, spouting all manner of lies and deceptions as easily as exhaling. Roger Quinlin had taught her that much when he'd stolen her five-hundred pound dowry. Two and a half years ago, on the day that her father had been arrested for treason, Mr. Quinlin had promised to hire a solicitor to find the best barrister for her father's defense. The only thing he'd needed was money. Since she was past her majority, she'd had full access to her own monies. Foolishly, she'd handed it all over to Mr. Quinlin. Instead of helping her, he'd helped himself, purchased a commission with her fortune, and disappeared the very next day.

When Lucan didn't respond to her question, Frances hissed, "I don't need your assistance. I don't need *anything* from the likes of you."

Something dark and wounded flashed in his eyes that almost made her regret her words. Instead of commenting, he pushed away from the post, flipped the silver coin with his thumb to the fishmonger, and placed a neatly wrapped fish in her basket before he started to walk away.

Then he paused to pay a flower girl for a cluster of violets and offered Frances an absent glance over his shoulder. "While I admire the stern workday countenance you employ to set an example for others, using a little smile in the market could do wonders for your basket."

He was talking about flirting. Flirting was one thing Frances never did. She'd seen how a friendly smile could give a man the wrong ideas. In her opinion, it was far better to know the character of the man beforehand. "I suppose you would have me remove my spectacles and bat my lashes as well."

Lucan turned to face her. Slowly, he revealed a grin that only hinted at the dimple lurking there. It hinted at other things too. *Scandalous things.* She was certain of it because a ripple of desire stirred inside of her.

"No, Miss Thorne, *always* wear your spectacles." He leaned forward, the brim of his hat close to hers. "They act like a veil, making a man wonder about the eyes behind them. A man starts to imagine being the one who'll steam up your lenses."

She couldn't breathe. His scent made her drowsy. In that moment, she was caught in the thrall of his words and mesmerized by his amber gaze. He could have kissed her, right there in the market, and she would have done nothing to stop him.

His gaze dipped to her mouth. "My advice to you is…keep your fichu pinned in place. Keep your hair in perfect order. That way, when you unleash your smile, it's all the more effective." He drew back. "Although, that is a mere supposition, since you've never smiled at me."

Someone bumped her shoulder, jostling the sense back into her. "You would only teach me charm and deception. No, thank you, sir. I would rather have nothing from you."

There it was again—that dark shadow drifted across his gaze but disappeared in a blink. Yet she knew very well that she could not be offending a man such as he for merely stating the truth.

He tsked, lifting his hand in an absent gesture. "Perhaps you'd prefer the tutelage of Whitelock."

"His lordship knows nothing of deception."

"I wouldn't be too certain, Miss Thorne."

His grave expression took her aback. She wondered at the source for a moment before her better sense returned. "Why bring the viscount into our tete-a-tete?"

"An unmarried woman should never entertain a gentleman alone, regardless of his rank or reputation."

She gasped. Instantly, she recalled the open window and the scent of him that had haunted her dreams. "Were you *spying* on me?"

"I might have been protecting your honor," he said, matter-of-fact.

"*You?*" Frances scoffed. She could think of nothing he sought to gain, but his comments ran close to besmirching

Lord Whitelock's impeccable reputation. "You would know nothing about men of excellent character."

Lucan nodded solemnly, as if sufficiently chastised for a lifetime of errant behavior. "Ah, but isn't a man who lacks all morals the first to spot others like him? It's sort of like one leper seeing another, I imagine."

Leper, indeed. She would do well to stay away from him. Yet when he took her arm just then, she didn't pull away. Instead, she allowed him to guide her through the ever-increasing crowd.

"Goodness in men is such a rarity that you should not mock it," she said, holding her basket out of harm's way.

As they traversed between two stalls, she was forced to draw closer to him. Her arm was now folded carefully beneath his. Their proximity allowed unfettered access to his scent, and she inhaled far more deeply than she normally would have done. She even found herself turning her head toward his shoulder for another breath. Not watching where she was going, she leaned into him ever so slightly. It took her a moment to realize that she was trusting him to deliver her to the other side of the hoard. What on earth was she thinking? What was it about standing too near Lucan Montwood that made her abandon her principles enough to rely on him for even the smallest of things? Her actions were unconscionable.

Then, with uncanny accuracy into the inner workings of her mind, he murmured, "If you seek the good in men, then you are looking in the wrong place."

"Are you speaking of yourself?" Miss Thorne asked.

Lucan was speaking of Whitelock, and he'd wager that she knew it too. Yet because he was feeling charitable, he did not argue the point. Not *that* point, anyway. "Do not be fooled, Miss Thorne. Not all serpents wear their skins so stylishly."

She surprised him by releasing a small laugh. "I'm certain few could."

"That sounded suspiciously like a compliment." *How rare and unexpected.*

Tucked up next to him, she stiffened. "Only you would take the meaning as such."

Still, she did not shy away from the touch of his hand at her elbow. Nor did she make a fuss when he slipped the basket from her grasp. Under different circumstances, they could be having a pleasant stroll through the park—*if* one were inclined to walk outside when the sun had only risen a bloody hour ago.

"Undoubtedly, you are correct." He sported a black cravat for the sake of mourning his *morning*. At this hour, he was usually in bed, often after a night of delicious debauchery.

The beast inside him rumbled, bringing to mind how hungry Miss Thorne made him. Unfortunately, his usual list of easily charmed beauties never quite sated that appetite. He hadn't minded it in the past. In fact, he enjoyed giving pleasure. No, he *excelled* at it. Feeding a woman's hunger was part and parcel with that sense of control he needed. He knew how to read a woman's desire, take the subtle hints of her body, and make her come apart again and again. And only then would he take his own pleasure.

Yet giving or gaining pleasure hadn't satisfied him lately. He wanted more. But more of what? More of the same wouldn't help—he'd already tried that with a pair of comely twins from Cheshire.

No, what he wanted was something else. Something that filled the vast emptiness inside of him. Something that likely didn't even exist.

"Your hand upon my arm is unnecessary," Miss Thorne said, breaking through his thoughts.

Lucan looked down at the fingers of his dark glove curled around her fawn-colored sleeve and wondered if he should mention that it had taken her a dozen minutes or more to mention it. If she'd truly wanted the removal of his hand, she'd have said so immediately. So, perhaps she hadn't minded too much.

Instantly, he thought about the booklet he'd removed from the agency yesterday. He carried it with him now and was tempted to reveal it just to test her reaction. This moment, however, was not the time for a more intimate conversation regarding her tastes in men and whether or not she preferred sketches or a man of flesh and blood. In fact, it would be better if they did not have that conversation. Because if it was the former, then he might be tempted to persuade her otherwise.

Reluctantly, he let his hand fall away. They were on the path that led to her street, and his time to offer a warning against Whitelock was coming to a swift end.

"You are fortunate that you are familiar with a serpent's skin. Some hide behind all manner of trickery. Like unimpeachable morals, for example," he said, peering through her lenses to see her smoky eyes narrow with understanding *and* irritation. "It would be good for you to practice a little charm to keep those other snakes from biting when you least expect it."

"You needn't carry my basket any further," she said, snapping her fingers with impatience. "I cannot afford the high price of it, if the cost is enduring your incessant warnings."

Unaccountably, her prickly nature roused the beast within him. He wanted to kiss that waspish mouth. Standing within arm's reach of her, he felt that low growl at the pit of his stomach again. Even though he was tempted to aggravate her more, instead he promptly deposited the handle into her waiting palm.

He curled his fingers over hers and leaned in. "Here is an instance where a little sweetness could earn you the turn of a favor."

Her gaze drifted to the dimple beside his mouth. The sight of his smile appeared to anger her further. "We wasps do not fear snakes. We have venom of our own, as you well know."

Then, without another word, she stormed off, leaving Lucan to wonder if he was beginning to crave her sting already.

Frances shifted the weight of the basket to the other hand as she marched up the stairs to her apartment. Glancing down to make sure she hadn't disturbed the contents, she caught a glimpse of purple and stopped.

Violets. Lucan Montwood had forgotten his violets in her basket. He'd likely intended to offer them to an actress at the theatre or to whomever was the most recent victim of that maddening dimple. Instead, he'd mistakenly left them with her. And yet…

Someone as calculated as he might have left them in her basket on purpose. Perhaps for the sake of making her wonder what sort of woman enjoyed receiving flowers from the likes of him. It certainly wasn't her. Perhaps he'd wanted to make her jealous. She laughed to herself at the ludicrous idea. Jealous of one of Lucan Montwood's paramours? Frances was more inclined to feel pity.

Although…he does have a certain way about him, she admitted with great reluctance. His charm wasn't altogether unappealing. Strangely enough, the true reason she hadn't forced him to release her arm when he'd first begun to guide her through the market had been that his nearness had comforted her. She couldn't account for it, but she'd felt…*safe* with him.

She scoffed the instant the thought took form in her mind. *What rubbish! Safe with Lucan Montwood?* She'd have a greater chance of surviving a week inside a pit of vipers than to spend an unguarded moment with him.

Reaching into the basket, she lifted the violets to her nose. Solely for the purpose of removing his scent from her nostrils, of course. Yet when she looked down into the basket again, this time she saw a familiar—and quite scandalous—booklet.

Embarrassment scorched her flesh from the tips of her ears to the soles of her feet. All she could think of was his smirk and that damnable dimple.

He knew the booklet was hers.

Perhaps he'd even suspected that her inner thoughts and desires were not as prim and proper as she was on the outside.

Oh dear. How could she possibly face her workday now without thinking of Lucan Montwood at every turn?

CHAPTER FIVE

When she dropped off the basket at her flat, Frances's father was still snoring in his bed. He'd come in late last evening, smelling strongly of ale. She didn't know where he'd found money enough for drink, but it was happening with such frequency of late that she'd stopped asking. He never told her the truth anymore.

So when he'd said that he'd come to a decision and that he would return to Mr. Youngblood's offices and beg for another chance, she knew better than to believe it. Still, a small seed sprouted to life against her better judgment. And as she walked to the agency to begin her workday, she sent up a swift prayer that starting now, their lives would take a turn for the better.

When Frances arrived early, as usual, even after her morning jaunt to the market, she was surprised to find the door already unlocked. Walking inside, she blinked, adjusting to the dim light in the shop. Automatically, she moved to open the shutters.

"Never mind with that, Miss Thorne," Mrs. Hunter said from deeper within, where her desk sat along the opposite wall.

Frances turned, puzzled by the coldness of the greeting. "Oh, good morning, ma'am. I didn't see you there."

"Disturbing news calls me here at this hour." Mrs. Hunter stood, her chair scraping in a shriek across the floor. Her plump face was devoid of any softness. "Disturbing news that involves you."

Frances immediately thought of the booklet and when she'd dropped it at Miss Farmingdale's feet. Perhaps Lady Binghamton *had* noticed. How could Frances have been so careless? Truly, she hadn't meant to ogle the backside sketch. In her own defense, however, it wasn't as if she'd been ogling an *actual* man's backside. Well, aside from Lucan Montwood's, but no one could have known about that.

Although, perhaps he suspected…

She adjusted her spectacles. "I'm certain there is a reasonable explanation—"

"Did you, or did you not"—her employer interrupted, raising her voice to operatic volume—"refer several of my own patrons to Mr. Harrison's School for those wayward boys, so that these patrons might employ tigers and errand runners, instead of finding them through my own establishment?"

Oh no. Frances cringed inwardly. She'd nearly forgotten about that. The referrals had occurred months ago. At the time, she'd never imagined that losing the profits from placing a mere half dozen boys would affect this agency. She couldn't have foreseen that Tuttle's Registry would have opened on the same street, reducing Mrs. Hunter's profits even more.

"At the t-time, w-we were short on available boys with experience," Frances stammered. "Mr. Harrison finds young men who are otherwise disadvantaged and gives them a chance at—"

"We find the boys. We train the boys. We place the boys in suitable positions. *That*," Mrs. Hunter intoned, breathing rapidly, "is what we are paid to do. That *we*, however, no longer refers to you, Miss Thorne."

Shaking her head, Frances refused to believe what she heard. "It won't happen again, Mrs. Hunter."

Her employer pressed her lips together. "Please bring your apron to me."

Frances went cold all over. Her limbs felt weighted and tingled as if they'd fallen asleep. Something inside of her dropped. It might have been her heart or her stomach—she wasn't sure—but it left her disconnected and in a state of disbelief.

"I've worked for you for two and a half years. I need this job. You know my father is unable to support—" She stopped to swallow a rush of suppressed tears choking her. "I need this job."

"Your apron, Miss Thorne," Mrs. Hunter said again but turned toward her desk. "Because of your behavior, I should not offer you a recommendation, but I have written one out regardless. You may take it with you, along with your half-week's wages."

Numbly, Frances lifted the apron from the hook—*her hook*—and handed it over. She'd defined herself by that apron. She'd been proud of that uniform and what she'd managed to accomplish in her mother's memory. Now, she suddenly felt naked. Her breath hitched in her throat, and a sob threatened to break over her as Mrs. Hunter put the letter and five shillings in her hand.

Frances refused to humiliate herself. Unsteadily, she rushed to the door, only to run headlong into Kaye.

Her best friend's usual bright smile fell instantly. "Frannie, what's wrong?"

"I—" The vowel came out as part of a sob, and Frances closed her mouth with a snap. For good measure, she covered it with her hand. Her breathing stuttered through her nostrils in a series of uncontrollable, loud, wet sniffs.

"Miss Thorne is no longer employed by the agency. Miss North, please allow her a small amount of dignity so that she may leave. And you may begin your work," Mrs. Hunter said, her voice quieter now but no less resolute.

Not wanting to endanger her friend's job as well, Frances left Mrs. Hunter's, hearing the door shut behind her. There would be no going back.

Even when she reached her lodgings, Frances continued to battle the tears. She'd replayed the incident numerous times until she'd assured herself that there was nothing she could have said that might have persuaded Mrs. Hunter to keep her.

Frances didn't worry about telling her father. Because if there was one thing Hugh Thorne was good at, it was leaving past jobs behind and believing that there was always another one waiting around the corner. She needed to hear that now more than anything.

Yet as she rounded the corner and headed toward the apartment, she saw two stocky Bow Street Runners escorting her father down the stairs. She rushed forward. A terrible sense of foreboding and déjà vu churned in her stomach. She'd witnessed this once before. "Father, what is happening?"

His skin looked sallow and sickly, like the color of the bath water after the last person in the boarding house had taken a turn. "Frannie. There's a good girl. Don't you worry. This is all a misunderstanding. They say I've collected a few unpaid debts. This will all be cleared up soon enough, I'm sure of it. A bunch of folderol over a five-pound note. Find Lucan Montwood. He'll know what to do."

She blinked, hoping this was a nightmare. That this entire morning was a nightmare. Surely, she was still abed and none of this was happening. But just in case it was, she asked, "How could *he* help? For all we know, this is his doing, or his family's doing, like the last time."

The runners passed her, keeping her father between them. He looked over his shoulder and seemed to force his lips to smile, even as his eyes filled with terror. "Not to worry, my girl. Your old da loves you. Soon enough, this will all be a memory. Montwood will find us on the right side of things."

Then he was gone. Just like that, disappearing into a waiting cart. The heavy, barred door fell into place with a harsh clank of iron.

"Miss Thorne," Mrs. Pruitt said, blocking the view of the wagon as it disappeared down the street. The older woman didn't even attempt a look of concern. Instead, she frowned and wagged her finger. "I run a respectable place, not a den of criminals. You have ten minutes to gather your things and leave before I have the runners come back for you."

Frances was too numb to feel shocked or hurt. Her mind was in a fog, where nothing connected or made sense. Still, somewhere in the soupy mire, she remembered one crucial point. "I paid our rent yesterday. You cannot force me to leave."

Mrs. Pruitt clucked her tongue and held out her stubby hand. "You paid for *last* week. Therefore, you still owe me for last night. That'll be sixpence."

This morning, Frances had planned to eat fish, potatoes, carrots, and peas, and her biggest concern had been arguing with Lucan Montwood in the market. Right now, she would give anything to go back to that moment.

Handing over the sixpence, Frances trudged up the stairs, her feet leaden. When she saw the market basket on the chest in the corner with the small bouquet of violets on top, she wanted to cry. A good cry too. A full collapse-into-a-heap-on-the-floor and wailing sort of cry.

But she did none of that. She was no longer a girl, after all. She was seven and twenty. Grown women did not have the luxury of giving in to complete terror and overwhelming misery.

Instead, she gathered her things, folding and packing as many as possible, taking extra care with the miniatures of her parents. Her sensible wardrobe was quite the asset in this circumstance. When she happened upon Lord Whitelock's card, she remembered his offer. Then, without waiting to see if Mrs. Pruitt would make good on her promise to call the runners, Frances grabbed her satchel and her basket and headed out the door in the direction of Mayfair.

Arriving at his favorite secluded spot in Hyde Park, Lucan pulled on Quicksilver's reins and dismounted. It was still early enough in the day to avoid being seen. The banks of the pond to his left were absent of nannies and their charges. Rotten Row was a good distance away. The fashionable elite, likely, were still primping in front of their bedchamber mirrors, deciding which new hat to show off today.

Leading his horse to a copse of trees, he drew a spyglass from the saddle pouch. Then, while Quicksilver munched on grass shoots, Lucan elongated the glass and turned his gaze toward Tattersall's.

In contrast to the park, Tattersall's teemed with gentlemen, milling about in a field of tailcoats and frock coats in various hues. Walking sticks pressed into the ground where Hessians plodded. And gloved hands frequently tapped the brims of top hats in greeting. The usual faces—horsemen and gamblers—were there, all vying for the chance to sniff out the new blood. Even Lucan's father, the Marquess of

Camdonbury, had made an appearance. Yet in such a crowd, it was difficult to find Whitelock.

Ever since the troubling conversation he'd had with Thorne the day before, Lucan had started to question whether there were others who might not have the highest regard for Whitelock. Luckily, after another encounter with Arthur— not surprisingly, near a confectionary—Lucan learned that Whitelock would be here this morning to bid on a pair of hunters to stock his stable in Wales. Since it was impossible to ask every one of Whitelock's acquaintances his honest opinions on Whitelock's character, Lucan decided to observe from a distance in the hope that an involuntary action would reveal even the smallest amount of animosity toward the viscount. If he could find a single person who'd talk, then perhaps Whitelock wouldn't be the only one holding all the cards.

Lucan appraised his father's appearance, noting the graying of his dark hair, the ruddy color of his nose, and the paunch of his belly, pushing at the buttons of a white-and-silver striped waistcoat. Perhaps he'd eaten too many glazed buns over the years. He walked with a cane as well, leaning heavily upon it. Lucan stared at the gloved hand curved around the silver crutch, certain that not many would believe the man capable of such violence. His father had always hidden his sadistic predilections well. In fact, it was in his nature to boast about good deeds, while casting the blame on others.

"Look at what you've brought on yourself," he'd bellowed, standing over a nine-year-old Lucan in a heap on the floor of the Great Hall. *"I've been generous with you. Do you think my own father ever allowed me to leave his presence with a mere*

*scratch on my lip? And you know what he earned from me in
return? A cold grave. You should be thanking me, ingrate."*

Ignorant, frightened child that he was, Lucan *had* thanked
his father that day. It had made him ill to utter those words to
a man he despised, and when alone in his room, he'd vowed
never to do so again.

Shrugging off the memory, Lucan adjusted the glass for
a broader picture. Baron Clivedale, the family physician,
crossed paths with the marquess but walked on without any
acknowledgment. Both men looked away quickly, as if they'd
never met. Which was strange, considering how Clivedale
hadn't once balked at the acquaintance when he'd come to
Camdonbury Place over the years. He was even the one who'd
examined Lucan's mother after her fatal "fall" and assured
the magistrate that there was nothing suspicious, despite
what Lucan had claimed.

Clivedale continued in the opposite direction but then
hesitated on the balls of his feet, turning his head. For an
instant, he went still before he pivoted slightly. Lucan followed his gaze and found Whitelock. Then Clivedale headed
directly toward the viscount. The men exchanged a slight
nod. Clivedale glanced from left to right in a nervous gesture. Curious, Lucan kept one eye on the baron and one on
Whitelock. The hairs on the back of his neck rose. He sensed
something was about to happen.

Clivedale retrieved a handkerchief from his breast pocket
and then stopped to cough into it. Whitelock bumped him
and then turned as if to apologize, placing a hand on the
baron's shoulder. If Lucan hadn't been schooled in the art
of sleight of hand, he might have missed the envelope that

Whitelock slipped into Clivedale's pocket, and the small leather pouch he retrieved at the same time. Anyone watching would see only the hand, reaching out to steady a coughing man, an insignificant exchange. In fewer than five seconds, both men parted like strangers.

But they weren't strangers. There were pretending. Just as Lucan's father had pretended not to know Clivedale.

Adding this peculiarity to an ever-lengthening list, Lucan's suspicions against the viscount's character escalated.

"*Why come to me and not Thorne?*"

"*I don't know Thorne.*"

Only now did Lucan realize that was the moment when he'd heard lie number one.

"*You don't know me either.*"

"*A mutual acquaintance alerted me to your plight. Instinct tells me that you would not want to allow an innocent to fall to his death.*"

Though Lucan understood that gossip spread quickly amongst the *ton*, he'd always wondered how Whitelock had arranged to have ten thousand pounds on his person only hours after Lucan had marched into the magistrate's office and declared Thorne an innocent man. The only way the viscount could have prepared his offer so soon would have been if he'd spoken to someone present that day…

The memory hit Lucan like the lash of a whip. As he was escorted out of the magistrate's office two and half years ago, he remembered being shoved past someone at the door. *Clivedale*.

But what did the physician have to do with all this?

Lucan was more puzzled than ever. The closer he looked into Whitelock's actions, the less sure of his own he became.

He'd agreed to repay ten thousand pounds to a man about whom he essentially knew nothing. And yet by all accounts, Whitelock was responsible for Lucan's two-year losing streak, but why? Why wouldn't Whitelock want Lucan to be able to pay him? What did he have to gain?

Until recently, there had never been a question of Lucan's repaying the debt. Yet earlier this year, when he'd become desperate, he'd cajoled his own friends into the bachelor's wager. Now, with both Everhart and Danvers married, Lucan needed only to wait a few months to pay off the debt. So why were those warning bells tolling in his head again? Perhaps it had something to with Miss Thorne and his need to stay away from her.

Just then, Arthur's familiar wheat-colored head appeared through the spyglass. He wove through the crowd of men more than twice his height. Out of breath, the lad stopped in front of Whitelock. After a short exchange of words, the viscount nodded. A slow, seemingly self-satisfied grin twisted his mouth as Whitelock left Tattersall's.

Lucan wondered what news Arthur could have brought that had the power to please Whitelock so. There was only one way to find out.

Frances fidgeted with the brim of the bonnet in her grasp. Having been escorted to Lord Whitelock's study some time ago, she'd worried over the same spot to the point of causing one of the woven straw pieces to come loose. Now, she focused on removing the single frayed strand without disturbing the others. It was a menial task but one that kept her mind off her worries.

Right now, she needed to fill her life with menial tasks. If Lord Whitelock did not renew his offer of employment, perhaps she could repair straw bonnets. She could set up an open-air shop in Covent Market and—

Her breath hitched suddenly. The staggered inhale came out of the blue, serving as a clear reminder that she had other matters occupying her mind, whether she wanted to dwell on them or not.

Her father had been taken away to gaol over a debt. She had no job. No home. Nothing in the world other than her satchel and a basket of violets, vegetables, and a smelly fish. The fish in question had been taken to the kitchen, where the butler had kindly offered to have it *watched over.*

Shortly after her arrival at Lord Whitelock's townhouse, a tea tray had been brought to her. The housekeeper and maids were as genial as the butler. Due to the state of Frances's nerves, however, she hadn't drunk any tea or nibbled on the assortment of pastries. Then, a quarter of an hour ago, a maid had brought in a fresh pot of tea and carried the old one away.

Not having eaten more than a few peas from the market on her way home—or more aptly, her *former home*—Frances was starting to feel the effects of anxiety roiling in her stomach. Even though she didn't feel much like eating, she was not doing herself any favors by starving.

Yet before she could pour a cup, she heard Lord Whitelock's familiar voice in the hall as he greeted the butler. "I understand we have a guest, Wimpole. And have you seen to her comfort?" There was a slight pause for the less audible, indistinct murmur of the butler's response before she heard the viscount again. "Very good."

Still worrying the brim of her bonnet, Frances faced the door. Soon enough, steady footfalls brought Lord Whitelock into view.

He smiled in his usual amiable manner, but as he drew closer, the flesh surrounding his mouth pulled into a frown. "Miss Thorne, it is a pleasure, as always, to see you; however, I note by your troubled expression that you have come for a purpose."

At his astute observation, she nodded. Inhaling a breath of resolve, she forced herself to maintain control of her hysterics. "I have, my lord. The situation I feared would happen with my employment *has* happened. I no longer work for Mrs. Hunter."

"Then you must allow me to renew my own invitation," he said, providing an acute sense of relief. "You have been invaluable to me, and I have great need of your services. My wife has not had any true companion for more than a month. She is looked after by the maids, but they have not the time to sit and read to her."

"And that is what you would have me do?" Frances asked but hesitated. Now was certainly the best time to tell him of her defects. "I must admit that my education is sorely lacking, specifically in the skills of a companion. I am fluent in neither Latin nor French. While I enjoy music, the pleasure I receive is filtered through an untrained ear. My own instruction was cut short when it became apparent that I have no musical talent. In addition, I have no artistic ability or any true appreciation, other than a rudimentary enjoyment of shapes and colors. I have never understood the meaning one is expected to derive from a painting or a sculpture."

As she spoke, Lord Whitelock's smile returned. "Nothing would give me more pleasure that to tutor you and further your education. Though I don't mean to be boastful, you'll find that my home in Lincolnshire hosts a collection of art that puts most galleries to shame. And as for your qualifications, you are desired primarily for your excellent tone and your pleasant nature. I have seen your penmanship and heard you read aloud, and I can assure you that you have already surpassed the tasks that will be put before you."

Nervous and with so much at stake, she fidgeted with the brim of the bonnet. "If you'll forgive me, my lord, I worry that reading a list of servants from a registry does not require the range of emotion that a sonnet does. I only say this because I do not want to disappoint you after you've been so generous with your offer."

"Your humility makes you even more valuable to me," he said with a slight edge of amusement, the creases around his mouth lengthening. "Of course, I would pay you handsomely. I am a generous master, but only because I value those in my employ. If you don't mind my asking, how much did you earn at Mrs. Hunter's?"

"After two and a half years, I'd begun to earn ten shillings a week."

At this, he balked. "Only ten shillings? For all the services you provided? That is unacceptable. If you'll forgive me for speaking of money—I do not wish to be vulgar—I pay my scullery maids ten shillings a week, and they have room and board as well. I hope this does not alarm you, but my wife's previous companion earned a pound a week."

A pound a week? That was unheard of! Frances felt her mouth drop open before she could collect herself. At the servant registry, she had been privy to more sensitive information, such as wages, and Lord Whitelock was renowned for his generosity, but she'd never known to what extent. He was greatly admired by servants and society alike, but now she understood why. He was more than a lord and master. He was a benefactor.

"Forgive me, Miss Thorne. You've gone pale. Where are my manners? Please, you must be exhausted from such a trying day. Take your rest while I pour you a cup of tea." Taking her elbow, he led her to a tufted chair near his desk.

Overwhelmed, she'd nearly forgotten for her training. A viscount should never pour *her* tea. "I—"

"No argument. I insist."

To argue now would seem ungrateful, not to mention insupportable behavior. Therefore, she bit her tongue and relished the feel of the soft chair beneath her. Even the furniture in his study portrayed him as a man who had the needs of others foremost on his mind. He made certain that the most comfortable chair was near his desk, so that his company would feel at ease.

"I cannot express my gratitude enough, sir," she said when he handed her the cup and saucer. Taking a sip, she cringed at the bitter taste. Obviously, the leaves had steeped too long, but she wouldn't dream of mentioning it. "There is another troubling matter of which you must be made aware. My own father, just this morning, was taken away by runners because of his debts."

Lord Whitelock was good enough not to show his surprise, just as he hadn't when she'd told him about her recent loss of employment. Not many men could be as skilled when presented with such news. Instead of gasping in shock or even arching his brows, he kept his amiable expression in place as he eased into the wing-backed chair opposite her.

Before her courage abandoned her, she continued. "I do not know the extent of his crimes, but of course I will inquire with the local magistrate later, when I visit him. Even now, I have no idea where they have taken him. I came here without thinking."

"And right you were to do so. A magistrate's office is no place for you." He steepled his fingers and glanced down at the teacup in her hand. Out of politeness, she took another sip. It was almost unbearably bitter. "Allow me to do you the favor of making the inquiries. In fact, if you would permit me, I could settle his debts."

Pay her father's debts and remove him from gaol? That would be…that would be… Well, in all honesty, that might not be the best thing to do.

She loved her father, of course, and didn't want him to suffer. However, if Lord Whitelock paid his debts, then Frances would need to repay those debts. She might very well be paying off her father's debts, in addition to any new ones he would likely incur, for the rest of her life. Of course, she would need to speak with her father to explain. "Though it pains me to say this, I could not accept such a favor. I have a firm belief that debt invites the ruin of scruples."

"I have often said as much, which is likely why I tend to err on the side generosity when it comes to those who work for me," he said, enticing her further. "I do hope that you will consider my offer. But I must warn you that since my wife has been without a companion for so long, I would require you to leave for my country estate at first light tomorrow. Under your particular circumstances, I understand if you would prefer to stay in town and remain close to your father…"

In other words, she could either accept his offer or choose to repair bonnets in Covent Garden.

Could she leave London tomorrow when she'd lived here all her life? Such a change would be drastic. She wasn't certain she could take much more change right now. Yet leaving for Lincolnshire—where she would earn *a pound per week!*— was the far more sensible decision. With that, she could pay off her father's debt in little over a month.

Frances opened her mouth to accept but was surprised by a yawn instead. "*Oh!* Forgive me," she said, thoroughly embarrassed. "I meant to express my gratitude once more but…I suppose I am more tired than I imagined." She tried again. "Please know that I am both honored to have been selected and delighted to accept the position as Lady Whitelock's companion."

Lord Whitelock glanced again at her teacup as she stifled another yawn. He seemed pleased by her answer in the way that he grinned. "You have eased my burden a great deal, Miss Thorne."

Reluctantly, she held her breath and took another sip, then because he appeared to be waiting for her to finish the brew, she did. But wished she hadn't because she instantly felt lightheaded. She leaned back against the seat to stop the dizziness.

"If you will permit me, I'll ring for Myrtle to show you to a room so that you may rest before dinner. In the meantime, I will inquire after your father on your behalf." Gentleman that he was, Lord Whitelock displayed no alarm at seeing her tired. Instead, he stood and walked to the bell pull.

After a frenzied few hours, Lucan paid the Fleet Prison gaoler two shillings to be led down to Hugh Thorne's cell.

The walls of the dank, narrow passages leaned inward, giving the impression of closing in bit by bit. Scant light filtered in through the high cell windows on the opposite wall, and no one had bothered to light the torches in the afternoon. Human waste ripened the air, the scent even more foul when accompanied by the echoes of sobs all around him. There was, however, a cool breeze, though its origins were undetermined. For all Lucan knew, it was a specter, silently roaming the halls of a more permanent prison.

The gaoler opened the door. Thorne sat on the floor in one corner, his chamber pot in the other. The sour stench of bile and vomit wafted through the cell.

Thorne lifted his head slowly, recognition bringing a moist sheen to his dark eyes. "You've come. I knew you would, my boy. I knew it wouldn't be long before you learned all, in that mysterious way you glean all the secrets you unearth."

"Only moments ago," Lucan answered, thinking back to the past hours' nightmare.

From Hyde Park, he'd traveled past Mrs. Hunter's shop. On the street there, he'd heard outraged whispers from a gathering of lady's maids on the pavement, gossiping about Miss Thorne's dismissal. Immediately, he rode to Mrs. Pruitt's rooming house, only to overhear the landlady's window-to-window conversation with Mrs. Bayer about the horror of having the runners appear at her door to cart Thorne away. *"It forced me to toss his daughter out on the street for the sake of decency."*

Decency? Lucan had been tempted to ask the old crow what was decent about throwing an innocent woman to the wolves. But he hadn't the time. He had to find Miss Thorne before she made up her mind to go to Whitelock for help.

Yet he'd been too late. According to Arthur, she was at Whitelock's townhouse now. Lucan would have to find a way to speak to her without risking the dissolution of his agreement with Whitelock.

"I would have come sooner. I would have stopped this," Lucan said to Thorne.

"Not this time, I'm afraid."

Lucan pinched the bridge of his nose. He'd been hoping this was a mistake. Hoping that Thorne would tell him that he'd been wrongly imprisoned again. Yet for months, Lucan had seen a drastic decline in Thorne. No matter how hard Lucan had tried to keep him afloat, Thorne had been determined to go under. "What happened? Tell me."

Thorne turned his hands over and stared at them, the same way he had in the carriage the day before. "It was at the tables at Lord Rowland's club. I came up short. He offered a loan. I thought the next hand would surely win. Or the next. Or…" His hands dropped into his lap and he looked up. "I couldn't repay it."

That's why Lucan had found him in a gaming hell in the middle of the day. "How deep are you?"

"One or two hundred pounds."

"Which is it?"

Thorne swallowed. "Two."

Bugger. "I don't have that sum right now, but I can get it."

"I don't want you to," Thorne said, shaking his head firmly. Slowly, he stood. "I've earned my place here. Not only by my unpaid debts but my despicable thievery." He rubbed the upraised flesh over his thumb where a T had been branded years ago. "I've earned this mark. I wasn't a thief when they gave it to me, but I am now. I don't know what kind of man I am anymore. I stole from my own daughter. She goes without food because of me. We've moved seven times over because of me."

"I can't leave you in here." It would be like letting the Marquess of Camdonbury win after all. "We'll find a place for you. A good job—"

"No. I deserve this cell," Thorne said firmly and then quietly added, "I…I *need* this cell."

Lucan was starting to lose his temper. He jabbed a fist into the air toward the tiny window. "Think of your daughter. She is out there right now"—jobless, homeless, and looking to Whitelock as if he were a white knight—"searching for the means to set you free."

"Stop her. Explain my mistakes. Tell her that I need time. But I don't want her to see me in here. She's seen me as a broken, feeble man for far too long." Thorne stepped forward, his expression earnest and not solely of a man wallowing in self-pity. "Take care of her. Watch over her. Although, I have a feeling you already do, in that mysterious way of yours. I still don't understand your methods."

Lucan lowered his hand to his side, his fist still clenched. "I listen, that is all."

"*I* should have listened," Thorne answered with a solemn nod.

This wasn't right. It went against everything inside of him to leave Thorne here, knowing that Frances was out there, suffering because of it. A woman as strong, bold, and independent as Frances Thorne ought to have security in the knowledge of her father's welfare. In Lucan's opinion, she deserved much more. Yet there was another part of him that believed in justice, and if Thorne was guilty—*because* Thorne was guilty—he deserved to be left here. For a time.

"I will return in a week."

Lucan would continue to watch over Miss Thorne. Not because he'd been asked to but because he wanted to…though he didn't bother to question his own reasons at the moment.

"No. Not even in a month. Give me"—Thorne drew in a breath—"*three* months, and then I should be ready to repay the debts I'll owe you."

Three months, then. During that time, Lucan would keep Miss Thorne safe. Even if she fought him every step of the way. "You have my word."

CHAPTER SEVEN

Lucan reached Mayfair early the following morning. At this time of day, only servants were about. In his usual method of gaining information, he listened carefully to gossip, keeping Quicksilver at a slow trot.

It wasn't long before he spotted a pair of maids carrying empty baskets and heading toward the market.

"It's a shame that Miss Thorne had to leave so soon," one said. "When I heard that his lordship hired her, I'd hoped for some of her lessons."

Miss Thorne was gone from London already? Lucan stiffened, and the action caused Quicksilver to stop. He dismounted and pretended to check his horse's flank as the maids passed by.

"Aye. Me as well," the other maid said. "But his lordship didn't want her ladyship to be without a companion any longer. I confess, the way he dotes on her ladyship almost makes me jealous. He is a very fine gentleman."

The maids were falling out of earshot. All Lucan heard in conclusion was a series of giggles. But the most important matter was that he was already too late to speak privately to Miss Thorne. Now, he would have to find her carriage on the road. He was little prepared for a journey, but it didn't matter. He would go now, without delay.

Hours later, Lucan spotted Miss Thorne's carriage outside of London. The curricle was not one of Whitelock's finest, which was likely because the viscount would travel behind her by a day or two. This left Miss Thorne to make the journey alone but gave Lucan hope of gaining the opportunity to speak with her about his suspicions without alerting the viscount.

Unfortunately, the first day offered no opportunity. The driver pushed the team more than fifty miles before the first stop. Lucan had been forced to slow and give Quicksilver a rest. By the time Lucan had arrived at the inn, it was only hours before dawn, barely enough time to feed his horse and brush him down. Then, the next morning, Whitelock's carriage had set off as the first rays of light blazed a thin line along the horizon.

After settling his account at the inn, the journey continued similarly, with Lucan trailing behind. It gave him time to think about the events of the past few days as if they were a chess game. All the pawns were gradually falling, one by one. Thorne was in prison due to a debt with Rowland, who was friends with Whitelock. Miss Thorne had lost her employment within the same week that Whitelock had offered her a position. And now, to Lucan, it felt as if the queen were exposed to the bishop.

As luck would have it, Lucan managed to catch up with the carriage as it arrived at the southern border of Lincolnshire, breaking the final night before the end of the journey. Unfortunately, the inn was full, and Miss Thorne had been forced to share a room with a pair of debutantes who were traveling toward Northumberland, again leaving Lucan without a chance to speak with her.

Then, good fortune finally smiled on him when he spotted none other than Arthur Momper waiting outside the tack room. The lad started chatting about his journey, how well he fetched the step for Miss Thorne, how Burt, Whitelock's driver, had let him manage the reins, and how—while Burt was having a pint—he was in charge of seeing to the horses. The lad beamed with pride.

As for Lucan, a new plan of action suddenly formed in mind. He would need to send a missive ahead to Valentine, the butler of Fallow Hall, in order to pull it off. But it was time to resort to drastic measures.

"Arthur, just how good are you at handling the reins?"

Leaving London, when her father was in Fleet, was the hardest thing Frances had ever done. Each time she thought of him there, all alone, she wanted to cry. But the more she thought about it, the more she wondered if *all* the tears were for him.

Even though Frances didn't think she was a selfish person, she realized that some of those tears were for herself. She was frightened but also filled with guilt for moving forward. How could she start anew before she'd properly mourned the life she'd had up to this point? And only a horrible daughter would feel the smallest amount of excitement about her new position as a paid companion! Yet a fair amount of trepidation lingered within her as well. So at least in that, she could forgive the inconsiderate nature of the thoughts that were not solely concerned for her father.

Before Frances left London, Lord Whitelock, true to his word, had made inquiries, and Frances learned where her father was being held. Unfortunately, she'd slept for the remainder of the day after she'd accepted his lordship's offer for employment. She'd never experienced such exhaustion. It was rather alarming. Apparently, she'd slept so soundly that she hadn't even removed her shoes. Upon waking, she'd felt peculiarly disoriented, her thoughts muddled. So much so, in fact, that she was not able to visit her father in prison before leaving. When she'd voiced her concerns, however, Lord Whitelock had informed her that her father had not wanted her to see him in a place such as that, and that he was relieved she was being well looked after.

That message sounded like something her father *could* say, she supposed. Yet she'd expected him to renew his request for her to seek out Lucan Montwood's help. Though, perhaps, that was not a message he'd wished to relay through Lord Whitelock. Therefore, she'd written to her father straightaway, informing him of her new employment and letting him know that she would be able to pay off his five-pound debt in five weeks. The viscount had even offered to post the letter for her. She wrote a missive to Kaye as well, letting her know not to worry.

That was four days ago, and now Frances was traveling to Lincolnshire. As the carriage slowed, she felt a tremor of apprehension. What if Lady Whitelock did not like her?

Moments away from beginning her new position, Frances peered through the window. The carriage approached a gray stone manor. Though, when the sun peered out from behind the clouds, the façade brightened, almost gleaming like silver. It was a vast, noble estate, and elegant in its monochromatic design. A large black lacquered door graced the front. There was no busy ornamentation, only high, sturdy walls, dotted with windows encased in a paler shade of gray. To her, the house emitted confidence and security, a haven from her worries. She liked it very much and hoped to remain here for many years to come.

Before the carriage came to a full stop, the door opened and through it rushed a large gray beast of a dog that might have blended in with the stone if not for his constant motion. He darted around the carriage, yawping excitedly, short ears flapping against the side of his head, and a skinny, curved tail wagging madly. Curious, she leaned closer to the window. She'd never seen such a large dog this close. He was the size of a pony, only much sleeker.

Then, abruptly, the dog stopped. With a quirk of his head, he stared up toward the driver's perch and, after a final *woof*, summarily sat down on his hind legs and waited.

A footman in dark livery came forward. A stern-faced man in similar attire stood to the side of the open doorway. She took the older man for the butler and was eager to make his acquaintance, as well as the housekeeper's. Frances would be working closely with them for the term of her employment.

Minding her foot on the step, Frances exited the carriage with all her earthly possessions in her grasp. She'd left the basket of food at Lord Whitelock's townhouse. But that was *after* she'd removed the violets and the booklet. She didn't know why she'd kept Lucan Montwood's flowers or pressed them in between the flats behind the miniatures of her parents. Perhaps she'd only thought to take a piece of London with her.

"Miss Thorne," the older gentleman said, drawing her attention. He bowed. "I've been instructed to escort you to the study."

"Thank you, Mr...."

"Valentine, miss."

Crossing the threshold, a large hall awaited. The stone walls resembled the exterior. On the far side, a colorful tapestry brightened the space, while overhead, a rather robust iron chandelier hung. The masculine simplicity of this manor appealed to her, but it also surprised her. To her, Lord Whitelock had seemed a much more refined, particular type of man. His townhouse was quite ornate, with curving sculptures, upholstered furnishings, and all manner of softness. This was the antithesis of his house in town. Since his wife resided here, Frances had thought the opposite would have been true.

Valentine relieved her of her satchel, her gloves, and her hat. The once-frayed straw brim was now smooth, since she'd had ample time on her journey to repair it.

Reaching the study, she noted the inviting warm colors—the brown leather-upholstered chairs, a deep burgundy and blue woven rug, the polished wood desk near the window, burgundy brocade curtains, and a hearth on the far wall large enough to fit the pallet she'd slept on at Mrs. Pruitt's boardinghouse.

"His lordship will be with you shortly," Valentine said before he left the room.

Lord Whitelock was here already? The viscount had explained that he would follow in a few days. But perhaps he'd only wanted to give her time to travel alone and sort out her thoughts instead. If so, it was quite considerate of him. Now that he was here, he would likely make the introduction to his wife himself.

Frances moved closer to the desk. A blank page lay on the surface with a quill resting in a stand beside a pot of uncapped ink, as if prepared to attend to business matters. Out of the corner of her eye, she saw a shadow cross the study door and automatically turned, expecting to see Lord Whitelock.

Yet it wasn't the viscount at all. It was Lucan Montwood.

She gasped. "What are *you* doing here?"

"I live here, Miss Thorne." Lifting one hand in an absent wave, he moved into the room. Wearing a hunter green tailcoat over a gold waistcoat and a pair of snug, buttery breeches, his self-assured gait bordered on brazen.

She tried not to notice the way each step seemed to accentuate every shift and clench of his muscles. Her throat went impossibly dry. She took a moment to swallow and to lift her gaze. "You live here?"

That hand—those long fingers—stroked the line of his jaw as one corner of his mouth curled up in a smirk. "I'm afraid that I must admit to subterfuge. You see, this is Fallow Hall, *not* Whitelock's residence. His estate is a few miles further north."

The words registered slowly. No wonder this place looked nothing like Lord Whitelock would live here.

Yet, she could easily imagine Lucan here.

"You've abducted me?" A pulse fluttered at her throat. It came from fear, of course, and alarm. It most certainly did not flutter out of a misguided wanton thrill. At her age, she knew better. Or rather, she *should* know better.

That grin remained unchanged, as if he could read her thoughts. "Not at all. Rest assured, you are free to leave here at any time—"

"Then I will leave at once."

"As soon as you've heard my warning."

It did not take long for a wave of exasperation to fill her and then exit her lungs on a sigh. "This is in regard to Lord Whitelock again. Will you ever tire of this subject? You have already said that you believe him to be a snake in disguise. I have already said that I don't agree. There is nothing more to say unless you have proof."

"And yet you require no proof to hold ill will against me," he challenged with a lift of his brow. "You have damned me with the same swift judgment that you have elevated Whitelock to sainthood."

What rubbish. "I did not set out to find the good in his lordship. The fact of his goodness came to me naturally, by way of his reputation. Even his servants cannot praise him enough. They are forever grateful for his benevolence. And I can find no fault in a man who would offer a position to a woman who'd been fired by her former employer and whose own father was taken to gaol."

"Perhaps he wants your gratitude," Lucan said, his tone edged with warning as he prowled nearer. "This entire series of events that has put you within his reach reeks of manipulation. You are too sensible to ignore how conveniently these circumstances have turned out in his favor."

"Yet I suppose I'm meant to ignore the *convenience* in which you've abducted me?"

He laughed. The low, alluring sound had no place in the light of day. It belonged to the shadows that lurked in dark alcoves and to the secret desires that a woman of seven and twenty never dare reveal.

"It was damnably hard to get you here," he said with such arrogance that she was assured her desires would remain secret forever. "You have no idea how much liquor Whitelock's driver can hold. It took an age before he was deep in his cups."

Incredulous, she shook her head. "Are you blind to your own manipulations? It has not escaped my notice that you reacted *without* surprise to the news of my recent events. I can only assume that you are also aware of my father's current predicament."

"I have been to Fleet to see him." Lucan's expression lost all humor. "He has asked me to watch over you. So that is what I am doing."

What a bold liar Lucan was—and looking her in the eye all the while, no less. "*If that is true,*" she scoffed, "you then interpreted his request as *'Please, sir, abduct my daughter'*? I find it more likely that he would have asked you to pay his debts to gain his freedom."

"He declined my offer."

She let out a laugh. "That is highly suspect. I do not think you are speaking a single word of truth."

"You are putting your faith in the wrong man." Something akin to irritation flashed in his gaze, like a warning shot. He took another step. "Perhaps those spectacles require new lenses. They certainly aren't aiding your sight."

"I wear these spectacles for reading, I'll have you know. Otherwise, my vision is fine," she countered, ignoring the heady static charge in the air between them. "I prefer to wear them instead of risking their misplacement."

"You wear them like a shield of armor."

The man irked her to no end. "Preposterous. I've no need for a shield of any sort. I cannot help it if you are intimidated by my spectacles *and* by my ability to see right through you."

He stepped even closer. An unknown force, hot and barely leashed, crackled in the ever-shrinking space. She watched as he slid the blank parchment toward him before withdrawing the quill from the stand. Ignoring her, he dipped the end into the ink and wrote something on the page.

Undeterred, she continued her harangue. "Though you may doubt it, I can spot those *snakes*—as you like to refer to members of your own sex—quite easily. I can come to an understanding of a man's character within moments of introduction. I am even able to anticipate"—Lucan handed the parchment to her. She accepted it and absently scanned the page—"his actions."

Suddenly, she stopped and read it again. *"As soon as you've finished reading this, I am going to kiss you."*

While she was still blinking at the words, Lucan claimed her mouth. The parchment crinkled. She heard an indrawn breath but wasn't sure if it was hers or his. All she knew was that the first press of his lips sent a ripple through her—her body clenching on a sigh of rapture as if she'd been waiting a lifetime for this. Her eyes closed.

This was no tentative kiss meant to test her response. Lucan did not ease away to beg her forgiveness. Nor did he ask her permission to continue. He was confident and sure. His lips firm but not hard. Coaxing but not demanding. He took command but yielded. It was exactly the way she'd always wanted to be kissed. It was as if this kiss were designed solely for her pleasure.

Somewhere along the way, his hand came up to cradle her jaw, and he stepped closer. Although, perhaps he'd done that first...She could hardly think straight at the moment. His scent filled her lungs, transporting her to a dewy midnight hour. She breathed him in deeper, opening her mouth to draw air as well. And then she tasted him on her tongue. His flavor was earthy and dark—a seductive elixir.

She'd never *tasted* a man before. Never slipped her tongue into a man's mouth. She'd never imagined wanting to. But the urge broke over her so suddenly that she was already engaging in the act before questioning it.

Lucan's mouth slanted, his flesh sliding along hers, stroking the sensitive inner walls of her mouth. *Oh yes*, her body sighed again. He made her legs tremble. Her hand slipped to his shoulder for support but somehow ended up curling around the back of his neck, pulling him closer. The kiss altered, turned hungry. She hadn't eaten since early this morning, so perhaps that was the reason. But she couldn't seem to stop searching for sustenance from him.

A low, growling sound rose up from his throat. Now, both of his hands held her face. He stepped between her legs, urging her bottom against the desk. Her trembling legs now ached, throbbing at the apex where they merged at her sex.

She felt empty there, as if a part of her had gone missing, and she needed it returned in order to stop the insistent, anxious beat of her pulse. Instinctively, she arched against him—

Then, just as suddenly as the kiss had begun, it ended.

Abruptly, Lucan took a step back and lowered his hands. She nearly lost her balance. He reached out to steady her with a hand at her elbow but nothing more intimate than that. She tried to read his expression, but for some reason she couldn't see him quite clearly. That was when she realized her lenses were fogged, her spectacles askew. She'd forgotten about the parchment in her grasp as well. Now, it was completely crumpled.

Removing her glasses, she faced the desk and laid the paper down before she rubbed her lenses with a corner of her shawl. She was barely able to catch her breath, and his labored struggle told her that she wasn't alone. She didn't know what to make of it. Any of it.

Frances replaced her spectacles. Glancing down at those words, she felt that ripple cascade through her once more. She had no idea what to say after experiencing a kiss like that. "You have exceptional…penmanship." *And the ability to scatter my wits completely.*

Lucan stood beside the desk, staring at Miss Thorne's profile. *What* had happened?

He'd wanted to prove that she might not be as adept at anticipating a man's actions or motives as she'd assumed. He'd meant to make a point by issuing an example. Instead, *he* was the one reeling from the lesson.

He'd lost control. Or nearly had.

Frances Thorne had surprised him. And he didn't particularly care for surprises.

He felt as if he'd taken a bite of that forbidden glazed bun. No, not just a bite. He felt as if he'd devoured the entire pastry. And now he wanted to lick his fingers to find any remnants. Wait…had she said something about *penmanship*?

Apparently, she wasn't going to mention the kiss or berate him for his advances. Which was fine with him. They could pretend it never happened. Or at least she could. *He* couldn't.

When he'd first begun to imagine what it would be like to kiss her—and he had to admit it had happened more often than not—he'd always thought of her as tightly wound, like a knot that he was meant to unravel. He'd even been prepared to take his time, to work his way beyond her stuffy exterior and those damned erotic spectacles. Yet in the end, it was she who'd undone him.

Penmanship? He nearly laughed. *That* was the most pressing matter on her mind? He was still trying to quiet the beast she'd awakened. The beast that cared little for control and only wanted another taste…

Now, as she started to smooth out the wrinkles of the parchment, he reached out and snatched the page from her. Then he stalked across the room to throw it in the fire. Unfortunately, there was no fire. The wadded-up ball merely pinged off the empty grate and sat there. It was far too anticlimactic. He needed to see that damnable page burn to ash.

"How did you convince the driver to bring me here?"

"*I* was your driver, Miss Thorne. Or at least, I took your driver's place in Stampton when he became too inebriated to continue."

Her slender brows furrowed. "A messenger at the inn informed me that Lord Whitelock's carriage required repairs."

"I needed a way to explain the change in carriages to avoid suspicion," he said with a swipe of his hand through the air. "Your cleverness forced my actions."

Lucan had made certain the man was foxed. Then, to lessen any ill will—should they cross paths again—he'd introduced the driver to the insatiable Nina. She'd been seeking bedsport with Lucan, but this time he'd not been tempted by her charms. Perhaps because she wore no spectacles, and her lips hid no overbite. Strangely, he found that combination entirely too tempting.

"That is right. You admitted to *forcing* a man to drink."

Strangely, she sounded more curious and less outraged than he'd expected. The Miss Thorne he knew would sooner sting him with her harsh judgments than bother to ask questions. She would stare him down with a flinty gaze so cold, he would believe that the color of her irises resembled the smoke rising from a pistol after a lethal shot. Instead, her irises resembled the gray, swirling smoke of a bedside candle being blown out. And when she glanced down to his mouth, it took all of his might to keep his distance.

"When a man has no control over his own actions, the smallest amount of persuasion is all it takes." They were speaking of the driver, of course, yet Lucan let his own gaze drift to her mouth to serve as a warning. "Do not worry for the driver's welfare, however. I sent him in Whitelock's carriage, albeit marginally delayed from your departure. In the event that you do not heed my warning, I wanted time enough for you not to worry about losing your position.

The driver should arrive at the manor in time to awaken and wonder how he'd reached his destination." Lucan had left Arthur Momper in charge. The lad assured him that he could hold the reins and reach the brake well enough to see them safely back.

"Such lengths for a whim…" She adjusted her spectacles, though her eyes shifted down to his mouth once more. Then, clearing her throat, she straightened her shoulders and faced him head-on. "Foolishly, I thought I'd arrived at what would be my home, when all along I am still miles away from it."

Lucan breathed a sigh of relief when the less approachable Miss Thorne he knew started to come forth. Wanting to increase her ire out of pure necessity and self-preservation, he threw in an offer he knew she wouldn't accept *and* that she would find offensive. "You are more than welcome to stay here at Fallow Hall with me…and my friends."

Her eyes turned flinty. "You are already going back on your word. At first, you said that I was free to leave once I heard your warning. So far, you have not convinced me of Lord Whitelock's deception. I find nothing suspect in his actions. Yours, however, are not so easily dismissed."

Was she finally going to berate him for the kiss? He opened his hands in a shrug, daring her to begin. Honestly, he was waiting for the opportunity to state that it was he, and not she, who had ended the kiss.

"You said my father did not want you to pay his debts," she said instead, disappointing him.

However, now that they were returning to the original reason for his bringing her to Fallow Hall, he needed to take care. What he had to tell her would be difficult to hear.

"Your father has asked that I leave him in Fleet for three months," Lucan said quietly and read surprise and disbelief in her expression. "He was sensible enough to know that if I'd paid his debts at that moment, he would only incur more. And he was sickened by his own behavior toward you, especially that he stole from you."

She gasped. "How could you know—"

Lucan did not press his point. There was no victory in her realizing that he spoke the truth. More than anything, he wished the circumstances in her life were different, simpler. "Thorne wants to be a more deserving father to you. He's a good man who's lost his way, that is all."

Lucan had lost his way once, shortly after the news of his mother's death reached him. Everhart and Danvers, being the decent fellows that they were, had taken him to a house of ill repute to drown his sorrows, amongst other things. An unsavory man named Richard Blight had been the proprietor at the time. The man enjoyed the drink he supplied, in addition to the favors of the women in his employ. He also used his fists in a manner that was far too familiar to Lucan.

Watching Blight raise his hand to a woman cowering at his feet had made Lucan lose his mind. He hadn't even known what had come over him, until Everhart and Danvers had pulled him off the man. Lucan was fortunate that they'd acted quickly. Blight had only suffered a few cuts on his face, a broken nose, and a few more missing teeth. But the truth was, Lucan could have killed him without needing to stop for a breath. It would have been easy. He'd kept seeing his father's face. Kept hearing his mother's whimpers. That sickening thud of her head hitting the floor.

So yes, he'd lost his way once. But he would never lose control like that again. He wasn't his father. Even so, because of that day, Lucan would never marry. Not with that monster lurking inside of him.

"Now is the moment where I usually issue a remark casting the blame for my father's circumstances on your family, for what your father did—"

"My father," Lucan interrupted with more vehemence than he cared to reveal. In prior encounters, he'd merely feigned a smile at her reminders, allowing her to believe what she chose. Now, with all that was at stake for her own welfare, he didn't want to be seen as the villain. He couldn't afford to have her believe he was the same type of cruel man. "Not me."

She lowered her gaze to the floor between them and drew in a breath. "True enough. And now it seems like the time to mention that my father had started to lose his way after my mother died. Not in the same manner he has of late, of course. He was a good steward, and we had a nice home. I had tutors and clothes. We even had a cook. But my father became absent, even when he came home at the end of the day."

"Losing your mother was hard for you both, I imagine," he said, feeling a connection between them.

Miss Thorne touched the brooch that held the ends of her shawl in place. "The illness took her far too quickly. Yet saying that makes me sound unforgivably selfish, doesn't it? I should be thankful that she did not suffer long. And I am...but had I known that our time was so limited, I would have done things differently. I wouldn't have left her side for an instant. I would have asked her thousands of questions. Memorized the sound of her voice…" Her words drifted off, and she cleared her throat once more. "Forgive me. You were telling me about my father. I haven't a clue as to why I began talking about my mother instead. I don't normally talk about her."

"Would you like to talk about her?" Listening just now, Lucan almost admitted to having had those same thoughts about his own mother and all the things he would change if he could.

Miss Thorne stared at him for a moment before turning away, issuing an awkward laugh, as if uncomfortable. "I almost believe you are in earnest, my lord."

"*My lord?*" Now it was his turn to laugh, albeit wryly. "You would be so formal, even now?"

She found the stopper for the ink and secured it in place. "Especially now."

"Good," he said with a nod. The last thing he needed was for her to make it easy for him to want another taste. "Now, returning to what I was saying about Whitelock."

"If you must," she grumbled. "But since you allotted me a small amount of time before I should be missed, would it be a terrible bother if I suffered through another one of your diatribes *after* a cup of tea and perhaps a small crust of bread? Or am I to be forced into submission by starvation?"

He enjoyed her wicked wit almost as much as he enjoyed steaming up her spectacles. "A choice between the two is a difficult one, indeed, but I prefer willing participants."

By the faint tinge to her cheeks, she understood his double meaning. Unfortunately, whatever response she would have made was left unsaid because in the next instant, he needed to warn her that they were about to have visitors.

Chapter Eight

"Do you like dogs, Miss Thorne?"

Puzzled by the sudden changes of their conversation, from her parents, to food, and then to domestic animals, Frances took a small moment to answer Lucan. "I do. In fact, I had a dog when I was much younger. Petunia Wrigglebottom was her name."

Though why she admitted the last embarrassing tidbit, she wasn't sure. In fact, she was speaking more freely than she ever did. It was almost as if his kiss had unraveled her as much as it had rattled her.

"Not simply Petunia?" He didn't bother to hide his amusement.

Frances pretended that the display of his dimple had no effect on her whatsoever. "I believe that any dog of distinction deserves at least two names."

His grin broadened, though why, she could not guess. "Earlier, when you were exiting the carriage, I wasn't sure if you would be afraid of the *Beast of Fallow Hall*, so I asked him to behave. Now, however, I'm certain he will want to make a proper introduction."

In the next instant, the large gray dog that she'd seen when she first arrived came bounding into the study, ears and tongue flapping and heading directly toward her. Since his head was as high as her elbow, and he likely weighed as much as she did, Frances doubted she would be standing for much longer. She braced herself, feet apart, but then Lucan stepped between them.

"I still expect you to be a gentleman," he warned, lowering down to his haunches to pet the beast, who in turn answered with a *woof* before licking the side of Lucan's face.

The low, robust laugh that followed surprised Frances. This was not the practiced laugh of a charmer or even the seductive laugh from moments ago. This was unguarded. She'd noticed how flawlessly he controlled his actions. He rarely revealed the inner workings of the man behind those amber eyes, like a true gambler. Which was the reason she'd never trusted him.

But hearing his laugh just now filled her with the peculiar impulse to know more about him. More than the fact that he kissed remarkably well.

The sound of feminine voices broke through her thoughts. Lucan stood. The tails of his coat fell into place. Only then did she realize she'd been staring quite fixedly at the strong lines of his shoulders, the narrowness of his hips, and his backside. Again.

Keeping a hand draped over the dog's scruff, he gently thrummed his fingers in time with ticking clock stand in the corner. "Miss Thorne, I do not mean to alarm you, but you are about to meet two of the most determined young women of my acquaintance."

Curious, her gaze locked on the open doorway. "Determined for what, precisely?"

"To see me married by year's end." He said the words with such gravity that a streak of alarm did indeed shoot through her. "They will see you here and begin plotting instantly, *especially* if you continue to ogle my person when my back is turned."

She started. There was no way he could have known—but then she noticed the reflective glass in the door of the clock stand and felt her cheeks betray her. "I was not *ogling* you. Not at all. You have a...a spot on your coat, and I was debating whether or not to tell you."

"Is it a large spot or a small spot?" He grinned.

She narrowed her eyes, feeling the tips of her lashes brush against her lenses. "Hideously large, like your ego."

"There. That is a better," he said, his voice low as the sound of conversation in the hall approached. "Keep in mind how much you despise me, and you will save us both."

The task would not be difficult in the least.

Two women stopped abruptly in the doorway and looked from her to Lucan before the weighted sound of a single syllable escaped them both. "*Oh.*"

They stood there for an instant before crossing the threshold. They were of the same height but different in figure and coloring. The first woman had hair the color of honey and a more slender figure, albeit with a slight rounding at her middle, where she rested a hand. The second was paler, her figure more voluptuous, and her eyes a bright, captivating blue. She spoke first.

"Montwood, you have returned." She beamed. "I'd worried that the diversion of London would keep you away."

This woman's evident fondness for Lucan caused a strange, dark stirring inside Frances for which she could not account.

"And miss an opportunity to gloat? I think not. There will be time enough for that later, however. For now, I would like to make an introduction." He glanced at Frances. Then his brows drew together in apparent puzzlement as if he were attempting to read her thoughts.

She assured herself that he couldn't.

"Calliope, Hedley, this is Miss Thorne, lately of London and new resident of Lincolnshire," he continued, studying her. "Miss Thorne, allow me to introduce Lady Everhart and *Mrs.* Danvers."

Frances exhaled. That dark stirring subsided as if it were nothing more than a breath waiting for release. She decided that was precisely what it had been. She also decided to ignore Lucan's uncalled for smirk.

Not only that, but his introduction intimated that they were all part of the gentry or aristocracy and that she belonged here, amongst them. While at one time that might have been the case, Frances did not want to deceive anyone. Her circumstances were much different now. Therefore, she dipped into a proper curtsy. "Lady Everhart—"

The one with the darker shade of hair lifted the hand hovering over her middle and smiled. "Call me Calliope, please."

"And you must call me Hedley," said the woman with the apparent attachment to Lucan. "Although I must admit,

I rather enjoy hearing the special emphasis that Montwood placed on *Mrs.* Danvers."

Ah, so Frances wasn't the only one who'd noticed.

Just then a man with dark, wavy hair and rakishly cut side whiskers appeared in the doorway. "And *Mrs. Danvers* you shall always be, sweeting," he said, his eyes locking on Hedley's as if there was no one else in the room.

Another gentleman followed closely, carrying a large basket. He was just as handsome as the first, but with pale, ash blond hair and an intense gaze that sought out Calliope, leaving no doubt that he was Lord Everhart.

Lucan politely cleared his throat before introducing her once more. Like their wives, the gentlemen gave her leave to address them with familiarity, as Everhart and Danvers. When she was younger and her father had worked for the Marquess of Camdonbury, Lucan had never offered a specific address for her use. He'd merely stated that she could address him in a manner of her choosing. Since *Montwood* had seemed too friendly, she'd settled on *my lord* and *sir*, as was proper and in no way intimated more than a mere acquaintance.

She would feel better if she could adhere to a more proper way of addressing his friends, as well, but to go against their wishes would be insupportable. Therefore, she gave them leave to call her by her given name, if they so desired.

The mystery of who she was and how she came to be here at Fallow Hall hung in the awkward silence that followed. Should she simply blurt out that she was to be the companion to Lady Whitelock?

"Lately of London?" Calliope asked, saving Frances the bother of blurting. "Then you must have traveled…this morning?"

"Yes, from the inn at Stampton."

Calliope nodded. "Are you famished? Traveling always increases my appetite. Though lately, I find that is the case whether I'm traveling or not." She laughed as her hand strayed to her middle once more. Then, slipping down onto one cushion of the sofa, she patted the place beside her in invitation.

Frances moved away from the desk. After the first step, a peculiar sense of separation came over her. She realized that she'd been standing beside Lucan all this while. Never once had she thought to move away. Yet she could not help but be drawn in by the easy manners of his friends and soon found herself sitting beside Calliope.

"After the walk from the market just now, I am fully prepared for the biscuits from Mrs. Dudley's teashop," Hedley said. She sat opposite the sofa, with her husband standing behind her curved chair, his fingertips resting lightly at her shoulder. They seemed to share a secret smile between them that spoke of contentment not only with each other but amongst their friends as well.

"I believe I have been nudged sufficiently," Everhart said as he moved toward the low oval table between them and set down the basket. Lifting the lid, he peered inside. "We have scones, pies, tarts, and biscuits enough to feed all of Lincolnshire."

"Or *one* rather large dog," Danvers added when the beast in question loped forward, sniffing the air.

Just then, two maids in aprons and ruffled caps entered the study from a side door. One brought in a tray of tea, cups, saucers, silverware, and serviettes, while the other carried a silver platter and a cake stand. Together, they made quick work of arranging the table.

"Thank you, Edith and Grace," Calliope said before they curtsied and left the room.

The dog sniffed the air once more, his tail wagging.

Calliope clucked her tongue. "I'm sorry, Duke, but I completely forgot your cheese."

When the dog lowered his head and issued a mournful groan, Hedley laughed. "You shouldn't tease Boris so. Look at the poor fellow."

Frances was puzzled by the different names they called the dog. Was it Duke or Boris?

"I suppose not." Calliope grinned mischievously and unwrapped a wedge of blue veined cheese. Instantly, the dog perked up. Then, to Frances, Calliope said, "Since he is closest to you, would you like to give it to him?"

Frances did not hesitate. She took the cheese. Only now, she wasn't sure how to proceed. She was already confused by which name to use. Turning to the dog, Frances held out her hand. The beast abruptly sat at Lucan's side and lifted his eyes to the man in question, as if waiting for permission.

"It's all right. You can have it," she said.

Even though the dog looked at the cheese with longing practically vibrating from him, he remained stubbornly fixed to the spot.

"Why, you sly devil," Calliope murmured. "Apparently, he is waiting for a proper introduction. Very well. Miss Thorne, might I introduce Boris Reginald James Brutus, also known as Duke."

That helped explain the different names. "Quite a mouthful," Frances said with a small laugh.

"Rafe and I call him Boris," Hedley added.

Calliope chose a strawberry tart for her plate. "He earned the name Brutus when my aunt visited. Her two Pekingese are now surrounded by four of his offspring."

Frances looked over at the beast. He didn't appear the least bit contrite. In fact, he almost looked proud. Hiding a smile, she wagged her finger at him and silently reprimanded the naughty boy.

"And Reginald James?" The dog's ears perked at Frances's question.

Lucan answered this and bent down to give his canine companion a solid pat. "I've always believed that a dog of any distinction deserves more than one name. Wouldn't you agree, Miss Thorne?"

Through her lenses, their gazes held for a moment. Since their kiss, she'd been pretending that it had had no effect on her, that her exterior was as practiced and controlled as his. Yet just now she felt a small ripple disturb the surface. Ignoring it, she turned to address the group. "And which name does he prefer?"

"That is the veritable puzzle of our friend. His preference alters from one person to the next," Everhart said with a shrug from the chair opposite his wife. "You may call him whatever you like."

Actually, Frances liked the name Reginald James, and he'd responded to it as well. However, there seemed to be the weight of expectation in the room, as each of them, no doubt, were wondering *why* she was here with Lucan. And if Reginald James was what he called the dog, using it might give rise to unwarranted speculation.

She held out her hand. "Here is your cheese, Duke."

The dog did not move.

She tried again. "Here is your cheese, Boris?"

Still, the same result.

"Surely, you don't prefer Brutus."

Apparently not, because he remained fixed to his spot. He did look up, however, toward Lucan.

Reginald James was on the tip of her tongue. Yet she refused to be coerced into using it. She wasn't going to be manipulated any longer by Lucan or even the dog that hadn't left his side. "Here is your cheese, *RJ*."

She must have said it with enough authority that the dog knew it was his last chance, because in the same instant he stood, loped over, gave her hand a lick, and gobbled up the cheese. Then, he crossed the room and found a cozy spot to rest near the hearth.

"Well, that settles matters, doesn't it?" Calliope asked. Although, when Frances turned, she saw that the question was directed to Hedley.

Hedley smiled in response. "It appears so."

Frances felt as if she'd missed something.

"Forgive them, Miss Thorne," Lucan said, his warning tone lacking amusement. "You have wandered into a den of newlyweds who would like nothing more than to pair off every man and woman of their acquaintance."

Frances straightened, her spine going rigid as she looked at her new friends. They grinned back at her without a word of denial. She decided a change of subject was in order. "And do all of you live here together?"

Everhart filled his plate with a scone and two tarts. "My wife and I will live at Briar Heath once the repairs are in order. Though with that estate in Northumberland, we've considered keeping a share of Fallow Hall as well, so that we may never be too far from our friends."

"My wife owns Greyson Park, not two miles down the lane," Danvers said, while Hedley was busy adding sugar to two cups of tea. "It too will need extensive repairs, however. Until a time comes when it is safe to inhabit, we will remain here, amongst friends."

Friends. It did not escape her notice that Lucan was part of this close-knit circle. Yet when she looked at him, expecting him to offer his reason for why he lived here as well, he said nothing. He merely lifted his brows as if challenging her to ask. She did. "And you?"

"I live here, as well," he said, without elaborating.

Danvers chuckled. "No doubt he is here to ensure that we hold true to our wager."

"A wager that I have already won, mind you," Lucan said, this time with an easy laugh. Then, for Frances's sake, he added, "My friends made a foolish declaration one night, vowing never to marry. Unable to resist, I proposed a wager. As you see, they have both married, leaving me the sole winner."

They wagered over marriage? Frances was confused. If they were manipulated, then why did they all seem so pleased? She hadn't suspected pretense in any of their welcomes or in their fond regard for each other. Yet how could it be otherwise? Frances decided to study them more carefully.

"Only if you last the year," Danvers taunted with a lift of a teacup in salute.

Lucan offered a smug grin. "It is only a matter of waiting a few months."

"More than six months," Everhart pointed out, absently brushing a few crumbs from his cravat.

Lucan's grin altered. The change was almost imperceptible, yet it appeared harder around the edges, as if fixed in place like a mask. "The time limit matters not, for I will never marry."

"*Woof!*" Apparently, RJ wanted part of the conversation as he stood up from his spot on the floor.

"The matchmaker has spoken." Calliope laughed as she poured tea and shook her head in mock distress in Lucan's direction. "I'm sorry, Montwood, but you're next."

"Matchmaker?" Frances asked, too curious by half not to learn everything she could about this group of friends who enjoyed teasing each other and gambling over marriage—*of all things*.

"Duke brought Everhart and me together," Calliope explained, handing Frances a cup and saucer. In turn, Frances passed the cup to Lucan before taking the next one Calliope offered.

"And Boris led me directly to Rafe. Actually, he caused me to crash into him." Hedley gazed up at her husband fondly. Then to Frances, she lifted her hands in a helpless gesture. "And…both you and Montwood call him RJ."

Frances's gaze snapped to Lucan's with such force that she nearly spilled her tea. He'd shortened the name to RJ too? She'd assumed he called him Reginald James.

Lucan offered an unconcerned shrug as he sipped his tea.

"I'm not looking for a match of any sort," she said to the group, making herself perfectly clear. "Even if I were, I wouldn't choose a man who abducted me."

Hedley gasped. "Abducted you? Montwood, is it true?"

Frances winced inwardly. She hadn't meant to blurt that out. All eyes went to Lucan.

"In a manner of speaking," he said without an ounce of contrition. "But it was not for selfish purposes. It was for Miss Thorne's own good."

Pfft, Frances thought just as Calliope said, "I'm certain that Frances can decide what is for her *own* good."

"Montwood, you should have asked her permission and then respected her choice," Hedley added.

Both women instantly became Frances's friends. Now, it was her turn to stare back at Lucan with challenge.

"Ah, yes. Blackguard that I am," Lucan said with a sly glance down to her mouth, "you could very well have found Miss Thorne in hysterics."

She adjusted her spectacles, trying hard not to think about that kiss. "I am not prone to fits. It would not have served me at my former employment if I were. After all, one cannot teach *Artful Defense* to young women unless one can respond appropriately in a situation of distress."

"*Artful Defense?*" Calliope asked. Surprisingly, in learning that Frances was a member of society's workers, Calliope's expression showed no disappointment, only curiosity.

"At Mrs. Hunter's Agency and Servant Registry, I occasionally trained young maids how to ward off unwanted advances—" Frances stopped suddenly and looked to her companions. "Oh, forgive me for mentioning such a topic."

"My brother taught my sisters and me boxing maneuvers." Calliope flipped her fingers in the air as if this were a common enough topic to discuss and not to worry.

Hedley leaned forward and took a biscuit from the platter. "What do you instruct them to do?" she asked Frances.

"Mainly, we advise them to work in pairs so that they are never caught alone. Housekeepers usually agree when the circumstance is warranted." Frances set down her tea so that she didn't spill it while explaining. "From there, we teach them to pay close attention to their opponents. Notice if he's wearing shoes or boots. Lord Lucan, for example, wears Hessians. A maid's slipper or half boot would likely be an ineffective deterrent."

Calliope and Hedley nodded, and then proceeded to scrutinize the gentlemen carefully. "And if they are wearing boots?" the former asked.

"Notice your surroundings," Frances answered, feeling more in her element. She'd learned similar instructions from her mother before her illness. "The *Artful Defense* is a method that often uses clumsiness as a tactical advantage. Perhaps a young woman suddenly becomes ungainly with, say…a hot pot of tea. If tipped properly, the scalding liquid can arc out at a good distance."

The gentlemen cringed.

"I've done that accidentally," Hedley admitted on a breath. "When we were in town, I poured for my new mother-in-law and completely missed the cups and soaked the carpet. I was mortified. Yet if I'd have known what you just told me, I could have pretended that I'd done it for the purpose of demonstration."

"I quite agree," Calliope said and picked up the scalloped-shaped sugar tongs, pinching them closed until they clacked together. "I'll never look at a tea tray the same way. What else do you teach?"

Seeing the fire poker near the hearth, Frances stood and crossed the room. She gave RJ a quick scratch behind the ears before lifting the iron from the stand. "Now, this could be a fire poker, a duster, a beater, or whatever is close at hand. Pretend that a man comes near in a threatening manner. This is when you suddenly become quite clumsy and pretend to drop it. But wait—you catch it in the last moment before it strikes the floor. *Dear me.*" She pantomimed losing control of the poker, only to catch it. "And then lift up sharply, catching the gentleman…off guard."

A collective groan tore through the gentlemen in the room.

"It reminds me of a trick Mother taught us girls to do with our fans," Calliope said. "If used correctly, it could break a gentleman's finger."

"I should like to learn that," Frances and Hedley said in unison. Then together, they laughed.

"Bloodthirsty lot." Danvers chuckled.

Frances took her seat and picked up her tea. This was such a pleasant break in her journey that she was nearly ready to thank Lucan for abducting her. Well, not quite. She had far too much sense to ever say those words.

Beside her, Calliope adjusted a small pillow and sat further into the curved corner of the sofa. "I see no injuries on Montwood, and he doesn't appear to be walking with a limp. Did you resort to any of your methods to subdue him?"

Leaning in, Lucan placed his empty teacup on the low table in front of her. His dimple flashed. "What *did* you do to subdue me?"

I kissed you into submission, she thought as she answered the challenging lift of his brows with a lift of her own. He was, after all, the one who'd ended it.

If she hadn't noticed how he'd been affected just as much as she, then his actions might have wounded her ego. She was sensible enough, however, to realize that if *he* hadn't broken away, then they likely would have been engaged in kissing when his friends arrived. Which could have turned into quite the conundrum.

"My person was never in any *real* danger." *Let him stew on that*. Besides, she knew how to defend herself. If he'd have done anything that displeased her, she would have stopped his advances. The only problem was, she imagined that Lucan knew precisely how to *please* her, even if she didn't know herself.

Calliope sighed. "While I am glad Montwood has behaved as a gentleman—aside from the abduction, of course—I'm also somewhat disappointed. This might be the first time that Duke was wrong."

As if summoned, the dog appeared again, loping across the room to sit between where Frances sat and Lucan stood.

"What does Boris have in his mouth?" Hedley asked, pointing to the cream-colored wad of parchment in his teeth.

Frances went still and watched in embarrassment as RJ dropped it directly into her lap. The page was unfolded slightly, revealing the last few words Lucan had written. *"I'm going to kiss you."*

Now, this was one situation for which she never could have prepared.

"What is it, Frances?" Calliope asked, leaning in.

"It…*uh*…appears to be paper," she answered, lifting it. "Something that RJ must have retrieved from the fireplace."

Hedley squinted. "That's strange. We haven't had need of a fire in here for weeks. It's been uncommonly warm. Not to mention, paper isn't the best source of kindling."

Helpless, Frances looked to Lucan. After her speech about being abducted and not needing to defend herself, revealing the words on this page would be quite damning. For both of them. And it was his fault. *He'd* written the note and then it tossed onto the grate.

Lucan looked at the wadded-up paper as if he'd never seen it before. "How curious. I do believe there is something written on the page. I wonder if it is something scandalous…"

"Is it an unsigned love letter?" Calliope asked, smiling fondly at Everhart.

"I'm certain it's nothing of the sort," Frances said. Lucan, *the scoundrel*, was only increasing their interest.

Lucan tsked. "How can you be certain without reading it?"

"It could be a ransom note for your recent abduction, Frances," Hedley offered with a trilling laugh, as if this were part of a parlor game. Everhart and Danvers exchanged a look without saying a word.

"Hedley may have a point," Lucan said before he plucked it out of Frances's grasp. Then he crossed the room to the desk and proceeded to smooth out the page. "There is a bit of dog drool to contend with, but I believe I can read the words. *Hmm*…It appears to be quite scandalous, I'm afraid."

"Those are usually the best sort of letters," Calliope mused. "What does it say?"

Lucan shook his head and proceeded to fold the page into a palm-sized square. "It's better that I not read it aloud. In fact, it would be best for all parties concerned if I made it disappear."

Frances shifted on her cushion, refusing to breathe a sigh of relief just yet.

"I remember this trick from our school days," Danvers accused. "You used to *borrow* one of my shillings."

"And one of *my* crowns," Everhart added, grumbling.

Lucan offered an unrepentant grin. "You were both repaid with entertainment, just as you will be once again."

Facing the group, Lucan displayed the folded square, nimbly moving it from one hand to the other with a roll of his fingers. He was putting on quite the show. And while Frances wished he would be done with it sooner rather than later, she could not help but admire the dexterity of those long fingers.

"And now, I will make this scandalous paper vanish," he said with a wink. "Do you believe it, Calliope?"

"Of course," she said with a laugh, humoring him.

When he asked Hedley, she gave the same response. And then he asked Frances. "What about you, Miss Thorne? Do you believe I can make this disappear?"

She fixed a grin to her lips. "Not for an instant."

"Ah, a skeptic in the room." Lucan didn't appear bothered in the least.

Everhart coughed. "There's more than one."

"Aye." Danvers crossed his arms over his chest.

"Then without further ado…" Lucan placed the paper in the center of his palm and closed his fingers over it, one by one. Then, turning his wrist so that the back of his hand faced the group, he swiped his free hand through the air as if casting a spell over it. "One…two…" And on the word *three*, he opened his hand with a flourish.

It was empty, of course.

"It's in your other hand, Montwood," Danvers said.

Lucan opened his other hand, revealing it too was empty.

After a pause, Everhart offered, "Then it's up your sleeve."

As if anticipating this, Lucan was already shaking his arms toward the floor. Then he shrugged and flashed his charmer's smile. "Everhart, your austere tone was so certain that I thought it was up my sleeve as well, but apparently it truly has disappeared."

"What a marvelous trick!" Calliope clapped and then gazed at her husband. "Forgive me, my love, but I'm glad you were wrong."

Hedley agreed. "Montwood, wherever did you learn it?"

"I spent my life in a traveling carnival, juggling and breathing fire…"

"Don't let him fool you, sweeting," Danvers said to his wife. "He knew those tricks even before our school days, but he would never tell us where he learned them."

Lucan sketched a bow, effectively concealing the dark shadow that crossed his expression. Frances noticed it, however. She wouldn't say anything, of course. Just like she wouldn't reveal that the folded paper was in his left pocket.

All the same, it felt as if part of his shadow had somehow swept over her as well. It was a shame that Lucan was a trickster and gambler, because for a small amount of time, she'd started to like him. But with his trick just now and the mention of the wager over marriage earlier, she was reminded how painful and soul-crushing it was to be deceived by his kind.

She'd promised herself years ago that she would only give her heart to a noble man, and if not, then to no man at all.

CHAPTER NINE

"As I mentioned before, it is my duty to check in on you. If anything is amiss, I will know. I will come for you." Lucan leaned back against the squabs, facing Frances. Less than a half hour ago, they were sitting in the study at Fallow Hall. Now, the carriage was inside the tall wrought iron gates of Whitelock Manor, yet still a distance from the house. The circular courtyard lay ahead.

While he felt marginally better in knowing that she could take care of herself with her *Artful Defense*, he would have preferred that she decline Whitelock's offer. There was something disconcerting in this entire ordeal. He still wasn't certain of Whitelock's reason for pursuing Frances. What secrets did the man keep? Whatever they were, no one else had an inkling of them. No one aside from Thorne and possibly Clivedale.

Frances folded her hands in her lap. "That won't be necessary, my lord. I free you from any obligation my father may have asked of you."

Catching the lingering doubt in her tone and in her phrasing, Lucan frowned. "That's the thing about obligations—only the person who made the request can revoke it."

"I'm certain my father would not have bothered to ask this favor of you, had he known to what lengths you would go."

The closer they came to the end of the long alabaster drive, the more anxious Lucan felt. He wondered how much she knew—if anything—about the history between her father and Whitelock. "*I'm* certain he would permit me to turn this carriage around and take you back to Fallow Hall in order to keep you from a man he abhors above all others."

Frances gave him a patient smile. "He does not hate Lord Whitelock. They were once rivals for my mother's hand, but the animosity between them ended when my father married my mother."

"Is that what your father told you when Whitelock began showing up at Mrs. Hunter's?" Lucan doubted it.

"I know my father. He does not harbor grudges." She swallowed and turned toward the window. "Nonetheless, I have chosen not to mention Lord Whitelock to him because reminders of my mother bring my father pain."

Lucan frowned. It was as he'd guessed—Hugh Thorne was not even aware of Whitelock's inexplicable appearance in his daughter's life. While Frances's motives were pure of heart, Lucan wished she'd have witnessed her father's acute dislike of Whitelock firsthand.

"It seems that you cast your own desires aside for the sake of your father quite often. You do not speak of your mother. You have not mentioned Whitelock. I can only guess that there have been many more instances."

"A gambler and practiced deceiver may not be able to understand this, but when you care for someone, you put your own desires aside. You do not manipulate that person with sly tricks. Nor do you selfishly scheme against your own friends in order to win a wager."

What she called *selfish*, he called *survival*. "Mark my words, if it wasn't for my trick today, there would be four people plotting and scheming against the two of us. Even you have to admit that the sleight of hand served its purpose."

"Entertaining or not, it was still deception." She pursed her lips in condescension. "Besides, you were merely fortunate that no one asked to check your pocket."

He stared at her for a moment, then shook his head in disbelief and laughed. He might have been showing off a bit earlier by demonstrating one of the parlor tricks he'd used to stay in the good graces of hosts who still invited him to parties, yet the one person he'd wanted to impress hadn't been fooled for a single moment. "You are quite the *knot*, Miss Thorne, full of twists and tangles. I find myself wondering if your abhorrence of my actions lies solely on my own shoulders or if perhaps I am paying for the sins of my father."

"I know you were not part of my father's trials. Your family's public disapproval of your defense of him speaks for itself."

That was something, at least. "Someone else, then? Was there another *selfish schemer* in your history who left such a dark stain behind that it can never be scrubbed clean?"

He knew there was. That cad Roger Quinlin came to mind. Lucan wanted to goad her into admitting it so that he could tell her that he wasn't like Quinlin either. But why should telling her suddenly be so important?

The simple answer was that he needed her to trust him under these circumstances. Yet he suspected that his *need* went a little deeper.

She narrowed her eyes. "You would do better to worry over your own dark stains."

"Ah, but yours are now under my keeping, as well." The carriage slowed. Lucan sat forward and took one of her hands. "Be on your guard, Miss Thorne. I do not trust Whitelock."

"So you have said." She snatched her hand free.

He didn't relent. This was too important. "Use whatever you can—fire poker, duster, beater, pen knife…"

She sat straighter. "I do not believe Whitelock will attempt to kiss me, so I need not worry."

At the mention of a kiss, the tension between them altered. Through her lenses, he saw those smoky eyes dip to his mouth. Abruptly, the carriage shrank, closing in bit by bit. He could smell the soap on her skin. See the milky white of her complexion, flawless aside from where a soft blush tinted her cheeks. Her nostrils flared as if she were drawing him in as well. Then she licked her lips, reminding him how soft and supple they'd felt against his own.

"You did not use your defense against me," he said, his voice hoarse.

She quickly looked out the window. "No, but I will in the future."

"Good." He felt a grin tugging at his mouth, pleased that he wasn't the only one plagued by their unexpected chemistry. Even though he knew he should keep his distance, he couldn't help adding, "Then I will see you soon and test your skill."

She jerked her gaze back to his, blustering. "I will not have you endangering my employment by calling on me here."

"You needn't worry. No one will know that I've paid a call. I know how to move about all sorts of places unseen."

"You believe that only because you haven't been caught yet. I'm not willing to put my future and my father's in jeopardy to satisfy your misguided assumptions," she accused. "I have lived in London my entire life, and I know when circumstances call for caution. Working for Lord Whitelock is not one of them."

Her arrogant belief in her ability to sense danger might very well the thing that put her in the direst of circumstances. "Since I know that it is your nature to turn obstinate, I did not force you to remain at Fallow Hall. I agree that you are more capable than any other woman in my acquaintance. *However*, I will keep watch over you, whether you like it or not."

Frances chose to ignore Lucan's threat and focus on her new life. She did not have the time to argue with him, or to examine the way his words caused her pulse to quiver. Instead, she left the carriage without a word and ignored the enigmatic pull that made her want to linger.

Whitelock's country residence was not a mere house or manor. It was a palace with marble floors, elegant crystal chandeliers, and walls lined from floor to ceiling with romantic paintings.

Upon her arrival, Frances met Mr. Greggs, the tall, stoic butler, and Mrs. Riley, the fretful, needle-nosed housekeeper.

"Dear heavens, Miss Thorne," Mrs. Riley said, busying herself with taking Frances's hat, gloves, and satchel and handing each off to a waiting maid. "We've been at sixes and sevens, not knowing what to do when our driver arrived without you not a quarter hour ago, and he not having full recollection of how it had happened."

Frances didn't want the driver to pay for what Lucan had done, and she quickly took the blame. "I apologize for causing you worry. I must have stepped into the wrong carriage. Fortunately, arriving at a neighboring estate, I soon realized my error."

At least part of it was the truth. As for the rest, she need not mention how she'd been *escorted* to the wrong carriage under false pretenses.

Then, after clucking around her like a mother hen to make sure all her limbs were intact, Mrs. Riley showed her around the estate. There were five floors in all, with the servants' quarters in the attic, the guest chambers on the second floor, the family rooms on the first, the main rooms on the ground floor, and the kitchens, laundry, butler's pantry, and housekeeper's office below stairs. Lord Whitelock employed forty house servants and sixteen more in the stables and on the grounds. She met nearly all of the house servants, priding herself on remembering all of their names.

Out of those, Nannette, Penny, and Bess—the first and second floor chambermaids, stood out the most. Each one possessed friendly manners and fresh-faced vibrancy that Frances hadn't often seen amongst the servant class.

"His lordship rescued me from a workhouse in the *dials*," Nannette said, tucking a glossy ebony tuft of hair beneath a frilled cap.

Penny's large brown eyes looked owlish against her pale features as she shared her story. "It was mid-winter two years past when Mum caught the fever. I buried my little sister the same week. I'd have been next if not for his lordship taking me in."

"I was left at a foundling home when I was twelve. I was too old, and they wouldn't let me stay," Bess said. She was a small bit of a girl with wispy mouse brown hair and a skittish demeanor, but when she smiled it was infectious. "His lordship rescued me the same as he did with all the others. I've been here three years now and worked up from the kitchens."

Just as she had when others had stopped to tell their similar stories, Mrs. Riley shooed them along, albeit good-naturedly. "You'll have plenty of time to speak of his lordship's kindness and generosity to Miss Thorne, but she's had a rough time of it today and deserves her rest."

On the second floor, the housekeeper showed Frances to her rooms. They were situated in the east wing, just one floor above Lady Whitelock's. The balcony windows hosted a view of the inner courtyard—a grassy knoll trimmed in conical topiaries with a curvaceous fountain in the center. Upon closer inspection, she saw that the statue depicted a reclining woman with a swan rising above her.

Now this, she thought, was something she would never see at Fallow Hall. Shaking her head, she thought it rather odd. Yet in the same breath, she did not doubt such a large statue and fountain held some significance. Lord Whitelock had said as much when he'd mentioned how his home hosted a wealth of art for her appreciation. And with earning a pound per week, she felt obligated to try.

Frances speculated that perhaps the artist had admired a woman's shape and likened it to a swan's grace and beauty— or perhaps the woman represented the earth and the swan was supposed to be the...

Frances squinted, unsure. She was starting to get a headache.

"Quite captivating, isn't it?" Mrs. Riley said as she moved to stand beside her. "His lordship has filled this house with such beautiful art. The fountain is a depiction of the myth of Zeus, who was so enraptured by Leda's beauty that he transformed himself into a swan to be with her."

The housekeeper's mention suddenly reminded Frances of the myth. From her own studies, she'd found the tale far from romantic. In fact, to her it had seemed more like Zeus had disguised himself to take advantage of an unsuspecting woman.

Yet for Mrs. Riley, she pasted on a smile. "It's lovely."

Frances turned away from the window and saw that her bedchamber was decorated in the same dramatic fashion as the rest of the house: Even her bedclothes were in a decadent white satin which shimmered in the light. The bed itself was immense, with its own vaulted ceiling attached to the four corner posts. Behind it, the curtains tied back to reveal a painting of woman dressed in gauzy silk and standing amidst a flower meadow.

Frances found herself sorely lacking in education here as well. She knew it was for her to admire and appreciate, but it did not hold her interest.

"His lordship is quite the collector," she said, turning away from the painting.

Mrs. Riley beamed like a proud mother. "Yes, indeed. He once told me that by furnishing his homes with beauty, those under his care could lead richer lives."

Frances offered an obliging nod before stifling a yawn. The long days of travel were taking their toll. While her chamber and the entire house was lovely, it was also a bit much to take in all at once. Quite honestly, she preferred the simplicity of Fallow Hall. Yet this was her home for the foreseeable future, and she would learn to get used to it.

"You must be eager to get settled," Mrs. Riley said, walking toward the door. "I've ordered water for your bath. Afterward, I'll send Diana to take your measurements for new clothes."

With such a generous salary from Lord Whitelock already, Frances opened her mouth to object. "That won't be necessary—"

"His lordship insists. In fact, he had four day dresses and two evening gowns made for Miss Momper." Mrs. Riley clucked her tongue. "Such a dear, sweet girl, we are sad to be without her, and her ladyship seemed to like her as well. Ah, but we cannot selfishly hold one of our own back when new opportunities arise."

"Was Miss Momper her ladyship's companion for many years?" Frances couldn't fathom a better opportunity than earning a pound a week.

"Not quite a year. Let's see…Since I've been here these past six years, there has been Cora, who is now housekeeper at one of his lordship's other houses. Then Molly, who found herself a husband, and they have a shop in London. And Betsy, who is now a companion to a baroness and touring the

Continent." Mrs. Riley looked heavenward with a sigh. "His lordship is good to us all. He'll be good to you as well."

Frances hoped so too. She wanted to free her father from gaol but through honest labor and a wage well earned.

Yet even with all of Lord Whitelock's accolades from his staff, she couldn't quite silence the doubt that Lucan had put inside her head. *Was* there a reason her father had never mentioned Lord Whitelock?

Find Lucan Montwood. He'll know what to do. And why had her father put his faith in Lucan, even after all that had happened between their two families?

These were two riddles she was determined to solve.

...

Chapter Ten

Lucan sent the driver back to Fallow Hall without him. Now
that Miss Thorne was under Whitelock's roof, more than ever
before Lucan needed to ensure her safety. Even though he had
no material reason to suspect Whitelock's motives regarding
her, the toll of those warning bells persisted. What precisely
was Whitelock's plan—both in regard to Miss Thorne and
also with the ten thousand pound debt? Lucan was starting
to suspect that they were connected. But how?

Until now, he'd limited his investigation of Whitelock
to what he'd gleaned from servants, eavesdropping, and listening for anything that would offer insight to the viscount's
actions. All he heard was praise. In fact, Whitelock's name
on anyone's lips touted accolades for him. Most of the perti-
nent information had come from Arthur Momper. Yet with
Miss Thorne living under Whitelock's roof, he wasn't about
to leave her safety to popular opinion or errant gossip. Lucan
would have to gain access to the house itself.

Using his spyglass from a safe distance, Lucan surveyed
the house for the majority of the day. He cataloged the

comings and goings of the servants and paid close attention to the doors that were used most frequently and the ones that were used the least. As in most households, the servants of similar stations kept company together. The stable hands and grooms had formed their own small community, as had the kitchen staff, the housemaids, the footmen, and the chambermaids.

Observing their interactions, Lucan began to wonder where Miss Thorne would fit, or if her position—working closely with the lady of the manor—would essentially segregate her. And worse, make her easy prey for the lord of the manor.

Lack of evidence notwithstanding, Lucan detested this arrangement. Frances did not belong here. He knew her well enough that she would not be satisfied with sitting and reading aloud all day long. She was a woman of action. He'd seen it in the way she'd demonstrated her lessons in defense. Her face had shimmered with life when she'd spoken of helping other women.

The image of her brandishing a fire poker in Fallow Hall's study earlier that day remained constant within him. He'd never seen her so happy, grinning, and laughing with his friends. She'd filled the room with her own unique vibrancy, so much so that even he—dark soul that he was—had felt it. He hadn't thought such warmth and joy would ever penetrate the walls surrounding his heart. The sensation was as intriguing as it was disconcerting. He wanted to feel more of it, yet at the same time he feared what would happen if he did.

But he'd given his word, and tonight, under the cloak of darkness, he would find a way inside the house. He would keep a diligent watch over her.

Walking near the tree line along the outer edge of Whitelock's land, Lucan spotted Arthur Momper's familiar sheaf of wheat-colored hair. He sat near the banks of a stream, head bent to his knees.

Purposely, so he wouldn't cause a fright, Lucan stepped on a twig. The boy jerked his head up, saw who it was, and quickly turned away to wipe his face dry. But it was already too late. Lucan had seen that he was crying.

"What's all this? Surely you don't miss the odors of London," Lucan teased, ruffling the boy's head.

"She didn't write. Henny said she would write and let me know when I could come live with her," the lad said, his voice muffled between his knees.

Lucan knew Henny and Arthur were close, so this separation was bound to be a blow. "She'll write. Don't you worry."

Arthur shook his head. "You don't understand. She said she would write every week. She promised."

"I imagine she has a lot of work to do now that she's managing the maidservants of an entire estate," he reassured.

The boy lifted his head. His red-rimmed eyes locked on Lucan. "She's all I have in the world, and now it feels emptier somehow. I don't know why, but I'm scared."

Lucan felt a chill pass through him. He remembered a time when he'd felt that same way, and shortly afterward, he'd learned of his mother's death.

Concerned, he sat down beside the bank and settled an arm around the lad's shoulder. "It just so happens that I know a few people in Wales. I'll send a missive, and we'll find her."

Arthur nodded and sniffed. Settling his chin on top of his knees, he stared out over the water. "Promise?"

"I promise I will do everything I can." And he would, because Lucan never gave his word lightly.

At the end of her long day, Frances walked up to the second floor to retire. She had just left Mrs. Riley in her office below stairs, where they'd shared a late supper and had spoken of Frances's duties, which included an afternoon per week of teaching *Artful Defense*. Since Lady Whitelock had been "out of sorts," Frances had not yet met her. The delay gave Frances a short reprieve to become acclimated to her new surroundings.

Holding a small brass lamp, she crossed through the gallery, shortening the distance to her chamber. Amidst the portraits of Whitelock's ancestors stood busts on pedestals, large urns filled with potted trees, and sculptures that gleamed bright white in the shreds of moonlight slipping in through the part in the curtains. Earlier, when walking through this room in the daylight, she'd felt an unpleasant discomfort at seeing all the faces in the portraits staring down at her. A few of her employer's ancestors looked downright menacing.

Yet now she felt perfectly at ease. There was something calming about the darkness in this particular corridor that she'd never felt before. The reason was likely because she'd lived in London all of her life. In town, one learned to be wary of dark places. Therefore, she never fully experienced the nighttime.

But there was something alluring about this quiet stillness. She could hear her heartbeat, the hushed whisper of her own breaths, the soft swish of muslin, and each rasp of her slipper soles on the floor. It was magical to be so aware and yet not feel guarded.

She lingered in the gallery, studying the sculptures in Whitelock's collection. The candlelight illuminated a pair of nude lovers, reclining. Well, *nearly* nude. The artist had cleverly shrouded the loins of the pair, carving a swathe of rippling fabric into the stone.

Frances didn't consider herself a prude. She enjoyed the human form…especially the male form. Nevertheless, that sense of uneducated uncertainty continued to plague her. Was she supposed to admire the alabaster breast of the woman and compare it to her own? And was she supposed to find more beauty in the sculpture? Then, of course, there was the man's body. The hard, muscular ridges and valleys were appealing. Yet how was she supposed to admire the form of a sculpture when she had no human reference with which to compare it?

Stepping around to view the statue from behind, she could not help but notice that her admiration was not stirred the same way it had been when she'd spied Lucan, fully clothed on a London street or even today at Fallow Hall. Wasn't this statue supposed to represent the epitome in male grace and beauty?

"You are quite the avid admirer, Miss Thorne."

Frances jumped. She spun around so quickly that her taper sputtered and flickered out.

"Careful," Lucan crooned, his voice emerging from the shadows lingering at the outer edges of the room. "Without a lamp how can your artistic perusal continue?"

It took a moment for her eyes to adjust to the dim light filtering in through the windows. The sculptures around her seemed to possess their own faint glow, soaking up the moon-light. And then she saw Lucan clearly—the glint of amber in his gaze, the flash of white in his smile, the darkness of his hair and eyebrows that made the shadows appear gray in comparison.

"What are you doing here?" she asked, still attempting to catch her breath. "I could lose my post if you are caught."

"As I said before, I'm too familiar with dark places to be discovered." He drew closer, never looking away from her. "Besides, I told you I would come."

Seven insignificant words and yet her pulse raced in her throat. Silly as it was, knowing that he'd come solely because he'd said he would touched on a tender wound that she'd carried with her for a long while.

"You needn't have bothered," she said, though her tone lacked any bite.

Lucan's grin broadened, as if he'd noticed. "You're glad that I'm here."

"Nonsense." She gave him her most condescending glare.

Unfortunately, it had no effect on him. He moved closer. Ignoring the sudden leap in her pulse and the warm tremor that coursed through her, she held her ground.

Reaching out, he slid her spectacles up the bridge of her nose. "There. Try it again. I might believe you this time."

"You needn't have bothered," she said again, the words coming out in a rush as his fingertips brushed her cheek. His nearness unsettled her, muddled her thoughts. "I know better than to have any expectations when a man gives his word."

He traced the rims of her spectacles in something of a caress. His breath was warm against her lips. "This shield of yours didn't protect you from becoming jaded, did it?"

"If I am, then it is for a good reason."

"Your position at Mrs. Hunter's forced you to learn things about the ways of some men that you should never have learned," he said with a convincing amount of sincerity.

She tried not to let it affect her. "I learned the hardest lessons outside of that agency—promises made to me over the years only to hear excuse after excuse for why they failed to be fulfilled."

"Your father loves you dearly."

She issued a sardonic laugh. "I have heard him say the words too often to be swayed by them. '*Frannie, my girl, I love you…*' is what he says to soften the blow. I don't think I could ever trust those words in the future."

She wished her experiences had been different, leaving her more receptive to the possibility of love. But such a wish left her feeling silly and naïve. Therefore, she dismissed it.

When Lucan opened his mouth to speak, she shook her head, interrupting him before he began. "Before you tell me that the foundation for my lowered expectations has no proper footing, I will tell you that my father wasn't the only one who used that tactic. The man I almost married did too. '*Frannie, my dear, I love you. Don't worry, I'll make good use of your dowry funds and find the best barrister for your father.*'" She still remembered the way Roger Quinlin had waved his hat in a salute as he rode off—and out of her life. "When he returned from Brighton a full year later, he brought his new bride with him instead of a barrister. Of course, I wouldn't have known that if he hadn't stopped by Mrs. Hunter's to inquire about hiring a footman for his new house in St. James. Needless to say, we were both uncomfortably surprised by our unexpected reunion."

"He was a toad." Lucan's fingertips strayed to her spectacles again. This time he traced the frame stem, his intense focus on following the path to her ear. His fingertips gently grazed the sensitive peak and then slipped behind to where the stems curved toward her lobe.

She shivered. "You don't even know of whom I'm referring."

"Roger Quinlin," he stated matter-of-factly, as if his mind possessed a catalog of every person in London. "Purchased a commission instead of paying his debts of honor. Thought he'd look right smart in uniform."

All right. Perhaps he did know Roger after all.

Lucan traced the other stem of her spectacles now. This time, he watched her. "You are better off without him, Miss Thorne. Rumor has it that he still allows his father to pay his debts, and he hasn't been a faithful husband to his wife. Some men have no honor."

She tried to ignore the sensations his exploration caused—the ripples that cascaded through her, the heat pooling low in her stomach. "And you pay all your debts?"

"All."

"And would you be a faithful husband?" The moment the words were out, she wanted to drag them back in. This conversation had taken a turn. It was far too intimate. And with their gazes locked, she wondered what he was thinking…and also if he would kiss her again.

His grin faded, and he drew in one breath. Then another. "If I made such a vow, I would honor it. However, you know of the wager. I will not marry now or ever. If I truly cared for a woman, I would be more inclined to keep her far removed from the likes of me. I have a dark soul, Miss Thorne."

He did not seem so dark to Frances at the moment. She could clearly see the light illuminated in his eyes. A trace of sadness lurked there, as well, deep within. She'd never taken the opportunity to see anything of substance in him. Yet now, she was beginning to see more. "If this woman truly cared for you, she would not stay away. It would be beyond her power."

Frances felt herself inching closer until the round brass bottom of the lamp she held pressed against her breast, serving as a barrier between them. She didn't know what was happening to her, but she couldn't seem to stop the desire to be near him.

Perhaps she *should* be wary of dark places, even here.

"I'm not going to kiss you again," he said firmly. Yet when he looked down to her mouth, he didn't seem entirely sure.

Her lips tingled. "I made no request."

"Yes, you did. You are," he accused her, lifting both hands to cradle her face. He held her still as he leaned in, not quite kissing her. Not quite touching her with his lips. But almost. "I never should have kissed you in the first place."

"That's correct. You only kissed me to make a point, after all." Unfortunately, she couldn't remember the point at the moment. The darkness was wreaking havoc with her sense of reason, casting a spell.

"I can still taste you, Miss Thorne."

A small whimper rose from her throat. His words shocked her. Thrilled her. "What do I taste like?"

"Temptation in its purest form." His mouth hovered over hers, lips parted.

Frances tried to seize whatever animosity remained between them before she lost all reason. "It was only a kiss."

He rubbed his nose along the length of hers, closing his eyes. "*Hmm...you sound like the voice in my head.*"

Her lips felt fuller now, plump and pulsating, aching to be fitted to his. The sensation made her anxious, jittery. She shuffled her feet, moving closer. She felt mesmerized by the night. Her free hand reached up to stroke the slender length of his fingers, feeling the ridges and the fine hairs of his knuckles.

"This is a test," he continued, his mouth shifting, poised to claim hers. "If I can resist you, I can resist anything."

Her chin tilted forward. She wanted to kiss him.

All of a sudden, he released her. It was so swift that she dropped the lamp. It fell from her grasp and would have crashed to the floor if not for Lucan's quick reflexes.

Instead of handing the lamp to her, he set it down on edge of the dais where the nearest sculpture lounged. Then, he took a step back and raked both hands through his hair. The amber light was gone from his eyes. Now they were dark and forbidding. And her pulse quickened at the sight of them.

"I don't understand what is happening," she said slowly, as if waking. "Perhaps, I am overly tired and overwhelmed by my circumstances and that combination has made me more susceptible to..."—*you*—"the night."

"A plausible excuse," he said on an exhale. "Let us both cast the blame elsewhere."

"Yet by all appearances, you were about to kiss me again. I have been kissed before today, and I know the look men have before they make an attempt."

"Do I possess that look right now?" His gaze lingered on her mouth in a caress she could almost feel.

She pressed her lips together to quell the ache. "You do."

"Then you have your answer." He turned and strode into the shadows. From a short distance, he asked, "You are well?"

Now, he was inquiring about her health? Frances's head was spinning.

She took a breath to regain her composure. Since her eyes had adjusted to the dark, she could see he stood near the half columns flanking the windows. "If you are asking whether or not I had maids sobbing on my shoulder with their tales of woe against the horrible Lord Whitelock, then the answer is no. He is adored by every person beneath this roof—"

"Not *every* person."

"Those who work for him," she amended, exasperated. "I am not so jaded that I find their stories suspect. The opposite is true. I'm finding that Whitelock is even more of a paragon than I'd first imagined."

"As you said earlier, sometimes we are jaded for good reasons. You, yourself, deal in ways to prepare young women to escape unwanted advances. I beg of you to give yourself the same courtesy. Be on your guard." He took a step forward so that the moonlight glanced off his features to reveal a furrowed brow, as if he truly were worried. "I will come again tomorrow night. Whitelock will arrive in the morning."

"How could you know that?"

He held her gaze before he turned away. "I pay attention, Miss Thorne. I pray that you do as well."

CHAPTER ELEVEN

Lucan sent a missive to an old card sharp in Wales the following morning. Any news about Miss Momper and her position at Whitelock's hunting box would arrive in a matter of days. Part of him wanted to travel to Wales himself to make inquiries on Arthur's behalf. Yet his obligation was here, watching over Frances. He would never forgive himself if he let anything happen to her.

Until recently, he'd always referred to her as *Miss Thorne*, even in his thoughts. He would continue to do so when he addressed her. In his mind, however, things had changed and not for the better. Some of her vibrancy or her alluring disdain—or whatever it was—had burrowed past the guards in charge of his control. She was a sly one. Her mouth could issue such venom, while her eyes, lips, hands, and body promised the sweetest antidote.

Lucan had always enjoyed women, but they'd never tested his control to this extent. How had he allowed this to happen?

He wasn't sure he wanted to know the answer.

"What are you doing, Montwood?"

Lucan lifted his gaze to see Everhart stroll into the breakfast room at Fallow Hall. His friend's tawny brows drew together in a puzzled expression.

"Are you going to eat it or not?"

Lucan glanced down to the glazed bun in his hand, poised near his mouth. Instantly, he lowered the untouched pastry to the plate.

"I went to the market early this morning and brought back some of Mrs. Dudley's pastries." He'd needed to test his control and put his mind at ease.

"Capital." Everhart removed a plate from the waiting stack on the sideboard. Then, reaching into the basket for a scone, he sat on the opposite side of the table. "These are far better than the rot from the kitchen."

The rot, also known as Mrs. Swan's cooking, was curdling and congealing in silver dishes on the sideboard. Fallow Hall's ancient cook no longer possessed the skill to prepare edible food. Even so, no one had the heart to sack her. She was part of this estate and had remained here through several owners.

Lucan, Everhart, and Danvers rented this property from Lord Knightswold—an old acquaintance who'd recently married. Because he'd wanted to start a family, he found that living in an estate named after fallow deer, but that also intimated a certain note of infertility, had lacked appeal. The amusing part was that now there were two women in *delicate condition* beneath this roof. And because his friends doted on their brides, they made frequent trips into the village for food when Mrs. Swan's cooking was unpalatable.

As usual, the kitchen fare was a far cry from inspiring temptation. However, that's what Lucan needed today.

Satisfied with his success in resisting the bakery bun, he pushed the plate away.

"Not hungry after all that trouble?" Everhart asked, setting the jam caddy near his plate.

Lucan shrugged and picked up his tea instead. "I've lost my appetite for pastries."

"But what about Miss Thorne?"

Everhart's question caught him off guard, and Lucan spilled the tea down the front of his own waistcoat. Then, clattering the cup onto the saucer, he stood and wiped at the mess with a serviette. "Pardon me?"

"Sorry. Unrelated topic." Everhart chuckled, his eyes bright with mischief. "I was inquiring about her welfare."

Lucan wasn't a simpleton, but he played along. "I imagine she is well."

"Quite the extraordinary young woman. She faced her *abduction* rather bravely." As if engrossed in his scone more than this inquisition, Everhart added a dollop of cream. "Although, I'm still not certain why you brought her to Fallow Hall. I imagine it has something to do with all that you never speak of."

Lucan walked over to the sideboard and poured another tea. "It does."

A short silence followed before Everhart asked, "We are friends, aren't we, Montwood?"

"Of course." Although, if Lucan were honest, he viewed both Everhart and Danvers more like brothers. They'd stood by him through the worst of his trials. Even when his blood family had cut him off, they'd remained. He would do anything for them.

"Then tell me this," Everhart continued. "In all the years that we've known each other, you've never once wagered against me. Or Danvers, for that matter. Not a true wager. Yet a few months ago, you cleverly manipulated us into a high-stakes game."

Still standing at the sideboard with his back to the room, Lucan stared straight ahead at the glossy paneled wall. He knew what was coming. "I did."

"If you are in need…"

"I would never ask you." Lucan could have asked, he knew. Yet he'd never wanted to put that strain on their friendship. Since Lucan wasn't certain how long his losing streak at the tables would last, he'd become desperate. The wager amongst friends had been his last resort. "You agreed to the wager. And you are content, are you not?"

"More than I ever imagined," Everhart said, a smile in his voice. "I should like the same for you."

Lucan laughed. "You would like me to lose."

In that moment, Everhart's chair scraped against the floor as he stood and Calliope entered the room. She greeted her husband with a glowing smile and a kiss upon his cheek before he withdrew a chair for her. Then, walking over to the sideboard to pour a cup of tea for his bride, he nudged Lucan with his elbow. "*Au contraire*, my friend. I want you to *win*."

Lucan wanted to win too. But they were speaking of two separate victories.

"Prepare yourself, Miss Thorne," Mrs. Riley said the following morning as they stood outside Lady Whitelock's door. "There is no way of knowing what to expect."

Frances barely had a chance to steel herself before the housekeeper turned the knob. Then she nearly gasped but managed to suppress her reaction by pressing her lips together.

The viscountess's bedchamber was not what she had expected at all. It came straight out of a childlike dream. Soft pastel silks draped in filmy layers served as bed curtains and adorned the windows as well. White furs covered the floor. Painted clouds and cherubic angels climbed the walls and ceiling. For Frances, it was too much to take in all at once.

Lady Whitelock moved as if she were lost in a similar dream. Lifting her arms up from the coverlet, she slowly moved them back and forth, the lace of dressing gown swaying.

"They're dancing," she said, her voice high and airy like a child's. In truth, she looked to be Frances's age. When Mrs. Riley introduced them, however, her ladyship issued no response but merely giggled.

When Lord Whitelock had explained that his wife was an invalid, this was not what Frances had expected.

The housekeeper then quietly introduced Frances to the mob-capped nurse before taking her leave. Mrs. Darby smiled reassuringly, the pale flesh around her blue eyes crinkling at the corners. "Her ladyship is having a good day. I'm pleased that you could meet her when her spirits are high."

Surmising that it was acceptable to speak freely, Frances did but kept her voice low as they stood in the far corner of the room. "Then she is not always like this."

The ruffles on Mrs. Darby's cap fluttered when she shook her head. "I'm sad to say that her moods are ever changing. Poor thing is bound by her pain. I've heard that she took a tumble from a horse, but that happened before my time here. Such a pity for one so young. An heiress as well as an orphan. The viscount married her during her first Season. They've only been wed eight years in all, and her ladyship has been in this state for six." Mrs. Darby turned to a tea tray sitting on an ornate commode and opened one of the drawers below. Lifting out a small brown bottle, she held it carefully in her hand. "This is the only thing that saves her. We add two drops to her tea each morning, each afternoon, and then again in the evening."

"Is it laudanum?" There was no label, but Frances remembered a similar type of vial in her mother's room that had eased her suffering.

"Laudanum has no effect on her," Mrs. Darby said. "This is a special elixir, provided for his lordship by a London physician. It is the only thing that will free her ladyship from agony."

Odd. There seemed to be an aura of mystery surrounding this medicine. Or perhaps the servants were not meant to know what they were giving their mistress. Either way, Frances found it unsettling. "And will I be required to give her ladyship these drops?"

"Not at all, dear." Mrs. Darby offered another wrinkly smile as she put the brown bottle away. "You're here to divert her mind with pleasant conversation and reading. She enjoys singing as well."

Frances cringed. Lord Whitelock had not mentioned singing as a requirement. "I do not sing."

"Not sing? All of her previous companions had lovely voices." The nurse looked at her with surprise at first and then gestured with a flit of her fingers. "Nevertheless, I'm certain his lordship hired the perfect companion. Sir is good to all of us, and we are happy to have a companion for her ladyship."

"How long has her ladyship been without?"

"Let's see." Mrs. Darby pursed her lips as she hesitated, seemingly counting the length of time. "Nigh on six weeks now. Miss Momper left for her new position in mid-May, and now here we are at the end of June. Poor wee thing"—she tsked—"had a terrible bout of sickness at the first of the year. I worried for her health. Thankfully, her coloring improved, along with her appetite, and just in time for her new position. Housekeeper at a new estate—can you imagine such an honor?"

"It is quite the honor," Frances agreed. Not many in service ever achieved such a high standing. Especially not one so young as Miss Momper. From what she'd learned, none of the previous companions to Lady Whitelock had been dependent relations of the viscount's, which was rather odd. Not to mention, none of them were older than four and twenty. At seven and twenty, Frances was the oldest. And she couldn't sing. Now, she was even more grateful that Lord Whitelock had given her this opportunity. She didn't want to disappoint him.

Later that morning, the man himself strolled into his wife's bedchamber. Frances closed the book of poetry she'd been reading aloud, albeit softly because Lady Whitelock's eyes had drifted shut some time ago. Standing from the bedside chair, Frances offered a curtsy. "Lord Whitelock."

The viscount smiled. "Miss Thorne. It does my heart good to see you here, especially knowing that you are away from the dire circumstances that drove you from town."

"I cannot express my gratitude enough, my lord."

His dark gaze held hers for a moment, but he made no direct response. "How was your journey? I understand there was an incident regarding the carriage."

"I mistakenly stepped into the wrong one, but fortunately, I arrived here with minimal delay." She hoped he wouldn't press further. While she hated to sound like a featherbrain, she would rather that than mention Fallow Hall or its inhabitants. Lucan did not seem like a particular friend to Lord Whitelock and, likely, it would be best to avoid any mention of him.

"For that I am glad. I wouldn't want anything to happen to you, as you are under my care now." Unexpectedly, the low timbre of the viscount's voice caused the hair at the back of her neck to stand on end. Lucan had said something similar, but her reaction now was quite different. Lord Whitelock's tone nearly had a possessive quality about it that unsettled Frances. Then, she assured herself that it was her imagination. Lord Whitelock saw her as the daughter of someone he'd once cared about and nothing more. He was merely looking out for her best interests.

"Her ladyship has an amiable disposition. We talked for some time." The thread of conversation between them, however, had changed numerous times. Lady Whitelock spoke as if she were flitting from cloud to cloud in a dream state, her words never quite forming complete thoughts.

"I look forward to having that same opportunity with you, tonight at dinner," he said, leaving no argument. "I have business matters to which I must attend throughout the day, so that is my only time. Most evenings will be similar. Of course,

I will not require you to dress for dinner until the clothes I have ordered for you arrive."

Frances didn't know what to think. Such a request was most unusual. She'd never heard of a gentleman dining with his wife's companion. Alone. Under different circumstances, she would advise any maidservant or companion to politely decline.

Yet as she opened her mouth to do just that, she realized that after everything he'd done for her, she could easily grant him his request. Besides, perhaps he simply preferred company and conversation while dining.

With a nod, she curtsied once more and left him to visit his wife. On the way out of the bedchamber, Frances reminded herself that she was no longer at Mrs. Hunter's. Therefore, she needed to stop being so suspicious. She was determined to work diligently and earn enough to free her father from gaol. A small part of her hoped that in working here, she would finally have her faith in men restored.

At the end of the day, most of Frances's prior concerns were tucked away. She did not dine alone with Lord Whitelock at all. In fact, they were joined by a neighboring farmer and his wife, Mr. and Mrs. Stubbins, in addition to the village vicar.

Whitelock put everyone at ease with his friendly manners. The conversation meandered around the table. There was mention of a fair in the village in a sennight. The farmer spoke of the likelihood of a bountiful harvest this season. The vicar remarked about the rain and the plump grapes in his small vineyard. Frances found herself enthralled and unable to keep from asking questions. Having lived in the city all of her life, farming seemed like an exotic adventure. She said as much and commented on how the closest thing she'd come to seeing a field was when she walked through the market. Soon thereafter, Mrs. Stubbins invited her to tour their fields.

Yet due to Lucan's questions, Frances was suddenly having uncertainties of her own. Nothing untoward had happened with Lord Whitelock, of course. However, she felt a distinct discomfort around him. She couldn't pinpoint the source of it. This afternoon when he had visited his wife, he was amiable and gentlemanly. Then, in the parlor before dinner, he was the perfect host to his guests, speaking briefly of his business and the people he was able to assist in one form or another. And yet, when he'd drawn her aside and asked how she was enjoying the comfort of her surroundings, he'd seemed almost eager for her appreciation.

Perhaps he wants your gratitude…Lucan's words kept reemerging in her mind, no matter how many times she tried to push them aside.

After dinner, Frances walked through the dark gallery on the way to her bedchamber. Distracted by her thoughts, she found her steps slowing as she neared the reclining sculpture where she'd encountered Lucan last night. Yet instead of admiring the art with her lamp, she found herself searching the shadows.

"Are you here?"

Unfortunately, her whisper fell into the void of silence that followed. Disappointment filled her. Though why she'd bothered to hope in the first place, she didn't know. She knew better.

With a sigh, she lowered the candle and continued past the statues and portraits. Then she drew in a breath and noted the familiar fragrance that was Lucan's alone. Her steps faltered. Slowly, she turned, willing her pulse to slow and the eagerness not to show in her expression. *He has come, after all.*

"I thought you'd prefer a moment alone with the sculptures," Lucan said with a low, seductive laugh from the shadows. "You'd seemed quite fascinated last night."

She drew a step or two closer to the sound of his voice. The lamp in her hand only offered a pool of light around her but did not illuminate the farthest corner where she'd seen him disappear last night. "It is my understanding that the purpose of art is to be admired."

"You were certainly doing your part. In fact, Whitelock's residence must suit your tastes quite well."

"Not true. You've misinterpreted my study. I was actually wondering what I was supposed to think," she admitted. "The few chances I've had to tour the museums, I've found myself at a loss for what to think. You see, my education did not include a study of artists or their techniques. Neither my mother nor my father had any fondness for it. Therefore, when I see a sculpture such as this, I feel that I cannot fully appreciate the meaning the artist meant to convey."

Again, silence greeted her for a moment. She shifted, wondering if he was studying the sculpture or *her*. And if so, was it in the same way that she'd studied him from the second-floor window of Mrs. Hunter's agency?

"For my opinion," Lucan said at last, "I think appreciation comes from being drawn to something inexplicably. Some prefer sculpture, others paintings…and perhaps a few enjoy sketches of men's fashions."

She lowered the candle to conceal her blush. "Certainly there are those who study sketches in order to learn more about the proper fit of clothing."

"Of course. Especially for those who aspire to become tailors or dressmakers. Is that your aspiration?"

Now would be the perfect time to pretend such a desire. Yet Frances did not condone deception. Not even her own. "No."

In the brief pause that followed, she could almost hear Lucan's grin.

"Then your need for understanding does not necessarily lie with clothing but with what it conceals," he said, teasing her. He didn't even bother to mask his obvious enjoyment over how the topic discomfited her.

She refused to confirm his suspicion. "And you? Do you find nothing worth admiration in this sculpture?"

"Until this moment, I hadn't realized that I see art in a similar fashion to yours. Having been surrounded by such portraits and statues all my life, I've never paid close attention. I too have toured the museums but more for the purpose of passing the time than for the sake of admiration."

His confession nearly made her smile. "I wonder if there are others like us."

Us? Now that was a peculiar thing for her to say. Stranger still was the pleasure she felt from the image it created, of the two of them touring the museum together, each keeping the other's secret.

"I suppose we are meant to acknowledge a thing of beauty," Lucan said before she could reconcile the turn of her thoughts. "Much in the same manner that I admire the way the lamplight caresses your cheek and weaves glossy bronze pathways through your dark hair."

A breath escaped her. She lowered the lamp again. "You could make the portraits blush with your practiced flattery."

"And if it *were* practiced, I would tell you that I had no intention of charming the portraits." After a short pause, he exhaled audibly. "The truth is, I was admiring the craftsmanship of the candlemaker. Their art is sorely undervalued, wouldn't you agree?"

She fought another smile. It would do no good to feed his ego. "I do. For without light, we would have nothing to admire."

"Clearly, you have not spent enough time in darkness."

An errant wave of longing rippled through her. Suddenly, she wanted his mouth on hers again. Wanted to feel his hands on her face, his body close to hers. She searched the shadows and was tempted to blow out the candle. Perhaps he would come to her then.

Lucan cleared his throat. "Speaking of light, have you come to any new awareness today? Is all as it should be?"

"I met her ladyship. Though I am told she suffers greatly from her ailment, she was quite at ease while I was with her." *In an odd sort of way.* Frances still wasn't sure if Lady Whitelock even knew she'd been in the room. "Then Lord Whitelock arrived, and we spoke of his wife and of my duties."

"Do your duties include dining with him?" There was an underlying edge to his tone.

She shouldn't be surprised that Lucan knew about her dinner, but she was. How often was he here? And how did he maneuver around the estate without being seen? "As he told me, he is too busy during the day and requested that I report to him at dinner."

Yet the conversation had never once turned to his wife this evening. In such mixed company, however, there likely hadn't been the opportunity. She would be sure to bring up her ladyship's good health the next time.

"You are finding reasons to excuse his behavior. I beg of you not to be so forgiving."

Frances was growing weary of these warnings, which, because of him, were beginning to weigh on her mind. "Is it not by some measure of forgiveness that I am speaking with *you*? Surely I could grant the same courtesy to a man who has never wronged me."

"And yet only a day ago, you professed that you did not cast the blame of my father's sin onto me," he scoffed. "I see you have changed your mind."

"No," she corrected. "I was speaking of my abduction. I do not appreciate deception of any kind. Nor does it please me to know that you are slinking about this estate, endangering my employment."

"Is it wrong for a man to honor his promise?"

"In your case, sir, it depends on the chosen method. Surely you could ask these same questions in a letter and be equally satisfied."

"I cannot," he growled.

"*Will not*, you mean."

"Very well then, I...will...not. I will not write to you, but I will see you. Each and every day."

His hard, stubborn resolve should *not* have caused a thrill to rush through her. But something hot and tingly eddied inside her nonetheless, stealing her breath.

"However," he continued, "you needn't worry that I will endanger your position here."

"Good," she breathed. Now that he'd agreed, they could part on amicable terms, perhaps even indulge in a brief good-night kiss. Surely there could be no harm in that...

"Unless—"

That single word was like a plunge into a frigid bath. "No. There is no *unless*. If there is ever cause for me to leave my post, then I will be the one to decide. And you will honor this decision, promise or not."

Silence answered her.

"I am not a schoolroom girl with romantic ideals about my employer, no matter what you might believe. I am asking you to trust me in the same manner that I have *trusted* you." The words shocked her. Had she spoken them of her own free will? She hardly knew what to make of the unexpected declaration.

The truth was, she'd come to rely on Lucan in such a short amount of time. Yet even admitting it to herself, she could hardly give credence to such an irrational notion. Most likely, it resulted from the uncertainty of her new environment. Seeing Lucan here in Lincolnshire offered a sense of separation from the roles they'd adopted during the course of their lives. In London, even after her circumstances had altered, she'd seen herself as the daughter of his family's steward, and he a member of the family that had accused her father of treason.

Here in Lincolnshire, however, the distance seemed to allow her a broader perspective. A clearer view. She caught glimpses of Lucan that reminded her of the boy who'd once fascinated her. Only now he'd turned into a man. A man who valued promises and honor. A man who'd risked the relationship with his own family to come to her father's defense. Such an act took a great deal of courage. For those reasons—and also perhaps because of his exceptional kisses—she was willing to allow his evening visits. But only under her terms.

"Then trust me enough to know that a stubborn woman does not always know what is best for her," he said with quiet resolve. While his tone hinted at tenderness, his words dripped with arrogance.

Stubborn woman? Hmph! She growled in frustration and, without another word, turned on her heel, sweeping out of the gallery. Lucan was far more agreeable when he was flirting…or kissing.

It was a shame her night had not ended with the latter.

Chapter Twelve

For the following week, Lucan rarely slept. Each night, he lingered in the gallery at Whitelock's manor, ensuring that Frances received no unwanted visitors.

He could not account for the sudden change in him—the urgent need to ensure her safety. It was different from the others he'd helped. It was in his nature, he supposed, to want to protect those who did not look out for themselves. Yet he wasn't even certain that Frances was in danger. Nonetheless, Lucan required daily confirmation of her safety.

And perhaps part of him merely wanted to see her.

During the days, he divided his time between his friends and locating Arthur Momper's sister. The nights were devoted to Frances. Today, however, was the village fair. With any luck, she would be there. Perhaps seeing her in the light of day wouldn't be as tempting.

Their exchanges had been brief during the past few meetings. Lucan didn't dare step out of the shadows as he had the first night. Seeing her in the lamplight was all the temptation he could bear. He had to keep his distance.

They spoke in whispered conversations. She would tell him about her days but merely the events. Not her own observations. He was beginning to wonder if she was starting to see cracks in the noble façade Whitelock had created. Was the surface of his flawless statue showing signs of deterioration or rot from the inside?

Standing beside him in the music room at Fallow Hall, RJ issued a grunt as if wondering the same thing. Absently, Lucan scratched the beast behind the ears, reassuring him that all would be well. "Until I have proof, I can do nothing."

"You wear that scowl more and more often these days."

Lucan turned away from the window to see Danvers's bride stroll in for her daily piano lesson. Unlike him, she wore a smile that gleamed brightly within her cornflower blue eyes. It was no hardship to grin in return. "It must have been a trick of the light."

Hedley eyed him with speculation. Having suffered in her youth as well, she knew the root of the darkness in him better than the others. And there was no deceiving her. "One would think you'd walk around gloating each day after having won your wager against my husband and Calliope's."

"You are all far too happy to inspire gloating. Truly, newlyweds are the worst losers." He feigned a grumble of disgust, but in truth, he couldn't have been happier for them. Nonetheless, he preferred to remain cautious about revealing too much of himself.

Perhaps that was one of the reasons he was drawn to Frances. She was wary of revealing herself too.

"Even Boris has noticed a change in you," Hedley said, petting the Beast of Fallow Hall, who would always be *RJ* to him. "He's been listless as well. I think perhaps he formed an attachment to Miss Thorne, and he misses her."

Lucan eyed his friend shrewdly. "He did not form at attachment to Miss Thorne. He barely knows her."

"He has this uncanny ability to know when the right person—"

"Hedley," Lucan warned.

She shrugged and sat on the bench. "We only want you to be happy. And it has nothing to do with the wager."

"Nothing, hmm?"

She laughed and began playing the scales with a great deal of flair. "Well, not in *my* case. My husband, however, might want your happiness *and* for you to lose the wager."

But he feared that happiness and losing the wager could never exist together. Because if he lost the wager and Hugh Thorne went to the hangman, then Lucan would never see Frances again.

The village hosted a fair in honor of Saint Etheldrea near the end of June each year. Lord Whitelock was good enough to allow the entire household time away to enjoy the afternoon. Penny, Nannette, Bess, and Mrs. Darby were amongst Frances's group. In the week since her arrival, they'd taken her in as one of their own.

"Many couples choose this day to be married," Nannette said as the church bells rang and a pair of newlyweds walked out from the chapel on the hill, beaming from ear to ear.

"I thought Etheldrea was a virgin saint," Frances whispered, confused. "She managed to persuade her husband to honor her vow of chastity throughout their marriage." Surely that couldn't be the intention of the couples marrying on this day.

"It has more to do with our strawberries, which are abundant in this village," Mrs. Darby said and then lowered her voice to a whisper and offered a cheeky grin. "Because the berries are covered in seeds, some believe they have a certain fertile power. Mark my words, by next March, the village will be full of babes, all fresh and new."

Behind the churchyard, small stalls and tents outlined the open green. Jugglers and performers milled about the crowd. Unlike a London festival, the air here smelled like sweet strawberries and the fresh hay growing in the surrounding fields. While Frances missed her father and Kaye and wrote to them each day, she'd discovered that she truly enjoyed living in the country.

The people were friendlier and smiled more. There wasn't any shoving or bustling, not even in the market. Her surroundings were idyllic too. The sounds were not of shouting and coarse language. Instead, she heard joyful cheers and children's laughter.

She could imagine having a family in a place like this, which was surprising for her. She'd never thought to entertain that notion again. Perhaps after a time, and after her father was situated, she might find a husband in this village. A widower who wouldn't mind a woman of her advanced years, or a shop owner in need of someone to assist him, or even—

Lucan Montwood crossed her field of vision.

He had an uncanny way of appearing just when she least expected it. Although, that wasn't entirely true. Lately, he was more apt to appear precisely when said he would.

There was something endearing about the way he held to his promise to see her at the end of each day. Of course, she didn't actually *see* him. After that first night, whenever she spoke with him, he remained in the shadows. Even so, knowing he was there filled her with a sense of peace but also restlessness too.

Eagerly, with each encounter, she waited to see if he would draw closer. The constant conflict inside her had kept her far too preoccupied. More often than not, she found herself thinking of him and wanting to see him again.

And now, here he was, lingering along the outskirts of the fair. His dark hair and a charcoal gray coat blended in with the shadows cast by the tents and stalls. He even wore a gray cravat. The color suited him remarkably well.

Loping beside him was RJ, his nose lifted high in the air as he took in all the fragrances, as if searching for his next snack.

Surreptitiously, she watched Lucan move, admiring the sureness of his gait and remembering the firm muscles she'd spotted beneath those tails that day in London. The morning seemed to grow warmer the longer she watched him. Even standing beneath the shade of a chestnut tree did not help. A droplet of perspiration slipped from beneath her bonnet and meandered down her throat.

"Miss Thorne, you must try this strawberry wine the vicar made," Nannette said, offering a tin cup. "It's delicious."

Overheated and needing refreshment, Frances took a sip and then another. The sweet flavor tasted like summer in her cup. "*Mmm*…lovely."

Above the rim, she watched Lucan lingering near a table laden with pastries. He held a shilling and flicked it with his thumb into the air before catching it. Standing near the corner of platters of strawberry tarts, buns, and scones, he leaned in. His coat stretched taut along the length of his back, displaying the breadth of his shoulders and the leanness of his waist. He closed his eyes and licked his lips. She felt the sudden desire to turn herself into a pastry.

Then, just when she thought he would flip the coin toward the baker, he straightened and shook his head before walking on.

She felt oddly disappointed.

"These strawberries are divine," Penny said, popping up in front of her. "You must try some, though perhaps you'll want to remove your gloves first."

"Oh, yes, of course." Not wanting to stain her best gloves, Frances slipped them off and tucked them away. Penny promptly filled her hands with warm, ripe berries. The scent teased, making her salivate. She took a bite. The sweetness burst in her mouth, flooding her taste buds. "They're like heaven, Penny. Thank you."

As she moved on with her group while they sampled jams, she wondered if Lucan had tasted the strawberries yet. She still kept her gaze on him.

Standing all the way across park, both he and RJ seemed to be watching something with avid interest. When she followed the path of their gazes, she saw a magician's stall with a wall of brightly colored ribbons behind him. A bevy of girls gathered around trying to guess his trick for a prize. But there was also a young boy with a messy mop of dark hair, jumping up and down, eager for the chance to win as well. The boy held up a shiny penny. The magician tried to shoo him away several times. Apparently, the man was only interested in having girls and young women at his stall. But after it appeared the boy wouldn't give up, the magician snatched the coin before waving his hands over the three bowls.

With a flourish, he presented a bean and summarily slipped it beneath one of the bowls. After maneuvering the bowls around and around, he gestured for the boy to choose. The boy pointed to the bowl in the middle. The magician's lips curled in a somewhat fiendish grin as he lifted the bowl. There was no bean beneath it. Left with nothing, the boy lowered his head and walked on.

That was precisely why Frances loathed deception.

To her surprise—and then annoyance—Lucan stepped over to the magician's stall, while RJ slipped away amidst the crowd. The girls, some of whom she recognized as maids at Lord Whitelock's estate, giggled and blushed at whatever he said in greeting. Frances felt the urge to instruct them about proper behavior. What saved her from marching across the knoll to do just that was the way Lucan turned his attention to the magician.

Lucan tossed a coin and the man caught it handily, that fiendish grin reappearing. As before, he presented the bean with a wave of his hand and then slipped it beneath one of the bowls. He moved them around at a dizzying speed. When finished, he gestured for Lucan to choose, but Lucan shook his head. Then he gestured to the magician's hand. A short argument ensued with the magician pointing to the bowls. Lucan turned to the surrounding coven of gigglers. After a short speech and an elegant bow, he appeared to be employing their assistance.

In the next moment, three of them reached forward and lifted one bowl each. There was no bean. Frances could hear their gasps across the park. The magician attempted a look of surprise and began searching for the lost bean until Lucan deftly captured the magician's hand to reveal that the bean had been there all along.

Shaking their heads, the girls stormed away from the stall. Lucan gestured to the wall of ribbons and the magician handed one over reluctantly. While Frances was impressed by Lucan's uncanny ability to spot the missing bean, she was also disappointed that he'd done all that to win a ribbon for one of the maids. Disappointed and…*jealous*. And not a mild sort either. As he left the stall and started crossing the park in the direction of the maids, hot, churning envy boiled in her stomach.

She hated herself for feeling it. He was a skilled deceiver and he'd just proven it. If she were smart, she wouldn't give Lucan a passing thought. She would forget about that kiss and the way it felt to stand alone with him in the dark. She would—

Just when she was about to turn away, she noticed that Lucan had passed the girls and caught up with the boy instead. With a tap on the shoulder, the boy looked up, wiping his nose on his sleeve. Lucan held out two closed fists and the boy pointed to one.

In the next instant, a bright blue ribbon appeared, waving in the breeze like a banner. The boy beamed. He lifted his face to Lucan's and received a nod. Then, as he took the ribbon, Lucan gave a penny to the boy as well.

Caught up in the boy's elation as he scurried across the park, she watched as he approached a man pushing a woman in a Bath chair, wearing a quilt over her legs. Proudly, the boy presented the ribbon to the woman, who must have been his mother, for she wrapped her arms around him and kissed him on the head.

Frances felt tears sting her eyes. Lucan had outmaneuvered the magician's trick solely for the boy?

Her heart fluttered in a queer sort of way. It wasn't as she'd suspected at all. In fact, Lucan was turning out to be far more than she'd ever guessed. She searched for him again, only to see him slip into a red-fringed fortune-teller's tent at the end of the row.

Unable to help herself, she made her excuses to the group and followed him. She encountered RJ along the way. He brushed beside her only long enough to receive a friendly scratch behind the ears before he moved on.

At the tent, she noted the sign hanging from a chain, indicating that the fortune-teller would return shortly. Frances listened at the flap for any sound but heard nothing. Perhaps Lucan had stepped inside and then left through another exit. She turned around to search the crowd just as a familiar long-fingered hand reached out and snatched hers, flesh to flesh. A rush ran through her as Lucan pulled her into the tent.

The flap closed behind her, blocking the daylight and muffling the noise of the crowd outside. It took a moment to clear away the splotches of light in her eyes. During that time, Lucan held on to her hand as if to steady her but kept a discreet distance. Behind him, two empty chairs sat at opposite sides of a small round table draped in deep velvets and silks. The air was thick and heady with incense. And they were completely alone.

Suddenly, the contact of her hand in his seemed far more intimate.

"You're following me, Miss Thorne."

Yes. She'd followed him because he'd surprised her and because she needed to know more about this man.

"Perhaps I want my fortune told," she said, her focus on the feel of his warm flesh against hers. She turned her wrist, shifting slightly to thread her fingers through his until they were palm to palm. The rough callused pads below his fingers elicited tingles through her body. A sense of longing stirred. It had been nearly a week since he'd last touched her. Until now, she hadn't realized how desperately she'd missed the contact.

Lucan tightened his grip. In that small gesture, he revealed so much. Perhaps he'd missed touching her as well. Then, stepping in front of her, he reached down for her other hand and lifted it. He turned her wrist so that her palm faced his gaze. But he wasn't looking at her hand. He was looking at her. There was not enough light to illuminate the amber in his irises. That must have been why they appeared dark, rimmed only with a thin halo of pale color. His thumb stroked the dewy surface of her palm, eliciting spears of pleasure along every nerve inside her.

"I see a long life of passion." Lifting her hand higher, his mouth took the place of his thumb, his gaze never leaving hers. The tip of his tongue traced the long horizontal line directly above the hollow of her palm. His teeth scraped the fleshy pad above.

She inhaled sharply. Her body clenched in a swift but almost sweet pain. A steady, throbbing pulse forced her to press her thighs together. Yet what she really wanted was to feel him…*there.*

"But not until you leave Whitelock's employ," he added before lowering her hand. While his gaze remained fixed on hers, his jaw hardened with resolve.

At seven and twenty, she was far more eager for passion than unwanted advice. She did not care for his tender manipulation. With a grumble of frustration, she slipped both her hands free and took a step back.

"Have you proof, then? Or are you still trying to poison my mind into seeing lechery where there is goodness?"

"Proof has a tendency to reveal itself past the eleventh hour," Lucan said, clenching his jaw so hard that a muscle twitched.

A frisson of apprehension tore through her at his dire warning. There was so much she did not know about his past. It was telling, however, that he'd publicly sided with her father instead of his own family. "If I knew the nature of your qualms, perhaps I could better listen to your warning."

He searched her gaze, his expression unreadable.

Believing that doubt was the cause for his delay in responding, she added, "I've spent a goodly number of years discovering all manner of sordid tales. I can assure you that I am the last person to defend someone when I believe them of wrongdoing."

"Then you are keeping a watchful eye, still, and have not been persuaded by the *appearance* of good?" His brows lifted, waiting for her answer. He even seemed to be holding his breath.

The unabashed concern she witnessed stole her breath. Was it possible that his warning did not come solely from an obligation to her father? That, perhaps, he cared for her? Though, after witnessing what he'd done for the boy, she wondered if he felt an obligation to protect everyone he encountered. There was no reason to believe she was anything special. But that's exactly what she wanted to believe.

She took a moment to weigh her response. "As of yet, I have not been swayed to either side."

"Though perhaps you are listing to my side now? Before, you refused to hear me at all." Lifting a hand, he grazed his knuckles along the edge of his jaw. A smirk toyed with his dimple.

He saw through her too easily.

"I heard you." Yet she wasn't ready to reveal the change occurring within her. "I credit the reason to your unpleasant tone. It has a grating quality that is impossible silence."

The full force of his grin flashed at her and in that moment, she wondered if he'd already noticed the change. "Then I will be cautious of what I reveal."

"And you are not cautious already?" she scoffed. "You reveal so little as it is."

Lucan propped a shoulder against the center pole of the tent and stared down at a crown he now rolled over his fingers. "Perhaps there is a reason."

"Of course there is a reason. We all have our own, do we not?" How could he look at her with such heat in one moment, concern in another, and yet still treat her as if she were a stranger? She'd confessed private thoughts to him regarding her mother and Roger Quinlin, albeit unexpectedly. Yet Lucan did not confide in her. He didn't even tell her the root of his suspicions against Lord Whitelock.

Frustrated by this, she prepared to leave. Turning, she peered through the gap in the tent flap to see if her exit would be noticed. Directly outside, she saw RJ blocking the way with his large body, as if standing sentinel. He turned his gray head in her direction, and she could have sworn that he winked at her. But no, that was impossible.

"What do you want to know?" Lucan asked from directly behind her. His hand closed over hers on the tent flap, drawing it away and turning her to face him at the same time.

His resolute expression told her that this was not an easy question for him. But apparently, he wanted her to stay. That alone touched her far more than it should have. She decided to go easy on him. "A few minutes ago, you gave a young boy a ribbon so that he could give it to his mother. Why?"

"You were watching me. And I thought you were too distracted by strawberry wine."

Ah, then he'd been watching her too. The knowledge made her feel warm. "You're distracting me *and* stalling."

"Am I such a curiosity, Miss Thorne?"

He was, and she wanted to know everything about him. "You knew the magician was hiding the bean and that the boy would have lost no matter which bowl he chose."

He shrugged, but there was a level of tension in the movement. "The man was a bully, amusing himself with the misfortunes of a child."

Suspicion filled her and she couldn't let the matter drop. "How did you learn his trick, and the other one you did at Fallow Hall?"

"My father." He took a step away and began to prowl around the tent like an amber-eyed lion in a cage. Anger rolled off him, giving her a glimpse into that darker part that he usually kept hidden. "But for me, there were more dire consequences than the loss of a coin."

"What were yours, then?" she asked in a whisper of dread. She didn't want to know, but at the same time, she *had* to know.

Another shrug. "The loss of a glazed bun. The loss of supper as well. Sometimes the loss of consciousness. Sometimes worse."

She felt sick. He'd been starved and beaten as a child. What could be worse? She didn't ask, however. If he wanted to tell her, he would. If he felt that he *could* tell her—if, perhaps, he saw her as a friend—then he would. Drawing in a breath, she waited.

"I was fortunate to escape," he said at last. "My mother, however, was not. As you know, she…died when I was in my fourth year of school."

Sudden awareness struck. All this time, she'd thought it had been an accident. All this time, she'd been so blind…

"Lucan, I'm so—" Tears gathered in her eyes and clogged her throat before she could compose herself. Quickly, she turned away before he could see her. Removing her spectacles, she blotted away the dampness with her fingertips. She felt his approach more than heard it. The security she felt at his nearness enveloped her, tempting her to close her eyes and simply fall back into his embrace.

But of course, she would not do that. Instead, she replaced her spectacles before facing him. She opened her mouth to tell him how sorry she was for the horror he'd lived through, but he pressed a fingertip against her lips, silencing her.

"You used my name without formality."

She wanted to shrug as he had done, but he was now holding her shoulders and drawing her near.

"I hope it was not pity that inspired you." He searched her gaze, seeing through her lenses in a way that made her feel undressed.

"My own error," she explained. "Since I rarely use the formality in my thoughts, it must have slipped." It wasn't until she glimpsed the appearance of his dimple that she realized what she had revealed. Drat her tendency to blurt! "Merely because thinking your entire name takes a great deal of effort...and therefore needs to be shortened. You have spent very little time occupying my thoughts. At all."

Lucan shook his head slowly. "And if I said the same, would my lies hold the fragrance of strawberries, as yours do?"

Her pulse beat wildly. "Have you eaten strawberries today?"

"I lived vicariously through each berry that passed your lips," he said, holding her against him now. "You're not easy to resist."

"But you do resist me, just like those pastries on the table."

The rasp of a wry laugh escaped him. "It isn't the same at all. In fact, you might be my downfall."

She saw his intent in the subtle shift of his posture and in the way his gaze drifted to her mouth. He was going to kiss her once more. At last.

Yet in that same instant, the tinkle of bells at the back of the tent alerted them to the fortune-teller's arrival. Swiftly, Lucan set Frances apart from him.

He bowed to the gypsy and slipped silver into her palm. "Please be kind to the lady."

And then he disappeared.

Chapter Thirteen

A scream broke through Lady Whitelock's chamber door the following morning. Frances rushed in. Mrs. Darby was leaning over a wild, clawing woman who only partly resembled the other-worldly lady who usually resided here.

"*Wantonness! Filthy succubus!*" the viscountess hissed, her body writhing off the bed.

Mrs. Darby, who outweighed her mistress by two stone, was struggling to hold her down. Her ruffled cap had fallen and hanks of graying hair stuck to her face with perspiration.

"What can I do?" Frances asked, beside her. A shattered teacup lay at her feet with a fan of liquid spattering the floor and the bedside table.

"Her drops. In the drawer. She needs her tea."

"*Tea! Tea! She needs her tea!*" Lady Whitelock screamed and then hysterical, high-pitched laughter filled the room.

At the commode, Frances jerked open the drawer to find the brown vial. With the teacup in pieces, she had to improvise with a water glass. "How many drops, Mrs. Darby?"

"Two. Only two," the nurse replied, panting from exertion.

Frances's hand shook as she lifted the dropper. She'd been warned about Lady Whitelock's spells, but this was her first time witnessing one. It was truly terrifying. She added a splash of tea to the glass, only enough for a single swallow. A bitter, somewhat familiar, scent rose as she moved to Mrs. Darby's side. A chill sliced through Frances, but she attributed it to the urgency of the moment and dismissed it.

"I'll hold her still. You'll have to pry her mouth open," the nurse told her. "Put your hand on her chin and pull down. You won't hurt her—she's stronger than she appears."

Lady Whitelock turned that feral gaze to Frances and bared her teeth. *"You're next, dearie."*

Frances hesitated. That was a mistake. Lady Whitelock snapped at her, trying to bite her fingers. Drawing back, Frances collected herself with a quick breath and tried to think of this as simply a part of her duties. She always managed to complete every task required of her. This was no different. It simply had to be done.

With a firm hand, she held Lady Whitelock's chin, drew it down, and then poured the tea into her mouth. Her ladyship coughed. Some of the tea sputtered out. Not knowing what else to do, Frances covered the viscountess's mouth with her hand until she swallowed.

"Move your hand before she nips you," Mrs. Darby warned, and Frances obeyed, taking a step backward.

Lady Whitelock's head thrashed back and forth, her chest rising and falling with shallow, rapid breaths. Then in a matter of moments, her white-knuckled grip on the bedclothes relaxed. Her spine eased down onto the bed. Her breathing turned, deep and even.

Mrs. Darby stood back and wiped perspiration from her brow. "And now she'll rest. Her ladyship is at peace."

"Is this what normally happens?" That bitter scent clung to her. Frances folded her arms in a measure of comfort. She instantly thought of Lucan, wanting to feel *his* arms around her. She wanted to feel safe. It was morning, but still she had the urge to run to the gallery and call out for him, hoping he would materialize at her will.

"Her ladyship suffers greatly when the pain is upon her," Mrs. Darby said, walking toward the door. "Now, I must inform his lordship directly about the episode."

"Is there nothing that can be done for her?" To live like this was no life at all. The viscountess either lingered in a dream state or was trapped in apparent agony.

The nurse breathed a heavy sigh. "His lordship does everything he can for her. It makes my heart ache to think of how much he gives but takes nothing in return."

Absently, Frances watched her disappear through the doorway. Again, Lucan's words sifted through her mind. *Perhaps he wants your gratitude.* A shiver ran over her skin, and she hugged herself tighter. Why *was* Lord Whitelock was so selfless and generous? Was it because he indeed wanted gratitude and for people to feel indebted to him? If that were true, then was his purpose for the flattery of his own ego or something more sinister?

Frances shook her head, disliking the direction of her thoughts. She was allowing Lucan's opinions too much free rein inside her head. After all, an important man such as Lord Whitelock could not deceive everyone. She knew how society worked. Whispers of scandal sprouted from small things—the barest hint of indiscretion—and she'd heard many while working at Mrs. Hunter's. But there had been no whispers about Lord Whitelock. Only servants who sang his praises for coming to their rescue.

There was no reason for her to imagine Lord Whitelock as anything other than a kind benefactor. And if the gratitude of his servants appealed to his ego, then surely there could be little harm in it. After all, his wife was incapable of providing him with praise or attentiveness. Even at his age, he was still a handsome man who doubtlessly missed the affection that only a wife could provide. Or rather, only a wife *should* provide…

Stop it, Frances. She would not discredit his benevolence simply because she'd been startled. Pushing her puzzled thoughts to the back of her mind, she went about cleaning up the mess.

By the time Lord Whitelock walked into the bedchamber, she was feeling more like herself. He looked over at his wife, resting peacefully now.

Then his dark gaze skimmed over Frances as he crossed the room. "How are you faring?"

"I am well, my lord," she said firmly, straightening her shoulders in an attempt to appear as if the episode had not shaken her. "However, her ladyship was in a great deal of agony."

"It is a difficult thing to witness for one not used to such trials." He reached out in a friendly gesture and patted Frances on the arm.

She smiled reassuringly, not wanting him to think she couldn't fulfill her duties here. "I wish I could have done something more for her."

"Mrs. Darby said you were remarkable."

Only now did Frances notice that Mrs. Darby had not returned with the viscount. The door was closed as well.

Suddenly, his close proximity and lingering hand on her arm disquieted her, and her previous thoughts interrupted.

She took a step back and gestured toward his wife. "Her ladyship needed our strength, and we came together for her sake."

"I can see your mother in you, Miss Thorne," he said with tender affection. At least, that was the reason Frances gave herself for seeing the unexpected grin on his lips. "Elise had a strong will and a feisty spirit. It's what called me to her. Alas, she chose your father, and our friendship ended. Yet I still hold her memory in my heart. I am pleased—perhaps selfishly so—that I can claim part of her spirit once more by having you here."

Frances felt another shiver slither through her, but did not reveal it. "I hope to serve her ladyship well."

"I'm certain you will serve us both very well indeed." He held out his hand in a request for hers.

When she complied, he covered it with his other hand and gently squeezed as if to comfort her. Yet she felt no comfort, only coldness and the desire to quit the room.

"Take the rest of the day for yourself. I should like to see you refreshed at dinner this evening."

She sank into a grateful curtsy when he released her. "Thank you, my lord."

Then without any further exchange between them, she swept out of the room, out of the house, and down the road that led to Fallow Hall.

Lucan rode Quicksilver toward Whitelock's manor. He needed to speak with the driver who'd taken Henny Momper to Wales. Because, according to the missive that Lucan had received this morning, Henny Momper had never arrived.

Lucan's friend in Wales had scouted Whitelock's property there and even met up with the caretaker. At that point, he'd learned that Miss Momper wasn't even expected to arrive for another two months.

Thinking of Arthur and the promise Lucan had made to him, Lucan felt sick with dread. The toll of those bells rang louder, deafening him. *Two months?* Then where was Miss Momper now? More important, why hadn't she written to her brother?

Compiling the list of all he knew about Henny Momper, which wasn't much, he tried to see things from a different perspective. Suspicion regarding the debt he owed Whitelock in addition to Lucan's near-obsessive desire to ensure that Frances was safe clouded his judgment. It was difficult to see past those elements, but he tried.

Whitelock had taken in Miss Momper and quickly elevated her to a position of companion for the viscountess. Then, Henny had left Whitelock's lair to begin a new position as housekeeper—a position at which she was not expected for two more months. And finally, she had not written to her brother—her only surviving family—since leaving.

None of it made sense. If Whitelock was as good as he made himself appear, then where in damnation was Miss Momper? Of course, her disappearance *could* merely be a misunderstanding. Perhaps she was off somewhere receiving training for her new post.

Instinct, however, told Lucan otherwise. Miss Momper could very well be in danger. Or worse.

That was the thought spinning webs in his mind when he rounded the bend and saw Frances walking on the road toward him. She stopped the instant she saw him. Her shoulders drooped on an exhale and her lips curved slightly upward, as if she was glad—or even relieved—by his presence.

Concerned, he dismounted instantly and strode to her. He noted the uncharacteristic waywardness of her hair. Fine, burnished bronze tendrils had broken free from the sensible twist at the crown of her head. The breeze lifted them like feathers, to brush against her cheeks and forehead. A sheen of perspiration on her face made them cling.

He stopped just short of taking her by the shoulders. If he took her by the shoulders, then he would likely haul her against him. And he might not be able to let her go.

They stood toe-to-toe nonetheless. "What has happened?" She shook her head. "Nothing—"

"Miss Thorne, do not pretend for one moment that I know you so little. We are beyond that."

She must have witnessed the doggedness in his expression because she slowly nodded. "We are. However, if it were a matter that I wished to keep to myself, no amount of coercion—kindly meant or not—could induce me to speak."

He knew that well enough. Lucan offered a stiff nod, not wanting to delay her explanation further. He was already imaging the worst possible circumstances, and he only needed a single word from her to head straight to Whitelock's manor and murder the viscount.

Frances glanced away. "To tell you the truth, I'm feeling somewhat unsure of myself. The experience I had just now has me in a muddle. I don't know what to believe."

"What happened?" When an opponent at the tables refused to meet his gaze, it was a telltale sign of withholding and the fear of giving himself away, either with a good hand or a bad one. Lucan didn't like not knowing what Frances's eyes would tell him. It left him to wonder what she *wasn't* saying.

"I was in the viscountess's bedchamber and…" Still, she didn't look at him. "Her ladyship had an episode this morning. She was writhing in agony. She needed her drops—the medicine the nurse puts in her tea—but I stopped cold. For the first time, I was faced with a circumstance in which I did not know how to react." Shaking her head as if in self-disgust, she finally met his gaze. "I am being paid handsomely for my job as companion. Far more than I deserve. And now I cannot resolve the amount of guilt inside of me. How can I take a salary without performing all of my duties to the best of my ability? Not only that, but I've been given the rest of the day off as well."

Lucan relaxed marginally. For a moment, he'd thought she was going to confess something else. There was no need for murder, after all, only reassurance. Reaching out, he grabbed Quicksilver's reins when what he really wanted to do was take Frances in his arms. But he wasn't in control enough to trust himself at the moment. "I'm certain you performed to the best of your ability at the time. Surely having never expected or encountered one of the viscountess's episodes, you can easily forgive yourself."

She shook her head. "My hesitation today could have been detrimental."

"If your friend Miss North were to come to you with the same concerns, would you forgive her and advise her to forgive herself?"

Her eyes lifted to the canopy of trees overhead. "Kaye? Of course."

"Then it is settled," he said and waited for the furrows of worry to smooth away from her forehead. Instead, she knitted her fingers. "Unless…" he added, "there is *more* to your experience that disturbed you?"

She blinked owlishly at him but quickly shook her head. "No. Of course not."

Her reaction alerted his suspicions once again. Yet instead of pressing further, he decided on another tactic. What she needed was a distraction to about this morning and the sense of failure. "Place your hands on my shoulders, Miss Thorne."

"For what purpose?" she asked but complied instantly.

He would have preferred a little hesitation on her part. Or he *should* have. With her hands on him, he was already abandoning his resolve to keep his distance and not test his control. Then, even though he had not asked her to, she stepped closer. Too close and yet not close enough.

"I've decided to abduct you again." Before he lost the battle within himself, he settled his hands at her waist and lifted her off the ground and up onto the saddle in one motion. With her legs draped over one side, she took hold of the pommel for support. Then, he slipped his foot into the stirrup and mounted behind her.

Through all this, she gave no argument. She never once ordered him to release her. Not even when he pulled her against the cradle of his thighs. The elicit pleasure he gained from having her close made him wish she'd issue a razor-tongued set-down. Then again, he rather enjoyed those from her as well.

With the reins in one hand and the other locked around her waist, he turned Quicksilver around and headed back toward Fallow Hall. "Are you comfortable?"

She'd been looking everywhere but at him since he first sat behind her. Now, she glanced at him from over the rims of her spectacles. A blush tinted her cheek. "Not at all, but I believe that is for the best."

He grinned at her sound judgment. "I couldn't agree more."

As they rode, her body moved in the rhythm of Quicksilver's canter, her hip pressing against Lucan's groin intimately. All he could think about was what it would feel like to have her moving against him like this, only straddling him. No doubt Frances Thorne would enjoy and excel in a position of power. The thought quickly began to drive him insane.

After a short distance, she murmured a sound of frustration. "I don't quite know what to do with my hands."

"Pray, do not ask me," he groaned. Right now he could be very explicit in his instruction.

His grip around her waist was firm enough that she needn't hold on to anything. In the end, however, she kept her grip on the pommel, one hand folded over the other. Gradually, she relaxed, leaning into the security of that arm, her shoulder nestled into his.

"When I first saw you riding around the corner," she began, "you looked equally as troubled. Might I ask the reason…or are we not quite beyond such familiarity?"

For him, they were. He shared with her more than he did with anyone else. More peculiar was that he wanted her to know about his life, even at the risk of telling her how he'd come to have such a dark soul. Perhaps he wanted to warn her away. Or perhaps the reason was more complicated than he wanted to think about at present.

One thing was for certain, if he wanted to continue to keep her trust, then he needed to share more with her. Not only that, but what he'd learned today might help her stay on her guard around Whitelock. "Conversation is a good distraction," he said, knowing it was best option. "When you saw me approach, I was concerned about recent news. You see, there is a tiger in Whitelock's employ. The lad's sister was companion to Lady Whitelock until recently."

Frances scrutinized him, her brow furrowed. "If you are speaking of Miss Momper, I have heard of her. She left the position to take another."

"She is the only family Arthur has left. Yet…she hasn't written to him in all her time away. He is worried. On his behalf, I sent a missive to Wales to check on Miss Momper's arrival at Whitelock's hunting box but learned that she never arrived. In fact, she wasn't expected to report for another two months."

Frances's expression altered from confusion to surprise and then to pleasure. "You are actually telling me your suspicions?"

One of them. He nodded. "I would not forgive myself if I allowed anything more to happen to you."

"Lucan, you are not at the root of my worries."

Just when he had a firm hand on his control, her use of his given name weakened his resolve. He closed his eyes, hearing the echo of it inside his head. Unconsciously, his grip around her waist tightened, fingers splayed. Her supple breast pressed invitingly against him. It was not until he felt her quick puff of breath against his jaw that he realized he'd drawn her closer. Desire filled every inch of his flesh. The satisfaction he craved was within reach. But now was not the time. Inwardly, he shook himself and repositioned her.

"Yet if I had made an effort to earn your trust in the beginning, you might have heeded my warning, and then I would not have felt compelled to abduct you…the first time." He added the last in order to keep to the truth because as for abducting her this time, nothing could have stopped him.

"I can see why your young friend would be alarmed." She hesitated, her gaze drifting as if she were lost in thought. "There could be a simple explanation, however. One does not advance to an important position of housekeeper without having had the proper training, after all. Likely, Miss Momper is in another of Lord Whitelock's houses as an apprentice."

He'd thought of that as well. But he wondered why she wouldn't have trained here.

"Yet why not the manor here?" Frances asked, as if their thoughts were interwoven.

They both fell silent, each lost in thought. The road beneath them gradually brought Fallow Hall into view, and Lucan felt a pang of remorse. Soon, he would have to release her. Worse, he knew that he couldn't allow himself the pleasure of her close proximity in the future. Because next time, they might not have the inconvenience of riding on the back of a horse in daylight. Hell only knew what he'd have done by now in the shadows.

"You care for the boy a great deal."

Lucan shrugged. "Anyone who met him would find themselves with a similar regard."

Having been spotted or scented by RJ, Fallow Hall's front door opened as they approached. Valentine stood there as RJ bounded out, yawping excitedly as he tromped around the horse in a circle. A footman rushed out to take hold of Quicksilver, and Lucan dismounted. Taking Frances by the waist, he lowered her to the ground. Not embracing her was a challenge. Thankfully, with their audience, Lucan found the strength to step back to a more appropriate distance.

RJ stopped near them, tail wagging and tongue hanging out of one side of his mouth in his canine version of a grin. He offered a low *woof*, his gaze traveling from Lucan to Frances and then back again. They both reached out to pet him at once, their fingers colliding. Lucan drew back. Then, surprising him, Frances reached out and grasped his arm.

Her expression was troubled again. "I just thought of this, but Lady Whitelock's nurse mentioned that Miss Momper had taken ill earlier in the year. They were all worried for her health, but I've been told that she recovered. You don't think that her illness has returned and she is lying abed somewhere and unable to write her brother, do you?"

Lucan absorbed this new information with dread. A dark suspicion filled him. He added this to what he already knew. Henny Momper had been elevated to a position of companion within a year's time. She'd taken ill, but recovered. And…she wasn't expected to arrive at her new post for another two months.

He cursed under his breath. "Later, I will speak with the driver to learn where he took her. I should have done that in the beginning," he said, unable to resist the urge to cover Frances's hand with his own. Was Whitelock the kind of man who would abuse his position and seduce a young woman in his employ? The question left him unsettled.

"Are you thinking the worst?" Frances asked.

"I pray that I am wrong."

CHAPTER FOURTEEN

Shortly after her arrival, Frances sat with Calliope and Hedley in the cheery parlor of Fallow Hall. There were no bold murals here or a clutter of imposing statues. Instead, silk wallpaper printed with orchids adorned the walls. A lovely shade of mauve dressed the windows and the upholstered chairs. A cream-and-gold striped camelback sofa sat in between a pair of tall windows, overlooking a garden in full bloom.

"Thank you for receiving me without notice," she said, ignoring their pointedly eager expressions. She knew what they were thinking. "I was offered the day to myself, and I thought how lovely it would be to see the two of you again."

"It was fortunate that Montwood happened by at the same time," Hedley said, her gaze bright with apparent curiosity.

"I'd say it was more of a peculiar coincidence," Frances amended. The man in question had left her in good company while he went to join his male friends. Obviously, he did not want to give the incorrect impression either.

Unlike Lucan, RJ seemed to prefer her company. The beast lay his head atop her knee, his eyes lifted in a plea for affection. She obliged him readily and earned the contented thump of his tail rapping against the table leg.

Seated across from her on the sofa, Calliope offered a knowing smile, as if RJ's behavior was some sort of mystical sign. "We are more delighted than we can say."

"It is true." Hedley passed her a plate of biscuits. "We missed our chance to see you at the fair, which was my fault entirely—I suffered a dizzy spell on the way, causing my friends to turn back."

"I hope you are well." Frances searched her friend's face for any sign of distress. Since her own mother had died because of an illness, she'd sometimes found herself worrying excessively over others. Coupling this announcement with her previous conversation about Henny Momper, Frances was quickly alarmed.

She saw no distress, however. In fact, Hedley appeared ebullient.

"Most assuredly. In the best possible way." At present, Hedley cast a glance over to Calliope before settling a hand over her own middle, providing a clue to the source of her joy. Apparently, *both* Calliope and Hedley were with child.

Relieved, Frances smiled. "Then Fallow Hall will be graced with two new arrivals. Please accept my greatest congratulations."

"Thank you, though I will be happier once my sickness ends. Mr. Hingston, the village doctor, assures me that his own wife, who bore him seven children, rarely suffered from illness beyond the first few months."

The conversation sparked a memory within Frances, niggling at the back of her mind. Yet before she could grasp it, Calliope spoke.

"We understand that Montwood was fortunate enough to exchange a word of greeting with you at the festival," Calliope said after a sip from her cup. "He mentioned that he'd spotted you preparing to have your fortune read. That is something I've always wanted to do. Tell me, was there a crystal ball filled with dark, swirling smoke?"

Frances laughed, recalling the silliness of the entire episode. "There was little magic, though smoke enough from the burning incense. The gypsy read my palm and suggested I would have a happy union and bless my husband with three sons and one daughter. I then explained that I was not married, not to mention past the age of a providing my fictional husband with such a brood. That was when she closed one eye, peered closer at my palm, and said, 'A king will decide your fate within a fortnight.'"

"A *king*—imagine that." Calliope was equally amused, though there was a trace of disappointment in her countenance, as if she'd hoped for different news. Perhaps regarding a certain gentleman they knew.

Frances had to admit that she'd been disappointed as well but only for the briefest of moments. Then she reasoned that a fortune-teller had likely assumed that Lucan was her betrothed when she'd walked in on the two of them in a near embrace. Therefore, she hadn't felt it necessary to offer insight on who her supposed husband would be.

Hedley offered a cheeky grin. "Are you acquainted with any unmarried kings, Frances?"

"None whatsoever. Nor am I likely to be. *However*, I am well acquainted with a Duke," she said as she scratched RJ's head. "Perhaps he could introduce me to one."

Eager to add his part to the conversation, RJ woofed and licked her hand.

"There you have it," Calliope said. "Our matchmaker has divined your tea leaves, and you will soon encounter your future husband. It is all settled."

"What is settled, my love?" Everhart asked from the doorway. Strolling in behind him were Danvers and Lucan. They all inclined their heads but then refused to allow Frances to rise and curtsy, stating that she was amongst their group now, and there was no need for formalities.

"Our new friend's marriage," Calliope answered with a wink to Frances. "She could very well become a queen in a fortnight."

Both Everhart and Danvers moved into the room, pulling additional chairs from the outer walls to sit beside their wives. Lucan took the vacant chair on the other side of RJ, and instantly began scratching the beast, his hand in close proximity to Frances's.

"A queen, hmm?" Lucan mused. "Was this the fortune you were told?"

She tried not to look at the dimple he flashed, tried not to let her pulse escalate—and failed on both accounts. "Not entirely."

"It's quite romantic, really," Calliope said. "A *king* will decide her fate."

"*Within a fortnight*, don't forget," Hedley added, passing the plate of biscuits to her husband.

"Montwood, you aren't by any chance in direct line to inherit a kingdom, are you?" Danvers asked, taking four biscuits before passing the plate to Everhart.

Frances did not miss the reference. Lucan's friends were misconstruing his intentions toward her. Since it was obvious that it was solely for the sake of fun, however, she didn't mind.

"I'm too selfish a creature to marry, as you lot know already," Lucan said with gravity enough to silence further comments. Instead, he received a laugh and a few chuckles.

"Do not be fooled by that hard tone, Frances," Hedley offered. "I happen to know his heart is complete porridge."

Lucan smirked. "Only if you are referring to *Mrs. Swan's* porridge, for it is tough and fibrous with a hard exterior—*that* could easily describe my heart."

Frances knew better. Until recently, she'd seen him as a ne'er-do-well who only supported her belief that mankind was corrupt and undeserving. Now, she saw the goodness in him, an integrity that was the foundation of his actions. He'd helped that young boy at the festival gain a ribbon for his mother but had not showcased his good deeds for all the village to praise him. In fact, he'd been embarrassed at her catching him.

Even in his first abduction of her, he'd claimed to want a moment to speak with her and to warn her. And soon thereafter, he'd kept his word and delivered her to her new employer.

Since then, she'd encountered him daily, and his concern for her welfare seemed genuine. He hadn't used their rendezvous for a more carnal purpose either. This both surprised *and* frustrated her. She even suspected that his all-important wager with his friends was nothing more than a lark. She could no longer imagine that he would actually gamble against his friends. Yet all in all…

All in all, she was beginning to believe that to restore her faith in men, she'd needed only to have looked a little closer at Lucan from the beginning.

Lucan's fingertips grazed hers, pulling her away from her thoughts. The touch was light but intentional. Her gaze met his. As if he noticed the shift in her, he shook his head. *"Don't believe them,"* the gesture said. *"I'm ruthless. I only take what I want."*

Frances should heed his warning this time. It was sage advice, after all. Because she knew, if he was so inclined, he could easily take her heart. Or worse, she might simply *give* it to him.

At Hedley's request, their party moved to the music room. Lucan sat at the piano, playing a waltz that Everhart and Calliope favored. This time, he did not add any of his usual teasing trills. He played with honesty, pouring part of himself into each note.

Over the glossy ebony sheen, he tried not to meet Frances's gaze but failed. The way the soft afternoon light caressed her face, she appeared enraptured by the melody. If the sound gave her such pleasure, he would play forever. Unfortunately, the score came to an end. With reluctance, he stopped as his friends applauded and rose from their seats.

"Exquisite." Calliope pressed a hand to her breast and sighed.

Hedley had tears in her eyes. "I've never heard you play more beautifully."

Lucan didn't understand why she was so moved until he saw her reach out and clutch Frances's hand. His friend obviously knew him better than he thought. And he wasn't fooling anyone other than himself.

"Have you ever heard Montwood play?" Hedley asked.

"No. This was my first opportunity, and I am more delighted than I can express." Frances smiled—a full blast of white teeth and that inadvertently sensuous overbite—aimed directly at him.

Lucan felt the force of it hit him square in the chest. The breath he was inhaling stopped, arrested inside of him. She did not gift smiles easily. They were hard won. "Do you play?"

"I'm afraid not," she answered with a small, captivating laugh. "When I was a girl, my tutor refused to return after it was clear that I lacked any talent at all. I love listening, however."

His fingers itched to continue playing for her right this instant, but he feared doing so would reveal more than he already had. Too much.

"Then you must hear more," Hedley offered, escorting Frances back to one of the chairs. "Montwood, of course you will play for her."

He had the frightening impulse to say *Every day for the rest of my life.* Instead, he found a way to breathe and gain some control. "I would be honored."

"Then it's settled. Montwood will entertain you while Hedley and I meet with Mrs. Merkel," Calliope said, linking arms with Hedley before they moved toward the door. "I quite forgot about the meeting I'd arranged with the house-keeper. We shouldn't be detained long, however."

Once they were in the hall, Calliope turned around and gave Everhart a pointed look.

Everhart abruptly turned to Danvers. "Ah yes, that reminds me. I have a new atlas that just arrived. It's waiting in the map room."

"A new atlas. How exciting," Danvers answered with a complete lack of enthusiasm—until Hedley cleared her throat from the doorway. "Indeed. It's highly important that I see it immediately."

All four of his friends left the room at once. It was comical that they assumed Lucan would somehow lose the wager in their absence. As if he had so little control. They didn't know that he'd had a dozen chances to make the most of being alone with Frances. And every night he struggled to remain in the shadows and *not* to close the distance between them.

"Do *you* have an urgent desire to see the atlas, Miss Thorne?"

The corners of her mouth curled up. "I am quite curious. It must be a rare and beautiful atlas."

Worth ten thousand pounds to them, was Lucan's guess. He resumed playing, albeit lightly in order to keep conversing. "They like you a great deal. Otherwise, they wouldn't have gone to such ends to leave us alone."

"With the wager between you, I imagine your friends want to believe you are incapable of resisting me." She glanced to the open door, amusement fading from her expression. "They do not know how simple it has been for you thus far."

How little she knew her own power over him.

"As simple as nailing my feet to the floor in order to keep from crossing the room. As simple as binding my hands to keep from reaching out for you. Yes, simple indeed," he said quietly, wanting her to know how difficult it had been each day and night.

By her surprised gasp, he knew she'd heard him. Yet he wasn't used to admitting such weakness. Therefore, he began to play a more elaborate piece, the music too loud for talking. She saw through him, regardless. He could tell in the way she watched him over the rims of her spectacles, her gaze never leaving his.

Sitting on the piano bench, with Frances as his only audience, he felt uninhibited. Usually, the only time he felt this way was when he played for himself, after everyone else had fallen asleep. But he wanted her to see who he was through his music.

Halfway through the score, he altered the tune and began to play one of his own melodies. It was new to him, and he wrote it only as the notes flowed from his fingertips. Unexpectedly, the words that Calliope and Hedley had taunted him with echoed in his head, rising above the music. A sharp note accompanied them.

A king will decide her fate...within a fortnight.

Why hadn't the fortune-teller gone with the obvious response and told Frances that she would marry a man with dark hair? *He* was the one who'd slipped her the silver, after all.

Of course, the gypsy merely told fortunes for money and entertainment. It wasn't as if the woman was a prophet. Yet he admitted, it still bothered him to think of it. He reasoned it was because Frances fit so nicely within their group and within these walls. Clearly, she belonged here.

Still watching him from over the rims of her spectacles, Frances hardly paused to blink at all. Her smoky eyes were focused solely on him, as if only he existed. In that moment, he wished it were true—that there was only the two of them. Here. Alone.

The melody dipped into the lower notes, a seductive arrangement he hoped she could feel. From across the room, he stroked her cheek and brushed her lips with the music. This was his only way of kissing her without losing control. As if attuned to him, Frances adjusted her spectacles and wet her lips. She *was* feeling it.

Shamelessly, he continued to caress her with each chord. He closed his eyes and felt the keys beneath his fingertips. But they weren't keys anymore. With each press, he imagined her skin, her throat, her breasts, her stomach, her hips, her sex…

The music altered again, delving deep, sinking lower. He lifted his gaze and connected with hers. She was flushed. Her breasts rose with the force of her inhalation. She shifted in her chair, pressing her knees together. He was breathing hard now. The melody gained momentum with firm, swift strokes of each key—

Until he recalled, quite suddenly, that they were not alone. The door was open, and his friends were nearby. He pulled back from *fortissimo* and eased into a soft *pianissimo* before rounding off the music with a far from satisfying trill.

Beside him, RJ panted, tail wagging, apparently pleased about something. Then again, the Beast of Fallow Hall was always in high spirits. Lucan wished he could say the same. At present, he felt surlier than ever.

Frances parted her lips to breathe. "I have never heard music like that before. It was almost as if I could…*feel* each note."

He felt a certain amount of pride in gaining that reaction, but at the same time, he wanted to continue what he started. Unless he wanted to lose the wager, however, he couldn't. "I will play for you whenever you wish."

"I would like that, Lucan," she said, her voice lower, softer.

Then, hearing footsteps in the hall, she glanced to the open doorway. So did he.

Lucan was tempted to cross the room and lock them inside. That way he could finally satisfy the yearning tearing him apart. Yet he'd already sacrificed his honor by wagering against his best friends. He would just have to sacrifice any other desires as well.

"Perhaps it would be best if we joined the others," he said.

"Then why are you looking at the door as if you intend to bolt it shut?"

"Miss Thorne, I was doing no such—" He'd intended to deny it. But when his gaze met hers, he knew that she saw the truth. "You are too perceptive by half."

His honesty earned him another smile and a blush before she dipped her head and began to clean her spectacles.

CHAPTER FIFTEEN

Frances returned to Whitelock Manor later that afternoon.

Leaving Lucan was more difficult than she imagined. Not to mention, she was still trying to sort out the sensations his music had evoked. Even now, it left her weak-kneed and eager to see him again. She was not too naive to understand the reason. It was desire.

Yet even more than that, her desire was focused solely on Lucan. The most frightening part of this realization was that her own scruples seemed to have gone missing. Here she was, trying to free her father from prison and looking for any remaining goodness in men, but she couldn't stop thinking about Lucan. What would she have done if he *had* bolted the door? She suspected that she would have surprised herself by walking directly into his arms. Was she truly considering having an affair with a man who would never marry her?

These thoughts continued to distract her when she joined Lord Whitelock for dinner in the evening. Frances gazed toward the windows for a measure of comfort. Beyond the billowing flounces of draperies and through the glass, the golden sun sank beneath the horizon, leaving a thin band of dark orange behind. Above that, striations of violet and deep blue merged into the night sky.

Inside, however, the immense dining room with its gilded adornment seemed suffocating, which was odd, considering that only she, Lord Whitelock, and two footmen were within.

"Is the fish not to your liking, Miss Thorne?" Lord Whitelock asked.

They sat in closer proximity than usual, with him at the head of the table and her place directly to his right. Before, she'd always been further down and left to converse with the viscount's guests. She wished there were guests here tonight.

"The fish is lovely." She smiled and then glanced at the footmen, offering a nod and knowing they would take the compliment with them down to the kitchens. "I suppose my thoughts are somewhat distracted since I learned that your other guests were unable to dine here this evening. I feel it is my place to take dinner in my room during such circumstances."

"Perhaps your previous employment leaves you mindful of the servants and their roles. Yours differs now. I expect you to be at ease in my company. Therefore"—Lord Whitelock gave a pointed look to the footmen—"I will send the servants out of the room for your comfort."

"It was not my intention to imply that I was ill at ease," Frances quickly explained. Unfortunately, it was too late. The footmen disappeared through the door, leaving her quite alone with the viscount.

"There. Now you must engage only with me." He turned to her and smiled. "Although perhaps this was your design all along. By holding your conversation captive, you've steered me into finding this one solution. Quite clever, but do not worry. I shall you keep your secret."

He made it sound as if she'd wanted to be alone with him. Yet it was said in such a teasing manner that arguing would have been seen as a petty endeavor. She decided it prudent to let the matter rest.

Rising slightly from his chair, he extended his arm and seized her wine glass, holding it out in an unspoken command for her to take it from him.

She did but carefully kept her fingers to the stem to avoid contact with his on the bowl. Obligingly, and because she needed a drink, she took a sip. A reminder that it was highly improper for him to serve her in any fashion waited on her tongue, but she bit down on it. Being a viscount, he likely knew that already. Still, she could not dislodge her own ingrained manners. "Thank you."

His dark eyes gleamed in apparent pleasure before he turned his attention back to his plate. "I understand that you only returned a short while ago. I hope you did not lose your way on my grounds."

"I did not restrict my walk to your grounds, my lord." Frances tried to keep the bite out of her tone. His pretending that he was keeping her secret left a sour taste on her tongue. She'd been under the impression that, when given time off, she was free to do whatever she chose with her time. "In fact, I spent the majority of my day with new acquaintances. Perhaps you know Viscountess Everhart and Mrs. Danvers?"

"Then I see that I needn't have worried for your safety," he said with enough sincerity that she felt a pang of guilt for her previous tone.

"I apologize if my absence caused you any alarm."

He took a lengthy swallow from his glass, watching her from over the rim. "It is merely my wish that you come to me first if ever you are in need of conversation or a tour of the countryside. There are days when I could use the pleasant distraction of your company to ease *my* burdens. This morning affected me as well."

Of course it had. Now, Frances felt uncharitable. Seeing his wife in such a state and having experienced many other episodes must weigh on him greatly. "In the future, I will come to you first."

Again, pleasure showed on his face. "I could ask for nothing more."

And yet, it still seemed like more of an order than a request. Frances shrugged off the sensation and thought back to her afternoon at Fallow Hall to lessen her disquiet. That was when she recalled Lucan's concerns for Henny Momper, in addition to setting Arthur Momper's mind at ease. Frances wanted to help as well. And what better way to learn where Miss Momper was than from the man who paid her salary?

However, she would have to phrase her questions carefully. After all, it would seem odd to inquire directly about the whereabouts of a young woman whom she'd never met.

"The countryside here is beautiful," Frances remarked with a glance out the window. "As you know, I've never been out of London until now. I was wondering if this county resembles where your hunting box resides in Wales."

"I find Lincolnshire more to my taste at present." His answer was all charm, revealing nothing.

She tried again. "I understand that Lady Whitelock's previous companion now resides there."

"Excuse me, while I call for our next course," he said and tapped his fork against the side of his water goblet. A footman appeared instantly and bowed after hearing the request. Then, as if they'd been waiting, the other footmen carried in a silver platter of partridge and a dish of glaze carrots.

After they were served, the footmen left again, and Whitelock regarded her with a steady gaze. "Forgive the interruption. Were we discussing my wife's previous companions or the country of Wales?"

"Whichever you prefer, my lord. I am eager to hear of both." She felt her smile turn brittle. Lord Whitelock preferred to keep a firm hand on the direction of the conversation.

The viscount cut into his partridge. "I found Miss Momper begging on the streets of London alongside her younger brother. When I learned they were alone in the world, I felt compelled to improve their circumstances. During the time of her employment, she did not disappoint me in her abilities. That was the reason I knew she was capable of being elevated in her position."

Frances shifted in her seat at his reprimanding tone. "It was noble of you. In fact, I've heard nothing but accounts of your charity in the way that you've helped so many. Your servants are fortunate indeed. Myself included. In fact, I often wonder where I would be if you hadn't appeared at Mrs. Hunter's when you did."

"You are generous with your praise. I am quite flattered," he said, watching the bite of glazed carrot slip past her lips. "The truth is that I found many of my servants by serendipitous events. Some were forced to endure the conditions of work-houses or were living on the streets. And of course, let us not forget the value of the registry."

"Do you seek out the less fortunate on purpose?" she asked. To her, it seemed like an odd question to find amusing, but the viscount grinned nonetheless.

"I enjoy all aspects of altering a person's circumstances—removing them from a dire fate, welcoming them into my home, and most especially in elevating their positions. I have great wealth, and I see no reason not to use it to my full advantage."

His statement struck an odd chord with her. To *his* full advantage? Didn't he mean to *their* advantage?

The conversation turned to his art collection and how much it was admired. He spoke at length of his various acquisitions. During this time, she wondered how to weave Henny Momper back into the conversation. At first, Frances thought of mentioning the illness of which Mrs. Darby had spoken. It could be an easy matter to express concern and garner information about whether or not his lordship knew of Miss Momper's health.

Then, quite unexpectedly, something clicked inside of Frances's head, like gears of a clock fitting together. Earlier, Hedley had mentioned that her illness caused her to miss the village fair. Yet her illness would assuredly not last much longer since it was because she was with child.

According to Mrs. Darby, Henny's illness had not lasted either.

Lucan said that she was not expected to arrive at Wales for two more months. When Frances began this position, both Lord Whitelock and Mrs. Riley had mentioned that Lady

Whitelock had been without a companion for six weeks. That was nearly two weeks ago. Therefore, Miss Momper had been absent for two months already.

Frances reached for her wine. Her hand shook. Had Miss Momper been with child?

Knowing nothing of Miss Momper's character or personal life, Frances couldn't be certain. However, the more she thought about it, the more it seemed like a possibility. That would explain her illness, and the reason she was not in Wales as of yet. Perhaps she was somewhere having the baby and not in training to become a housekeeper. Perhaps Lord Whitelock had found out about Miss Momper's delicate condition and sent her away. Although, that still did not account for her not writing to her brother.

When Frances had lived in London, she would have come to this conclusion sooner, if not immediately. Yet here, in this idyllic setting, she wanted to see only the good. Was that a selfish mistake on her part? She clung to that dream in the hope of having a brighter future for herself. She didn't want to be cynical and jaded. Instead, she wanted unfettered joy and perhaps even…love.

"The painting in your chamber is one of my particular favorites," Whitelock said, drawing her back into his dialogue on art and unsettling her further.

"It's…lovely." She swallowed nervously. The wine and rich foods did not mix well with her trepidation. Her stomach churned, and her temples began to throb. And the only thing she wanted was the comfort of Lucan's embrace. "Pray, forgive me, but I've a sudden headache. Would you mind terribly if I retired?"

Unmasked disappointment hardened Lord Whitelock's features, but he inclined his head and rose to assist her. He hesitated, bending down to speak near her ear. "I'm feeling even more generous than usual, Miss Thorne. I believe another afternoon away from the manor would set you to rights. Therefore, tomorrow, once you've concluded your duties, you are free to roam."

"Thank you, my lord," she said on a breath of relief as the chair slid from the table. At last, she stood and stepped away from him.

He smiled at her. "With that settled, I offer myself as your guide. I would be more than happy to take you on a tour."

"Actually, I was going to request tomorrow afternoon away because Lady Everhart and Mrs. Danvers have invited me to shop in the village," she said in a rush. It was a complete fabrication, of course, but she felt a spark of pride at thinking of such a plausible excuse without any forethought.

"Ah. A disappointment, to be sure," he said, holding her gaze. "Some other afternoon, then, and *soon*."

She backed up a step toward the servants' door. "Yes, of course, sir." And with a quick curtsy, she made another escape.

Shortly after Lucan had parted with Frances that afternoon, he and RJ found their way to Whitelock's stables. He'd timed it carefully. This was the time that the grooms congregated near the south of the estate to watch the maids gather the laundry that had been hanging all day. A familiar sheaf of wheat-colored hair disappeared behind a loft amongst the rafters overhead. And then Lucan saw the driver in the tack room. The man looked at him with surprised recognition, obviously remembering him from the night he'd gotten drunk in Stampton.

Devising an excuse for coming here, Lucan tossed him a leather coin purse. "I found this shortly after you left the inn."

The driver snatched the purse out of the air. With a skeptical frown, he weighed it in his hand. "A lot of trouble for a few shillings."

"I could have left it with the butler at the main house, I suppose," Lucan said, pausing long enough to note the look of alarm that the driver tried to conceal, "but something tells me you wouldn't want Whitelock to know of your evening. I thought I would do you a small favor."

The man narrowed his eyes. "In return for…"

Lucan wouldn't insult him by prolonging this game. "I'm looking for a young woman who used to be employed here as companion until recently. She has family who are worried for her welfare."

Just then, Arthur swung down from one of the rafters overhead, hanging upside down. "What have you got there…Is that a *dog*? Blimey!"

Lucan found it interesting that the driver was not in the least bit surprised by the boy's sudden appearance. Which meant that Arthur spent a good deal of time here. And if Arthur spent time in the stables, then it was likely his sister had come here as well.

Absently, he introduced RJ to Arthur and watched as the lad dropped easily down from the beam into the driver's waiting hands. Seeing the protectiveness from the driver—an action one might see from a father—offered Lucan another insight. As Arthur approached, the Beast of Fallow Hall began wagging his tail with such eagerness that it nearly threw him off balance. All the while, Lucan kept his eye on the driver. The man watched the exchange between Arthur and RJ, his stance indicating a readiness to rush forward if the need arose.

"Arthur, you're just in time. I was just asking where this man took your sister," Lucan said, knowing that the lad was too distracted to hear him. As for the driver, Lucan had a hunch that the direct approach was the best path to take.

"I could lose my post." The driver swallowed, but there was more than nervousness in the action. In his eyes, pain lingered.

"I'm not even here." Lucan lifted his hands in a shrug. "And Arthur isn't here for this conversation either. Are you, Arthur?"

In answer, the boy giggled as RJ licked his face. He wasn't even paying attention.

This must have satisfied the driver somewhat, because he shifted closer. He scrubbed a hand over his face and looked to the door one last time. "I drove Henny to Shalehouse, where all the *companions* go for their training."

Ah. The familiarity of his address was tinged with bitterness—possibly from unrequited love?—and told Lucan that Miss Momper was the last person this man had wanted to drive to Shalehouse and never see again.

If each of the companions went to this one single location for their training, then it could be assumed they had all been elevated to the position of housekeeper. Just how many housekeepers could Whitelock require?

Then again, everyone knew the man had property all over Europe, like a lepidopterist collecting butterflies and pinning them to a board. Lucan hoped the viscount didn't collect companions in the same manner.

Hmm… Disturbed by that thought and worried about Frances, Lucan found himself hoping that Whitelock's spotless reputation was earned and that these dark assumptions were only a product of his own concern and perhaps even a deeper, unnamed emotion.

Stepping forward, Lucan extended his hand to the driver. "Thank you for watching over my friend in his sister's absence."

The man shook his hand and glanced down to Arthur. "He's like my own brother."

Or like a son, Lucan imagined. With a nod, he turned to leave. Before he slipped away, he ruffled Arthur's hair and called RJ to his side. Then once he'd sent RJ home, Lucan made his way through the narrow hidden passages of Whitelock manor.

When the dinner hour approached and the servants were busy in other parts of the house, Lucan slipped into Whitelock's study and carefully searched through his papers and ledgers for any clue to the evidence he had on Thorne. There were separate books kept for each of his properties, which included many in Europe and even a farm on the coast of China. Unfortunately, Whitelock was careful to the point of appearing boring on paper.

Frustrated, Lucan slipped through the passageway again and climbed the narrow stairs to wait for Frances. He didn't have to wait long.

Frances stepped into the gallery and placed her lamp on a crescent table near the archway. Leaving the security of the light behind, she crossed the room, heading straight for his shadowed corner.

"Lucan, I must speak with you."

As of yet, he'd given no indication that he was here. *None other than being here, each night, waiting for her in the same spot.*

She came to the reclining sculpture of lovers and hesitated, searching the shadows. Then, as if certain of precisely where he stood, she continued her trek, albeit slowly. "I know you are here," she whispered.

"How?"

She lifted her hand, reaching out in the darkness. "I can feel your presence. This room changes when you are in it."

"Do I make it a dark and frightening place?" Unable to help himself, he closed his fingers over hers. The touch sent a rush of indescribable yearning through him. He drew her near and had the sense of sinking slowly, his body melting into her embrace.

He worried about the depths of his feelings toward her intensifying in such a short time. Surely, the reactions she elicited within him should cause him to want to disappear through the passageway instead of lingering, waiting for her.

She shook her head, the distant lamplight providing a halo of gleaming bronze around her hair. "Dark perhaps but not frightening. In fact, I feel quite safe with you."

A sweet ache spirited through his heart, awakening it to impossible imaginings. If she knew what nightmares lingered inside of him, she would never feel safe with him. "Your tender, foolish words surprise me. Where is your level head, Miss Thorne?"

"Firmly atop my shoulders. The words were not meant as a declaration, merely an observation." But when she spoke, she belied those words by threading her fingers through his. "I believe I know what your suspicion was earlier. I have put it all together, and I think that Miss Momper might be with child, and that is the reason for her absence.

"If it is true," she continued, "then likely, she formed an attachment to a young man, either on the grounds or in the village on her afternoons away from work."

Apparently, she hadn't jumped to the *same* conclusion Lucan had. She was still blinded by Whitelock's shiny snakeskin. "That is one option," he said.

She looked over her shoulder as if afraid of being overheard. When she turned back, she kept her voice low. "In fact, she might have been dismissed for it. Whenever I mentioned her name this evening, Lord Whitelock did not appear pleased."

Alarm shot through Lucan. Instantly, he set his hands on her arms and drew her deeper into the shadows.

"I shared my suspicions in order to keep you safe, not for you to put yourself at risk," he scolded softly, barely resisting the urge to pull her against him. "How did he react when you mentioned her?"

She shrugged, oblivious to the panic running amok inside of him. "His lordship repeatedly changed the subject, but in a way to make it clear that I was rising above my station by asking about his personal business. I should have known better—I did know better."

"*Your station,*" Lucan growled. "I wish you would put those thoughts out of your mind."

Beneath his hands, she stiffened. In the dim light, he saw her purse her lips. "How does knowing my place and embracing my altered status deserve your anger? You have nothing to do with it."

A fair reminder but not one that improved his mood. "It's common knowledge that Whitelock's wife—the very one that caused you such worry earlier today—was an heiress to a fortune earned by trade. There is not a drop of royal blood in her line."

"For some, bloodlines matter little."

Lucan didn't know why, but he was suddenly incensed by that remark and how she'd spent so many years scraping by on her own earnings. "You, however, are the great-grand-daughter of an earl. It is well within your grasp to marry a duke, if you are so inclined."

"I am not inclined to marry a duke, an earl, or even the second son of a marquess," she hissed. "*If* I marry, it will be to a man of whom I will prove to be an asset. A widower, per-haps. Or an elderly shop owner."

He gripped her tighter. Pulled her closer. "And if I choose to marry, it will never be to a woman who wears spectacles and tempts me beyond reason."

In that same instant, he claimed her mouth. His lips pressed hard against hers. His tongue swept past her teeth. This was not the slow unending kiss he'd imagined earlier when playing the piano for her. This was born of frustra-tion and pure, raw hunger. He growled low and deep, a clear warning that she was dealing with a feral beast. Yet instead of pushing him away, Frances clung to him.

Her hands slid up between them until her fingers dove into the hair at his temples. Finally, she slanted her mouth beneath his, urging him deeper. An equally hungry sound rose from her throat as her tongue parried with his.

He'd never kissed any woman like this before, with a complete lack of finesse and no carefully weighed control. There was no thinking involved. It was all basic animal need that pushed him now.

And he needed Frances. Desperately. If the blood pooling and pulsating in his thick erection wasn't proof enough, then the near-painful tightening of his bollocks was. This had been building since he'd first kissed her, taunting his control all the while.

She broke away from the kiss, pressing her cheek against his as she gasped for breath. "Touch me, Lucan."

He shuddered at her low, throaty command and kissed her again. He gripped her waist, tilting her hips toward his. The only distance between their bodies was a thin layer of clothes. Yet even then, he could feel her enticing heat. The firm swells of her breasts molded against him. His hands twitched, one battling to inch upward and the other wanting to find the hem of her skirt.

Touch me…but if he did, it would be for his own pleasure, not hers. He'd never touched a woman without cataloging her preferences and ensuring her satisfaction before he took his. He didn't trust himself to do that now. *Now*—when it mattered most. *Now*—when he had the urge to take her against the wall, thrusting deep until his hunger abated.

Lucan moved away from Frances so swiftly that he had to take hold of the wall for support. He didn't dare look at her.

"Please know that I would love to touch your entire body—every delectable inch—with my hands *and* my mouth, but not while you are here, beneath Whitelock's roof." Damn, he was shaking all over. Even his voice shook.

"And if you abducted me just once more?"

Lucan pressed his forehead to the tapestry on the wall. "I'd never let you return."

"Never is a long time, Lucan. Think of your wager, after all." By the sound of her breathy laugh, she must have thought he was teasing.

"Ah yes, the wager. I'd nearly forgotten." Insanely enough, it was the truth. "Besides, you are not one who can adopt such a worldly perspective."

"At my age, do you think I am still naïve to the arrangements men and women decide upon?"

Now it was his turn to laugh. Did she think he knew her so little? "I know the persuasive power of desire and how it mingles with curiosity to create an irresistible concoction. That heated brew is inside of me now…and you. Yet no matter what you might profess at this moment, you are not the type of woman who could make such an *arrangement*. The light of day would bring regret."

"And what type of woman am I, then?" she scoffed.

"The kind that frightens me, Miss Thorne." He looked over his shoulder to see her grow still in the shadows. "Because whether you know it or not, you require a certain depth of feeling before entering into an affair. And what scares me is that I could oblige your every need but at great risk to us both."

Her soft gasp filled the space between them. Such a small intake of air, and yet he felt himself pulled by the force of it. He'd all but confessed how much she meant to him. How she alone tempted him beyond reason. How he would marry her and love her for the rest of his days if circumstances were different.

She took a step toward him. "Lucan, if we were to—"

"I will be away in the morning," he said quickly, interrupting her so that she could not say more to tempt him. Or before he could confess any more of his feelings. He'd already said far too much. "My aunt sent me a missive and requests my company. Should you need me for anything, I will return by afternoon. And as usual, I will be here for you in the evening."

"Every evening...for how long?"

For as long as it takes to keep you safe. Forever, if need be. "You know the answer."

Aching with reluctance and unfulfilled desire, he slipped through the passageway door.

CHAPTER SIXTEEN

Frances spent the morning reading poetry to Lady Whitelock. Not surprisingly, after Lucan's heated kiss last night, her tone was far more passionate than usual.

The viscountess was in a dream state again, floating in and out of awareness. Mrs. Darby sat in the corner with her needlework, while Nannette lingered near the hearth, dusting the row of porcelain figurines on the mantel.

Frances could not stop thinking about Lucan and the startling words he'd spoken.

You require a certain depth of feeling... I could oblige your every need.

Was it true? Did he care for her beyond what had begun as his promise to her father? The notion seemed to turn her heart and lungs into vapor, floating like the wispy clouds in the sky today. It was difficult to catch her breath.

She closed the book as the clock in the hall chimed the luncheon hour. Both she and Nannette slipped away, leaving Lady Whitelock in the nurse's care.

"It's sad, isn't it?" Nannette said as they walked down the back stairs toward the kitchens. "With her ladyship forever in such a state, Lord Whitelock must be lonely. Henny used to say as much too. She'd go around sighing all day long, half in love with his lordship."

Startled by the news, Frances paused on the stair. "Surely not."

"It's true. They all do—the companions, that is. That's why they don't last," she said with a nod, as if her life's experience had made her an expert. "They spend all that time alone with his lordship, forgetting that he's just a right nice fellow, and believing something else. I'm sure once he's aware of it, he has to find them another place in order to save their feelings."

An icy chill swept through Frances, forcing her to grab the handrail for support. Miss Momper had been in love with Lord Whitelock? The suspicion that the young woman could be with child resurfaced. Then, linking those two thoughts left Frances with an unwelcome realization.

No. She truly did not want to believe Whitelock capable of such an atrocity, of preying upon a woman in his own employ. She wanted to believe that he was good and kind. That he wasn't a lecher like so many others. Yet hadn't she felt uneasy in his presence lately? Certainly, that made it a possibility. Could it be that her own arrogance and belief that he was as good as rumor promised had blinded her to his true nature?

"He's been so generous," Nannette continued, "that we'd all do anything for him."

Perhaps he wants your gratitude... Lucan's words ran circles in Frances's head. It had taken a great deal for him to admit his suspicions too. He usually kept his thoughts and feelings locked tightly away, yet he'd offered her a few glimpses, demanding nothing in return. At first, she would have discounted every word from his lips, but thinking back, he hadn't lied to her. Nor was he a man who'd sully another's character for no reason. He was honorable and...she'd already admitted to trusting him. If he believed she should be wary of Lord Whitelock, she would trust that too.

At the bottom of the stairs, Nannette placed her hand over Frances's arm. "We really like you here and want you to stay. And...well, I just hope *you* don't fall in love with his lordship as well."

Frances shook her head with resolution. "That would be impossible."

"It's only impossible if you're already in love with someone else." Nannette smiled, her eyes sparkling. "Are you?"

"In love?" she scoffed. In love with Lucan? What a notion. She desired him, yes. But love?

Love required a certain level of trust, of knowing that your heart was in safekeeping. As she absorbed her own thoughts, a rush of panic flooded her. Years ago, she'd vowed never to open her heart again. Never to leave it vulnerable. Men were undeserving, selfish and lecherous...

Except for Lucan. He was noble, honorable, caring, generous, and everything she'd ever wanted. *Everything.*

Dear heavens! *Was* she in love? The floor seemed to tilt beneath her feet, and she reached for the wall to steady herself.

The answer was clear. "Yes. I believe I am." Very much indeed.

Twenty miles from Fallow Hall, Lucan entered the Flame and Spit. Inside the pub, there were a half dozen patrons, all hunched over their tankards, including its proprietor, Aunt Theodosia.

Theodosia laughed when she saw him and slapped her hand down on the oaken bar. Brackets of wrinkles surrounded her mouth, displaying a lifetime of smiles, while the fan of creases by her clear blue eyes held a few sorrows. He knew that most had come during the years when her younger sister, Lucan's mother, had suffered abuses.

He couldn't help that he thought of his mother every time they met. And from the tears shining in his aunt's eyes as she opened her arms wide for a hearty embrace, it was clear that she was thinking the same thing. He hugged her tightly, lifting her over the half door that kept her customers away from the ale. Her famously flaming plait of red hair held more silver now and swung over her shoulder as he set her down.

"Let me look at you," she said, brushing the road dust from his shoulders and not entirely meeting his gaze.

Lucan knew it was because he had his father's eyes. That's what she said hurt the most when she saw him. "I'm past the age of growing taller, Aunt."

"I know. I just like to make sure you're still in one piece." She poked him here and there, turning him around until she was satisfied that he wasn't at death's door. "No holes from duels at dawn or anything?"

"Not today." He grinned.

She pinched his chin. "Don't tease an old woman."

"I wouldn't dare." He earned forgiveness by bussing her cheek. "If you merely needed certainty of my existence, a note would have sufficed."

She shooed him, directing him to a table in the corner before she stepped behind the bar again and pulled two pints. Then, once she was sitting on the bench nearest his, she touched her tankard to his and was silent. It was their usual toast to his mother, marking her absence.

"You were the best thing she ever did," Theodosia said after a moment and shook her head. "Your brother... Well, word tells me that Vincent is very much like your father. Not to mention, eager to inherit. His debts are mounting. He wants to sell off the land and the house that was part of your mother's dowry. But I hear your sodden cuss of a father already did."

This news took Lucan by surprise. That land was worth a goodly sum. Game of all sorts filled the forested acreage. Fernwood Glade had been left untended but had served as his own refuge many times over the years. Whenever he needed a place to escape his inner demons, he went there. Yet it was early spring when he'd last visited. He wondered who the new owner was. More than that, he wondered why his father would have sold it after all this time. Typically, he'd enjoyed using the land as a taunt against both Vincent and Lucan, threatening to burn it all to the ground, leaving nothing of their mother behind. Of course, Vincent thought little, if anything at all, of preserving their mother's memory. Like most in line for the title, he only wanted the property.

"Then Father had better hope that Vincent isn't *too* like him." It was a well-kept family secret that the Marquess of Camdonbury had poisoned his own father in order to gain the title. Of course, he hadn't been tried or hung for that crime either, because Clivedale had been his friend then too. "Besides, Father never cared for the house after the marriage contract was signed. He only wanted the dowry, the land, and the heir."

"But the best came later," Theodosia said, patting his hand with affection.

Lucan recalled how his mother had said things like that. She'd endured years of abuse, and there had been nothing he could do about it. His only consolation was that she did not have to suffer any longer. "I'm better off without Camdonbury and his heir. After all, debt and murder follows the family line."

She took a hearty swallow of ale. "Not if the title ended up in the right hands."

"That is an old argument, long buried. Besides, I hear Vincent has found himself a bride," Lucan said with a shudder. He already planned to do his best to warn her away, the same way he had with Vincent's previous candidates.

Theodosia offered a noncommittal grumble over the topic being put to rest. "I also heard mention of wager."

"Did you now? Considering you run a tavern, I'm not surprised." Now it was his turn for a few gulps of ale. He knew she was referring to *his* wager, but he didn't want her to know the desperate state he was in.

"Ten thousand pounds…Quite a sum." She whistled. "You know if you need any money, I still have my dowry tucked away. A little land, a little house, and *hmm...*about thirty thousand in silver."

"Don't say that too loudly, Aunt," he said with a chuckle. "I bet not many of the patrons know you're an heiress."

"Eh...I've had my offers, but marriage isn't for likes of me." She took another long swig, her gaze taking in the clean but worn tables. She'd once said that she could build a fancy place, but who would she get to come to it? She couldn't tolerate the *Quality*. Not even before her sister's death. "Just so you know, whatever I have is yours."

"I'm not a borrower or a beggar. At least a wager has honor." And honor was what separated him from his father.

She smiled at his vehemence. Resting her forearms on the table, she curled her hands around the base of her cup. "All right, then, down to the other reason I called you here. I wanted to tell you that your old family physician stopped by two days past. Smarmy cuss. He didn't recognize me. Not surprising. I'm hardly the same *accomplished spinster* that I used to be in my former life. But *I'll* never forget the man who'd claimed that your mother took a fall, and it was all an accident."

Lucan set down his tankard with a clunk. He wondered what would bring a cautious fellow like Clivedale to Lincolnshire. More importantly, did it have anything to do with Whitelock and their secret exchanges? "What was Clivedale doing here?"

She tilted her head in a shrug. "It looked like he was meeting a fellow. He waited for a few hours and when no one came, he left a coin on the table and walked out. But then I happened to look outside and see him slip into a black carriage, which had all the shades pulled down. Though the painted crest on the door had mostly worn away, I noticed enough to spark a memory."

Lucan sat forward. "And?"

"Laurel leaves in a bird's talons"—she paused—"I believe that's part of Viscount Whitelock's crest."

Lucan kept his breathing calm and even, concealing the internal jolt that started off a series of guesses tripping through his mind. But still, he had nothing concrete. Not yet. "Perhaps Clivedale is the viscount's physician."

"Then why meet in secret?"

Why, indeed. "The next time Clivedale shows up here, send me a missive. I'd like to chat with him."

She agreed but scrutinized Lucan with her shrewd gaze as if she saw the gears of his mind turning. "Clivedale was a friend of Camdonbury's for a time, starting before your grandfather's death. Then again, Camdonbury always preferred friends with no scruples. And with Clivedale having apprenticed as an apothecary, I'm sure that made his friendship quite valuable."

"I never knew that about Clivedale," Lucan admitted.

"Aye. That tidbit was forgotten when your grandfather wound up poisoned as well."

Lucan thought back to that day at Tattersall's, the exchange he'd witnessed and the way they'd pretended not to know each other.

"Tell me, Aunt, what do you know of Whitelock?"

"That he's too good to be true. Never heard a bad word so much as whispered about him. No one is that crisp and clean on the outside without a wrinkled soul on the inside," she said with a sage nod, pursing her lips. "Of course, having an invalid wife likely helps his impeccable reputation. It wouldn't serve him to meet with an unscrupulous man like Clivedale. Not out in the open."

Could Clivedale still be dealing with poisons or…

Lucan stilled. Even though he knew nothing about the viscountess, he recalled Frances mentioning the drops she'd had to put in the viscountess's tea. Suddenly, Whitelock's farm on the coast of China seemed neither boring nor benign. Considering the location, it was likely an opium farm, which wasn't illegal, but it certainly raised questions. Was Whitelock an opium-eater? It seemed unlikely. The man was far too sharp-witted.

Was it possible that Whitelock kept his wife drugged on opium? If so, was his reason to keep her an invalid or to gain sympathy for having such a wife as a burden?

Perhaps it was both.

"It's no secret that Clivedale's wealth has increased exponentially over the years," Theodosia hissed.

Gaining riches by providing a discreet service? It was possible. Or perhaps he earned his money by blackmailing those who sought his services.

Now it was Lucan's turn to scrutinize his aunt. "You've been keeping watch on his dealings all this time?"

"I've been waiting," she said, her voice a harsh growl. "One day, he will find himself in a position of distress. He will have made a vital error and nothing will save him from the hangman's noose. That is when I will play my hand—*a confession for his life*. You see, I still have friends in London. Influential friends, who might be willing to offer Clivedale a bargain.

And then the truth of what your blackguard father did to my sister will finally be revealed."

She let out a breath. Tears, once again, glistened in her eyes.

Lucan squeezed her hand. "You are a formidable woman."

"Be glad that I am on your side," she said with a raspy laugh, breaking the tension of the moment. "So tell me about this wager."

He'd wondered when she would return to this. There wasn't any use in trying to outmaneuver her onto a different topic. Therefore, he gave her an abbreviated version, leaving out the fact that Hugh Thorne's life depended on his winning, as long as Whitelock accepted the money.

"And when you struck the bargain, you were confident you'd never marry?"

He thought of Frances instantly. *Never* lasted a long time. He imagined it would feel even longer now. Already, he was planning a swift gallop back. He knew he was tempting fate as well as his control, but he couldn't deny the overwhelming need to be with her. "Of course."

"But now you've tasted forbidden fruit, and you're not so sure."

She couldn't know that, he told himself, but he risked a sideways glance. Smug as can be, she nodded.

"Your spies have failed you this time," he said with authority. Besides, it was more like tasting a forbidden glazed bun.

Those brackets fanned out over her cheeks when she grinned. "Fine. Have it your way, but I'd like to meet her sometime. Perhaps you could…*abduct* her and bring her here."

Lucan frowned. So then, her spy was someone he knew, someone who knew all about Frances, and the comings and goings at Fallow Hall. "Who is it, Aunt?"

She laughed and patted his cheek. "Aw...you're such a lamb to believe I'd ever tell."

CHAPTER SEVENTEEN

Before Frances left the manor that afternoon, Lord Whitelock had insisted that his driver take her to the village, claiming that he refused to allow anything untoward to happen to her. Yet she suspected that he simply wanted to keep an eye on her.

Soon thereafter, she found herself in his carriage. Instead of directing the driver to the village, however, she asked Burt to take her to Fallow Hall. She explained that she was set to meet up with her friends there and that he should not wait. Unfortunately, when they arrived, he refused to leave until she offered a time for him to return for her—at Whitelock's request, of course. After agreeing upon three hours, Frances was glad to see the carriage rumble out of the drive. Then, like before, when she arrived at Fallow Hall, the front door opened, and RJ bounded outside. Valentine stood at the door.

"Miss Thorne," the butler began, "I'm afraid that Lady Everhart and Mrs. Danvers have just left for the market and to visit the poor with their husbands. It will likely be some time before they return."

Frances stopped short. She glanced over her shoulder to see the carriage shrinking in the distance. "Oh. Are *all* the residents of Fallow Hall away?"

One corner of Valentine's mouth wrinkled, hitching upward in something of a grin. "There is one other here. I believe he just arrived."

She suspected he knew that she wanted to see Lucan most of all, but the butler gave nothing away. "Perhaps I could wait in the music room?"

Valentine inclined his head and led the way. Coincidentally, Lucan was just descending the main stairs as she entered the hall. They both stopped, arrested. His hair was slightly damp and clung to his temples. His dark cravat was tied in a simple knot as if he'd dressed in a hurry. The lapels of his smoky blue coat rose and fell with his breaths, and it seemed to take an age before he spoke. "Miss Thorne, I did not know you had plans to travel to Fallow Hall today."

"I quite surprised myself." But the truth was, she needed to see him. She needed to be alone with him, even for a few minutes, hours, days, years…an *eternity*. She would gladly take them all. "I hope you can forgive the intrusion."

"You are more than welcome here," he said quietly without a hint of teasing or flirtation. His words left little doubt of his being in earnest. "Always."

A tender, terrifying thrill stirred to life inside her breast. At any moment, her heart could take flight, zip over the banister, and crash into him. If such a thing were possible, she believed that he would catch it. "I have just now discovered that your friends have gone to the village. Valentine was showing me to the music room."

Something hot flashed across Lucan's gaze. "Not to the parlor or to the study?"

"I'm rather fond of the music room." *And you*, she thought. "Perhaps I could hear you play again, my lord."

Lucan didn't look away from her. "Valentine, please see that a tray of refreshments is sent to the music room."

After descending the rest of the stairs, Lucan walked beside her down the corridor, both of them silent. And when they entered the music room, they paused just inside the doorway. With the house so quiet and with Lucan standing so near, her desire to merely have a moment alone with him took new form. She recalled the last time they were in this room together. The air seemed charged with the memory as well. Even the breath she took was warm and sultry.

Lucan's sleeve brushed her bare arm, and the action caused her flesh to tighten, not only in that spot but all over her body. He looked down at her as if he'd felt the contact as well. His pupils were dark and round, rimmed with gold. "Should I play for you, Miss Thorne, or…" He paused mid-question, leaving innumerable possibilities at their disposal. "Have you come to continue our previous conversation from last night?"

She nodded in answer, wanting both. Her body trembled in anticipation. "I believe we left off at your belief that I do not know my own mind."

"Clearly that was short-sighted of me." His hand cupped her elbow, his fingertips caressing her lightly. Then, he escorted her away from the open door and toward the row of chairs. He could kiss her here without anyone seeing them…

She lifted her gaze, licked her lips, hoped. "Quite."

"I also recall trying to keep my distance, but clearly that method has not aided my self-control whatsoever," he confessed, lowering his head. His hand reached up to cup her cheek. "In fact—"

Unfortunately, the distant clink of glassware from down the hall interrupted. A maid would soon arrive with their refreshment.

Lucan glanced over his shoulder. "It is a good thing we are not alone, or else I might forget myself entirely."

"I would like that."

He closed his eyes and, with a heavy exhale, moved to the piano.

Reluctantly, Frances sat in her chair while Lucan began to play. They said little more by way of conversation. All her thoughts were centered on waiting for that tray to arrive, waiting until they would be truly alone. At any moment, she was likely to explode from the anticipation.

"Did you have an enjoyable visit with your aunt?" she asked, fidgeting in her chair.

Lucan nodded. "She is eager to make your acquaintance."

"You spoke of me?" This surprised Frances. She knew that Lucan was a private person and couldn't help but wonder what it meant that he would speak to his aunt about her.

"To be honest, she already knew about you and how you came to be at Fallow Hall on that first day. Theodosia has a mysterious way of knowing too much."

"Rather like her nephew, I suppose," Frances said affectionately, not caring that her tendre for him was transparent.

He studied her intently, his expression unreadable. "Of course, you could very well be cross with me for not mentioning you to her first."

She swallowed down a sudden rise of exhilaration. "That would be a bold assumption on my part, wouldn't it?"

"Let it never be said that either of us is guilty of making bold assumptions." He laughed wryly and then glanced at the door. His notes took an ominous chord.

In the next moment, Grace brought in a tray of lemonade and a dish of strawberries, which she told Frances were the sweetest because they were the last. Frances thanked her and set the tray on the window seat nearest the piano.

Once they were alone, Frances poured Lucan a glass and moved to stand beside him. "Don't stop playing. Allow me." She brought the rim to his lips.

Lifting his gaze to hers, Lucan drank deeply, emptying half the glass. When he finished, she lingered near, stroking his hair, and then bent to press a kiss to his head. His hair was cool and damp against her lips. The music he played spilled over her, filling her head with an idea that would surely be shocking, but the risk was worth it, no matter the consequences.

Placing the glass back on the tray, she moved across the room. Without hesitating, she closed the door and turned the key in the lock. Her mind was made up. She knew what she wanted. Looking over her shoulder, she saw Lucan raise his brows.

"The breeze from the windows closed the door," she explained.

He glanced at all the closed windows and then to her. His dimple appeared. "I can see that."

On her way back, she unhooked her mother's brooch and slipped the fichu from around her neck. "It is a little warm for this," she said, folding the gauzy square of fabric before she set it down on a table.

As she returned to his side, his gaze drifted appreciatively over the newly exposed skin, the modest swells rising above the neckline of her simple blue dress. She stepped behind him, brushing her hands over his shoulders as he played. Leaning down once more to kiss his head, she breathed in his comforting scent.

"You feel rather warm as well," she whispered, slipping her hands down his lapels and underneath to feel the hard contours of his chest. "Would you like me to remove your coat?"

He pressed his lips to her cheek, her jaw, and nuzzled her just behind her ear. "You are impossible to resist. Remove any article of clothing that you like, either on my person or yours."

"What a scandalous thing to suggest. Think of my reputation," she chided while her hands skimmed his torso. "However, if you continue to play, I doubt anyone will suspect."

The sound of his amusement vibrated through her, cascading down through her body. She slipped his coat free, one arm at a time, while he continued to play with minimal interruption. Kissing his temple, she pressed her cheek against his as her hands roamed down his arms. The fine lawn of his shirt was damp in places and heat radiated from him. Wanting to cool him, she untied his cravat and let it drop to the floor.

The melody he played turned urgent, matching the quick work of her fingers on his waistcoat buttons. This, too, she pulled down over his shirt sleeves, one side at a time. She could see the dark hair of his chest through the open collar of his shirt and even through the linen.

"What do you plan to do, Miss Thorne?" he asked as she ogled him shamelessly.

Pulling the tails of his shirt free, she lifted it, exposing his hard, lean build, inch by inch. "I am developing my appreciation for the human form. Your melody is inspiring me."

Soon, his shirt was on the floor. She'd already given up folding every article of clothing. She was getting impatient and overheated. And at last her gaze touched him. He was no statue of marble but somehow looked harder, firmer. There were no soft lines chiseled into his form, yet his muscles moved with grace and ease. From his corded throat to his broad shoulders, and from the defined musculature of his arms and chest to the ridges of his stomach, he was perfect.

Twisting her arms behind her back, she unfastened the short row of buttons between her shoulder blades. She slipped her dress from her shoulders and let it fall to the floor. Having no maid of her own, she was used to such maneuvers, yet Lucan appeared transfixed by them.

His gaze roamed over her. "You are quite adept with your hands."

It wasn't true. She was nervous and her fingers had fumbled over the buttons. Being here in this room in the light of day, alone with him, and undressing them both was the most audacious thing she'd ever done in her life. But no amount of maidenly apprehension could stop her. She wanted him, she loved him, and she refused to go another day without him.

"I'm certain not nearly as clever as you are." Even though she was thinking about his sleight of hand tricks, by his sudden rakish grin she realized she'd implied something else altogether. Frances imagined that she was correct about that too. She wanted to find out.

Her petticoat unbuttoned similarly, and she slipped it off as well. Encouraged by his hungry gaze, she ignored her trembling fingers and unfastened her short stays. Even in nothing more than her chemise, stockings, and shoes, she still felt far too hot.

Lucan continued to play, every note a caress. Desire rippled through her, tightening her own flesh. Her nipples rasped against the damp cotton of her chemise. Lucan's eyes lingered there, and he swallowed as if he could taste her. Moving one hand off the keys, he pulled her over to stand in front of him, between his thighs. At the same time, he slipped one strap down her shoulder. The blue ribbon border of her chemise clung to the taut crest of her dusky nipple. Then he leaned forward, pulled it down with his teeth, and devoured her breast.

His music covered the gasp of her pleasure. She clutched his head, threading her fingers through his dark silken hair. Sliding down the other strap, she offered herself to him. He feasted. His hot, ravenous response revealed that he was just as eager as she was. The music was all around her now, inside of her. Her pulse was the stroke of each key. His mouth was the melody.

On a growl, he stood, pushing the bench behind him and lifting her to the piano top in one motion. Parting her legs, she pulled him closer. Her hips were just above his waist, and it gave her the perfect access to kiss him. Still holding onto him, she indulged in his mouth, delving deep with her tongue, tasting the dark, exotic flavor of him, drinking him in.

"One of us must play. And I'm afraid my hands are otherwise engaged," he said, lifting her knees to remove her slippers. Then he placed her stockinged feet on the keys. Hers was not music at all, but more of a clash of notes.

Again, he proved his skill by playing a beautiful symphony over her flesh, making her writhe. He kissed her throat and laved her breasts. And with a gentle shove, he urged her to lie back. The ebony piano top felt cool against her skin. But in the next instant, she felt Lucan's kiss on her stomach. His lips brushed over her flesh, followed by his tongue. He was greedy, touching her everywhere, tasting her, stroking every part of her. His urgency aroused her, making her tremble with need. She ached with it. How had she been able to live without experiencing the force of his passion and her own for so long?

The springy hair of his chest brushed against her bare thighs. He traced her nipples in feather-light touches that made her arch against his fingers, begging for his caress. She covered his hands, pressing his palms to the pale swells of her breasts. He nipped her stomach with his teeth as his hands kneaded her flesh. Then his kisses roamed lower. His hands drifted too, leaving no part of her without his touch. He stroked her hips, her thighs, and the sensitive flesh behind her knees, teaching her about pleasure, making her feet restless on the keys. He nudged her legs wider.

Frances watched his kisses drift downward. She could feel his hot breath against her sex. Then his mouth claimed that part of her in a hard, heated kiss. Her hips arched off the piano. Her feet pressed down on the keys with a discordant crash, but it was the sound of ecstasy to her. His tongue rasped against her flesh, slipping through the swollen seam of her sex. He murmured unintelligible hungry sounds that made her tremble all over. She was lost to pleasure. Sunlight poured in through the windows, bathing her. She felt the heat of it inside as well, pulsing low and fast, matching the flicks of his tongue, eliciting an insistent throbbing pulse. At seven and twenty, she'd explored her own body a time or two. Curiosity had gotten the better of her. But it had never felt like this. Her own ministrations had left her unfulfilled and frustrated, eager for something more.

"Yes. More," she groaned, lifting her hips higher. She knew he would understand—that he was everything she'd ever wanted.

He growled in response, sliding a finger deep inside where she was wet and ready. She felt her body clench around him and then the vibration of his next growl against her sex. Ripples of pleasure expanded and multiplied, like a stone skipping across the surface of a lake. The ripples grew stronger, turning into waves, washing all the way through to her fingertips and toes. And then he drew on that bud of flesh, suckling, his tongue flicking once more—

She cried out, arching higher, seeking…and suddenly ecstasy rushed over her. The sound of her climax was still echoing in the room when Lucan lifted her to him. Holding her, he lowered her onto the bench so that she straddled him. She could feel him shaking, even through her own residual tremors. Meeting his gaze, she saw nothing remaining of his carefully guarded self. Instead, she saw a hunger so intense that it sent a wanton thrill through her.

"Do you have any hesitation at all?" he rasped, his hand poised between them.

She shook her head, certain. "We are beyond that."

He ripped open the fall of his breeches. His thick flesh jutted forward, standing tall and solid like a sentinel. Adjusting her spectacles, she barely had time to admire this part of him before he lifted her hips and positioned himself at the damp entrance of her body.

"Now is not the time for study." In other words, there would be time later. This was only the beginning.

Slowly, he filled her, inch by inch. At her age, she needn't worry about a barrier guarding her virginity. Still, her flesh burned where her body stretched to accommodate his girth. She held on to his shoulders. Her face close to his, their open mouths shared breaths. They were sharing everything now. She never knew this was what she'd been missing all along. Yet even so, she knew that making love wouldn't be this powerful with anyone else.

He closed his eyes, his face tight with near anguish. "The way you feel... *killing me.*"

She resisted the urge to smile but pressed her lips to his. He guided her hips down the length of his shaft and then up again. Each time, her wetness coated him, making her movements easier. And soon she was moving of her own accord.

"*Frances. Frances. Frances,*" he crooned against her lips in a way that was more potent than any *I love you* she'd ever heard.

She rode him slowly, sliding down to the hilt. There, she stopped on a gasp as a spasm of pleasure jolted her. She hadn't been expecting that. Beneath her, he moved his hips, thrusting, eliciting another spasm. Her body clutched his. He urged her faster, lifting her, tilting her hips forward so that she rubbed against him. Again, pleasure spiraled through her, coiling, tightening. She was close already. Overcome with sensation, and fearing that she would give them away, she pressed her mouth to his. Instantly, she came apart. A low keening moan escaped her as her body clenched. Lucan kissed her in return, pulling her down hard, thrusting deep, burying himself inside of her. He groaned too, his body quaking as he found his release.

Mouths open, they gasped for breath. Against the short hairs of his chest, her nipples ached. She felt sore and tight all over but still never wanted to separate from him.

Frances dropped her head to his shoulder and nuzzled his neck, pressing her lips to him and tasting the salt of his perspiration. "You don't think anyone suspects what we've been doing in here, do you?"

Lucan pressed a kiss to her head, her neck, and her bare shoulder. She could feel his flesh still pulsing inside of her. He stroked her back with one hand and touched the piano keys with the other. "I'm certain they imagined that your delectable sounds were caused by your strenuous efforts to open the door."

She shifted on his lap. "But they couldn't possibly have heard me."

His flesh twitched, and he grinned. "Of course not."

"You shouldn't tease me so," she said, trying to sound cross, but it was impossible. She loved him too much. "Besides, what about you and the way you said my name over and over again?"

"I'm afraid I have to give you the blame for that as well. You forced me to abandon the last shreds of my control after all."

She saw the truth in his gaze and felt as if she were glowing from the force of her smile. "Then, you're finished resisting me?"

"I don't suppose now is the time for any declar—"

"No. Don't." She covered his mouth with her hand. "I did not come here expecting any declaration. I know that winning your wager is important to you. And because you are important to me, I want you to win. It is just that I couldn't imagine not being with you, like this."

He gently lowered her hand and kissed her fingertips. "But, Frances, you must realize that—"

He was interrupted this time by the unexpected barking of RJ down the hall.

"They have returned." His hissed an oath under his breath. In an instant, he reached back into the pile of discarded clothes and found a handkerchief. As she lifted away from him, she winced. He carefully but efficiently cleansed her sex and pressed a quick kiss to her lips. "We will speak more later."

"Yes," she promised, believing they would come to a satisfying arrangement. She stood. Already she felt empty without him. Yet they needed to dress—and with haste.

In no time, Lucan was fully clad and assisting her with her buttons before helping to replace the pins she'd lost. Then, just as they heard voices in the hall, Frances placed the brooch in her fichu.

"I don't look like we've just engaged in wild, amorous congress, do I?"

Lucan poured her a glass of lemonade. "Perhaps you should drink this to cool your cheeks. I'll open the windows."

"Very good. I'll get the door." She sipped as she crossed the room and quietly turned the key. When she opened the door and rushed back to her seat, but the door slammed shut with the force of the breeze coming in through the window.

She couldn't help but laugh.

Lucan resumed playing the piano as she crossed the room once more. This time when she opened the door, their friends were standing on the other side.

"I've been having a terrible time keeping this door from slamming shut," she explained, feeling another rush of heat to her cheeks. "With the windows open, I might need to put a chair in front of it."

Everhart, Calliope, Danvers, and Hedley all looked at her with speculative grins. But as they walked inside, another gust of wind blew the door shut. Frances looked up and offered an unspoken *thank-you* to the heavens.

Lucan was at odds with himself. He couldn't repress his joy. He felt victorious and at the same time completely at peace, even though he'd lost complete control. Making love to Frances had been an experience like no other. He felt changed, in a way that he'd never imagined. Everything seemed clearer, brighter. The shadows he carried with him had receded for the first time.

Yet he'd just lost the wager.

Frances might not think so, but he would correct her later. They would be married, and soon. His mind turned with all he must do. First, he would need to free Thorne from Fleet and then remove him from the country so that he was out of Whitelock's reach.

Lucan would come up with a plan and enlist the help of his friends. Pride had kept him from sharing part of his life with them. Pride and fear. He'd been afraid of their rejection all this time, believing that if they knew how dark his life had begun, they would no longer welcome him as a friend. Yet if a person as remarkable as Frances could see past all of that, he suddenly felt confident that they would as well.

When they entered the music room, he tried to keep his gaze on the piano keys because, surely, if anyone saw him look at Frances, they would discover a stranger residing in his skin. Then soon enough, they would know the reason.

"It was such a warm afternoon that we decided not to go the market after calling on the neighbors," Calliope said, easing down onto a chair nearest the windows. "Had I known you were dropping by, Frances, I would have stayed here."

"My visit was of an unexpected nature." Frances glanced at Lucan as she took another sip.

Hedley looked from Frances to Lucan and slowly grinned. "I'm delighted that Lucan was here to entertain you."

Frances sputtered, coughing on lemonade. Lucan stood immediately and stepped out from behind the piano. Apparently seeing him out of the corner of her eye, she gave him a hard look.

"It is fine. I'm not choking on another seed this time," she rasped, attempting a charade for his friends to cover his instinctive response. Apparently, she thought she was saving him.

Everhart cleared his throat. Danvers looked entirely too smug. Calliope and Hedley both beamed. His friends knew he'd lost the wager. Perhaps not what had occurred moments before they arrived, but his intentions toward Frances were impossible to hide.

Yet Frances—as clever as she was—did not seem to realize how different he was with her than with anyone else.

He silently laughed at himself and shook his head. What a fool he'd been all this time to think that the wager would never apply to him.

CHAPTER EIGHTEEN

Frances returned to Whitelock Manor, against Lucan's wishes. But when Whitelock's driver had arrived at Fallow Hall, she was almost relieved to depart. Trying to pretend that she wasn't bursting with love and happiness in front of their friends had been next to impossible. All she'd wanted to do was wrap her arms around Lucan and stay close to him. Forever.

She'd left with the promise that they would talk about their plans later that evening. Yet the moment the carriage separated her from him, she realized something important—what she had with Lucan was honest and true. And perhaps he knew her better than she knew herself. She wanted more than an arrangement with him. She wanted a life.

Now standing in the main hall at Whitelock Manor, she stared at the painted clouds on the domed ceiling. They resembled the ones that she'd seen from the music room window earlier.

"Miss Thorne, if you have a moment," Viscount Whitelock said, catching her lost in a daydream.

She instantly sobered. "Yes, my lord?"

"Take a walk with me to my study," he said, gesturing with his open hand toward the hall. "There is a matter I should like to discuss."

Frances felt a jolt of uncertainty when she noted that Lord Whitelock's expression bore displeasure. With her goal of freeing her father from Fleet only weeks away, she couldn't bear to lose her post. "I hope I am performing to your satisfaction, my lord."

With his study just down the hall, they were inside before he answered.

"I could not hope for better," he said, closing the door behind them. "However, it has come to my attention that you have been seen in the company of Lucan Montwood. Since you are under my care, it falls to me to offer a kind warning."

Heat rushed to her cheeks before she took a moment to realize that Whitelock couldn't have known the intimate details of this afternoon. And it was unlikely anyone could have seen her with Lucan in the shadowed corner of the gallery each night. Therefore, it had to have been when they were on horseback together. Since there didn't appear to be any fondness between the two gentlemen, and one of them paid her salary, she tread carefully while still respecting her own privacy.

"I appreciate your concern, my lord."

As expected, the viscount approved of her words. "Have you formed an attachment? I only ask because he has no income other than gambling. I'm not sure if you are aware, but gambling debts are considered debts of honor. Left unpaid, and a gentleman can be cast out of society, even out of his own family, and without means."

Just as Roger Quinlin had fled London after purchasing a commission in order to escape his debts, which his father had paid for him. Yet this had nothing to do with Lucan. "Yes, I understand, but I cannot see how this relates to—"

"Montwood has such a debt," Whitelock interrupted. "In fact, I've learned that he intends to fleece his own friends with a wager."

She smiled. "That wager was nothing more than a lark."

"I'd hardly call ten thousand pounds *a lark*."

Ten thousand pounds? Her mouth opened on a gasp. They'd never mentioned that amount when they'd spoken of the wager. But this was absurd. She didn't believe it. For her, that would be equal to ten thousand weeks of labor. Her head was spinning. "A wager for that amount is unheard of, I'm sure."

The viscount took her elbow and escorted her to a chair. "Unfortunately, it is true, my dear."

No. It couldn't be. She rejected the very notion. Lucan wouldn't do something like that. Not to his friends. He wasn't a man who would have such a debt and then not honor it.

Refusing to sit, she stood in front the chair and faced Whitelock. She knew the real Lucan now. And yet…she knew how important the wager was to him. "How did you come by your information, my lord?"

"Lucan Montwood borrowed the money from me." Lord Whitelock's expression turned gentle and apologetic.

Her world came to a sudden halt. The blood in her heart froze. The warmth of her skin turned cold and clammy. She slumped down and put her face in her hands, her stomach churning. "From you?"

"Sadly, yes," he said, stroking her shoulder as if to reassure her. "I have been accused of being too generous at times. It is my own failing. I only warn you so that you are not too generous with your favors. It would not be prudent for an intelligent woman to involve herself with a man who cannot support her, as you no doubt already know from experience."

Though she bristled to hear it, she could not deny the truth. After all, her father was in gaol for his debts. Suddenly, she felt like a fool for putting her faith in the wrong man once again.

The shred of hope that she'd clung to—that she'd found a noble man in Lucan Montwood—dissolved into dust. *A wager for ten thousand pounds…fleecing his friends…*and all the while, Lucan had cast a shadow of suspicion over Lord Whitelock. The only reason he would want to do that would be to distract her, so that she didn't look too closely at his own character. It was a magician's parlor trick to make the audience focus on one hand while the other worked the trick.

She'd fallen for deception once more. "If you'll forgive me, my lord, I would like to retire. My headache seems to have returned."

Frances felt a keen, sharp pain beneath her breast as she left the room. She knew that her heart was shattering. This time, there would be no way to mend it.

After spending a few hours writing letters and speaking privately with Everhart and Danvers, Lucan strode into the foyer at Fallow Hall. "Valentine, I need this letter sent out post haste."

The letter was addressed to Theodosia, asking for her assistance—or rather, the use of her connections in London—in order to have Hugh Thorne released from Fleet. He knew that he'd given his word to Thorne to allow him three months to sort himself out, but now circumstances were different. Thorne was at risk from far more than sitting in a cramped cell. Once Lucan confronted Whitelock about his suspicions, there was no telling what the viscount would do.

If Theodosia's friends declined, then Everhart had already offered to press his connections. And Danvers knew of an empty house where Thorne could hide out until this matter with the evidence against him was sorted.

The butler inclined his head. "Will there be anything else, my lord?"

Lucan was confident that after he spoke with Frances, she would return with him and leave Whitelock Manor for good. "Yes. Have the Raven chamber prepared." In his opinion, it was the finest room in Fallow Hall. Not only that, but it was near his suite of rooms.

"Very good."

Lucan watched the butler carefully. "Was that a grin, Valentine?"

There it was, that twitch at the corner of his mouth. "I'm certain it couldn't have been, sir. The shadows in the foyer are quite deceptive at times."

Hmm… In recalling his last conversation with Theodosia about her spy, Lucan eyed him shrewdly. "Tell me, have you always worked at Fallow Hall?"

"No, sir. As a younger man, I worked at Thistlemane."

Ah. Now, he understood how his aunt was receiving information. Thistlemane was an estate not far from where his mother and aunt were raised. "Do you keep in contact with the people of that area?"

That smile flickered again. "Not as often as one would like."

Lucan settled his John Bull atop his head and studied Valentine. He couldn't believe he'd been blind to it all this time—the glint in his eyes and the way his last comment was edged with longing. However, Lucan supposed it took a man in love to recognize the symptoms in another.

"My aunt is a remarkable woman."

"I couldn't agree more, sir."

Shortly afterward, Lucan left for Whitelock Manor. The sun had set, and the dinner hour for country dwellers approached.

Once at the manor, he slipped through the passageway and climbed the narrow stairs to the gallery. Surprisingly, Frances was already there, waiting for him. She was sitting in the dim light of a single lamp at her feet.

"Shouldn't you still be at dinner?" he asked, curious about the change in her schedule. Then again, perhaps she was as eager to see him as he was her.

"I wasn't hungry."

He peered around the gallery to ensure they were alone. It was still early enough that a servant might make a final pass, but when he was satisfied, he knelt in front of her and took her hands. They were like ice. He brought them to his lips to warm them. Then he looked into her face and noticed the puffy flesh around her eyes.

He was instantly alarmed. "What has happened? Are you unwell? Did that blackguard—"

"*Blackguard?*" she asked, her irises hard and flinty. "You would accuse the man who loaned you ten thousand pounds of unscrupulous behavior?"

Slowly, he felt the cold seep into him, and he removed his hands from hers. "How did you hear that?"

"The generous man who loaned you the money so that you could gamble it away told me," she said, already damning Lucan. She didn't even ask for a denial or reason. "It is no wonder that you have spent all your time trying to persuade me to see the ill in him."

Lucan loathed Whitelock and his methods. First, he made Frances feel as if she were indebted to him, and now he wanted to poison her mind so that she couldn't see the people who truly cared for her. Who loved her.

"Do not be fooled by what you learned today. It is true that I am in debt to Whitelock for ten thousand pounds, but the nature of the bargain that I made is that I was never to speak of it. *He* was to adhere to the same bargain."

Lucan wanted to tell her everything now, but his need for her to trust his words above Whitelock's made his tongue stubborn.

"I can think of only one reason you can never speak of it and that is *shame*," she accused, her voice breaking.

He longed to haul her into his arms and reassure her. All she had to do was trust him. Instead, he stood. Turning on his heel, he faced the back of that damned sculpture. Something in the vicinity of his heart was tearing apart. The pain of it made him want to shout loud enough to shatter the windows.

Yet, somehow, he managed to keep his voice low and even. "Yes, Miss Thorne, you should have known better. I am the type of man who is all charm and no substance."

"Your self-deprecating comments will not make me fall in love with you again. I am finished loving you," she hissed.

His heart seized. Joy and agony hit him at once. Her confession nearly brought him to his knees. Steeling himself, Lucan clenched his fists and looked straight ahead. Her words would forever be caged in his mind, torturing him.

"Finished so soon?" He tried to make light of it, but his tone was harsh. "Might I ask when it began so that I am able to mourn it properly?"

"I doubt you could. It is my own burden to know that love does not come from a place of sound judgment, nor did my actions earlier today." Her breathing staggered and the candlelight wavered as she stood. Then, she stepped around to face him, pushing her spectacles up along the bridge of her nose. "I put my trust in you. I felt safe with you, but it was all part of a deception. I was naïve to think I was worldly, that I knew better. Though perhaps, I do now."

Seeing his own anguish mirrored in her lenses, it panicked him. He couldn't let this be the last thing between them. He took hold of her arms. "Don't say that, Frances. Please. You don't understand everything. Whitelock is trying to manipulate you."

Frances took a step back until his hands fell away. "That is far too convenient of an answer."

"You're right. I don't know for certain about Henny Momper. I will find out more tomorrow when I travel to Shalehouse. However, I do know that Whitelock is hiding things from society," Lucan said, agony clawing at him. "He has underhanded dealings with a physician whom I know is untrustworthy. Whitelock also owns property in China. It is entirely possible that it is an opium farm. He could be keeping his wife an invalid to suit his own purpose."

"Enough!" she shouted. "Don't you hear yourself? You have no proof of any of it. This is all speculation, conveniently aimed at a man to whom you owe ten thousand pounds."

"I know what it sounds like, which is precisely why I've kept it all to myself. But you've turned me inside out. I am a desperate man—desperate to make sure you don't choose a cunning devil over me." He shook his head, taking a step toward her. "Choose me, Frances."

She looked stricken. Tears streamed down her cheeks. "Lucan, I don't—"

"Wait. Before you decide, there is one thing I know for certain." He swallowed hard, hating that he was telling her this way. But this might be his last chance to get through to her. "When I spoke with your father, I learned that there was a reason why he never mentioned Whitelock to you. It's true that they were once rivals for your mother's hand, but Whitelock lured her into being alone with him. He did something despicable, *heinous*, to her… Then, later that same summer, she married your father."

"It still doesn't prove anything. And how could you mention my dear mother in such an unforgivable manner?" She swiped at her tears with a closed fist. "I never want to see you again."

Then she rushed away, taking the light with her and out of his life.

He returned a short while later, but he did not bother her with a renewal of his plea. Without a word, he left RJ to stand guard at her door and slinked back into the shadows.

CHAPTER NINETEEN

Lucan left that same night. His path was lit only by the moon. He rode hours without a break, as if demons were on Quicksilver's heels.

Shalehouse was inside a small parish, hidden away near the outskirts of the Brindle Forest with no other surrounding villages for miles. It was suspiciously secluded. The house itself was more of a farm and less of a manor. It certainly didn't appear to be a place that a noble would send his staff for training—if that was truly what Whitelock did.

Tying Quicksilver to the branches of a twisted yew, Lucan skirted through the predawn shadows toward the house. With the morning as warm as it was, the kitchen windows were open, revealing lamplight spilling out onto the garden. The scent of porridge and ham drifted outside. An older man and woman sat at a rough wooden table, their cups and bowls set before them, a stack of papers nearby.

Lucan crept low, crouching near a honeysuckle as he overheard bits and pieces of conversation. He concentrated, tuning his ear to the rustic accents.

"In that letter, it seems Cora's done well for 'erself, wouldn't ye say? Managing a fine 'ouse, she is. Couldn't do no better," the man said as he shuffled paper.

"That boy o' 'ers is nigh on three years now," the woman added. "The farmer what took 'im came by here yestermorn and said 'e wouldn't mind another like 'im. So if the next girl o' 'is lordship's bears an 'ealthy boy, we'll know just where to put 'im."

The next girl of his lordship's? Lucan felt a jolt of panic rush through him. If this was the house where the driver always brought the companions, then it sounded as if it wasn't for training at all. But who was Cora—one of the first of Lady Whitelock's companions?

If that was true, then Whitelock had been sullying his employees for quite a while. At least four years, if the first boy was three.

"Couldna been more surprised that Molly found 'erself a husband. Right stubborn minx. Wanted 'is lordship or nuffin. They all want to please 'im, e'en after 'e's done wi' 'em," the man continued. "I just learned that she runs a shop in London now. 'Is lordship bought it and even let Molly put 'er 'usband's name on it. *Tuttle's Registry.* Sounds right fancy, once you say it."

Tuttle's Registry. The shop that had opened down the street from Mrs. Hunter's. So Whitelock now had his own servant registry. He would have a never-ending supply of unsuspecting maids in the future. Not only that, but he likely helped force Frances from her employment.

Though Lucan had sought to find proof, this news was far worse than he'd ever imagined.

"We could do wi' a bit o' 'elp in the kitchen. Mayhap 'is lordship could send a cook from the registry. Or send us a cook with a babe in 'er belly," the woman said with a laugh.

The man laughed too but then tsked. "Such a shame the last one didn't live through the birthin'. *She* was a fair cook. Ah, but 'tis for the best since 'er babe woulda been a girl. Saved us the trouble, she did. Rest 'er poor soul."

Lucan didn't need to hear her name. He already knew. Henny Momper was dead.

Leaving the same way he came, only with a heavier burden, he made it back to Quicksilver. Only now, with dawn creeping low in the sky, did he notice that the yew tree stood beside a small graveyard. There were several older stones, sinking in the soft ground. But there was also one wooden cross that hadn't yet weathered. All the marker read was MOTHER AND CHILD.

Anguish and injustice flooded him. Arthur Momper had lost the only family he had left. Whitelock, in his lecherous seduction, had stolen Henny Momper's innocence *and* her life. He was worse than Lucan's father. At least the Marquess of Camdonbury was terrible at disguising his monstrous nature, while Whitelock was far too good at it. Hell, even the older couple had sounded as if they admired him.

It was more than Lucan could take. He was going to confront Whitelock once and for all.

Like his mother, Lucan had been unable to save Henny Momper from a monster. But he was determined to save Frances. He loved her and refused to let her come to harm. Even if she didn't choose him in the end.

CHAPTER TWENTY

Frances had not slept at all. The morning offered no reprieve for her aching heart either. She'd arrogantly clung to the idea that she could easily spot the cads and bounders. Yet it was all too clear that she was a horrible judge of character. Not even being cynical had kept her safe from anguish.

Foolishly, she'd given her heart to Lucan too soon, like a cloud set adrift amidst the heavens. Sadly, she'd discovered that it was merely a painted façade—a creation contrived by a cunning deceiver. Summarily, her heart had fallen back to earth, landing hard enough to cripple her.

The worst part was, she still wanted to believe Lucan. Her broken heart yearned for him. Especially after she'd discovered RJ standing guard outside her chamber door this morning. Just when she thought she'd spent all her tears throughout the night, the moment she saw the lovable beast, she sank to her knees, hugged him, and wept some more.

Afterward, she led RJ to the back stairs in order to let him out. Since it was Sunday, the entire household typically attended church services. Therefore, she didn't need to worry about being caught. At the garden door, she gave RJ one final pat and sent him on his way, certain he would know the path back to Fallow Hall.

Climbing the stairs, Frances went to Lady Whitelock's bedchamber. She could use the distraction of Mrs. Darby's conversation. However, when she entered the room, the nurse was not there. The viscountess slept peacefully in her pastel silk bed. Frances had always assumed that she was never left alone, but obviously that wasn't true. Yet not wanting to return to her own chamber, Frances decided to sit in a corner chair and wait for Mrs. Darby's return.

Soon enough, however, Frances felt her eyes grow heavy. As her lids drifted shut, she recalled how she'd sat in her mother's room like this. It was a comforting thought, and soon she found herself lost in a dream.

"Come here, my angel," her mother said from the bed, beckoning her from the corner chair and trying to lift her arm from the coverlet. But the strength had all but left her.

Frances crossed the room and sat on the edge of the feather mattress. Automatically, she withdrew a cloth from the bowl waiting on the nightstand and cleansed the perspiration from her mother's face. "What is it, Mother?"

"There is something I need to tell you," she rasped, her face pale but full of determination. "Be on your guard, always. My greatest fear is that I will not be here to protect you from life's cruelties."

"Don't speak like that, Mother. You're going to be well again." But they both knew differently. *"You've already taught me so much…"*

"There is more." Her mother clutched her hand, squeezing it tightly and shaking from the effort. Even her voice trembled.

"I had...a dear friend who trusted the wrong man. She believed he was good and honorable, only to have her naiveté stolen in the most vile manner imaginable for a young woman."

A glacial cold crept over Frances as she saw the horror in her mother's eyes. In that instant, she knew what had happened to her mother's friend. Yet the word was left unspoken. In fact, not many women ever dared to whisper about that particular evil. No woman could recover from such ruination, she was sure.

"I will be cautious," Frances promised.

Her mother released a slow breath. "Good. My wish is for you to know only love."

Frances lay down beside her and was quiet for a while, thinking. "In the end, whatever happened to your friend?"

"She married the kindest of men who cherished her in spite of everything. She married for love."

"Just like you and Da."

Her mother pressed a kiss to her forehead. "Yes, my darling. Exactly like your father and me."

Frances awoke with a start. She blinked, her eyes adjusting to the room. When she saw the furs on the floor and the cherubs overhead, she realized she must have fallen asleep in the viscountess's bedchamber.

What she thought had been a dream was actually a memory. Only now, years later, Frances realized something she'd missed before. Her mother had never once mentioned her friend's name but spoke of the *naïve girl* as if they were close. Close enough to be the same person? Could it be that her mother hadn't been speaking of friend at all but of herself instead?

Even before the question whispered through her mind, Frances knew the answer. Her mother had been diligent in teaching Frances to pay close attention to everything and everyone around her and to keep a wary eye on every man. Now, she knew why.

Frances covered her mouth on a sob, fearful of waking the viscountess.

She recalled Lucan's warnings. And she thought of how she'd discounted her instinctive uneasiness around Whitelock, time and again. How could she have been so stupid?

Then, another suspicion came to mind. Rising unsteadily from the chair, she opened the drawer where Mrs. Darby kept the brown vial. Turning the lid, she opened it and inhaled. The fragrance was cloying but also unbearably bitter…like the tea she'd drunk at Whitelock's Mayfair townhouse.

Frances gasped. The tea…

Soon after she'd finished the tea that day, she'd fallen into an exhausted, hazy sleep. Had Whitelock put these drops in her tea?

A cold chill ran through her. Dear Lord, was Whitelock truly drugging his wife with opium, like Lucan had said?

And Whitelock had drugged Frances too, but why?

"Elise had a strong will and a feisty spirit. It's what called me to her. Alas, she chose your father, and our friendship ended. Yet I still hold her memory in my heart. I am pleased—perhaps selfishly so—that I can claim part of her spirit once more by having you here."

Frances felt ill. Bile churned in her empty stomach, rising up her throat. Whitelock had raped her mother. Had that been his intention when he'd drugged Frances? Yet thankfully, she remembered that when she'd woken at his townhouse, all her clothes had been in order. She'd even had her shoes on. So then if his design was to get her away from London in order to *claim* her, then why bother drugging her after she'd accepted the position?

At the time, her only plan had been to speak with her father first and to tell him that she was going to work for Whitelock. Even though her father had his flaws, she knew without a doubt that he would have warned her away from the viscount. However, because she'd been drugged, she'd never had the chance. That must have Whitelock's reason that day.

Hearing distant voices, Frances put the vial back in the drawer. She walked to the door and cupped her ear to it. She could hear the two distinctive tones. One clearly belonged to Lord Whitelock, while the other sounded almost familiar. In fact, the voice nearly sounded like Lucan's. Surely not. Lucan despised Whitelock.

"*Unless you have come to pay your debt,*" Whitelock said, "*this borders on dissolution of our agreement.*"

"*I believe the agreement was for both parties to remain silent. From what I know, you have not upheld your end of the bargain.*"

It was Lucan! She knew his voice like a melody inside her heart. But what was he doing here? A shiver rushed through her, raising gooseflesh on her arms.

"*Sampson! Hershell! Take hold of this man,*" Whitelock called, summoning his valet and the footman. "*Greggs, send for the magistrate. This man is trespassing.*"

Frances opened the door quietly. The voices sounded close, as if the men stood around the corner near the stairs. When she peered out into the hall, she saw Nannette frozen and wide-eyed in the doorway of the servants' stairs. Frances held her finger to her lips and earned a stiff nod.

Other than the two of them, this hall was empty. Frances crept forward.

Lucan grunted, as if struggling. "*You have many men who owe you favors, I'm sure. Otherwise, the evidence against Thorne never would have been lost so conveniently.*"

Evidence against her father? Frances stiffened. What could Lucan be talking about? Their conversation sounded like they were speaking of the Marquess of Camdonbury's accusation against her father. But since he was acquitted…

No, not acquitted, she remembered. Her father had been released because the evidence had been lost. But what if it hadn't been lost…

"*And it can be found again with ease,*" Whitelock answered in a dark, threatening tone that she'd never heard before. "*It is surprising, however, that you haven't figured out how, with a small manipulation, your name proves equally as guilty of the treasonous offense.*"

Guilty of the offense of coining? No. Frances was certain Lucan never had a part in his father's scheme.

"*There is nothing to support the claim. Even at that time, I hadn't lived at Camdonbury Place for years.*"

"*That matter is easily cast aside when your recent, crippling finances are taken into account. In fact, you've had little money since you were cut off from your family. I believe most of society is aware of your current insolvency. And once the evidence reemerges, soon everyone will believe that you and Thorne worked together. Besides, what better way could you have planned to punish your father for your mother's death than to have him appear guilty of treason?"*

"Then your bargain from the very beginning was to ensure I went to the gallows beside Thorne. You made this arrangement with my father."

Frances covered her mouth on a gasp. Why would Lucan go to the gallows beside her father?

"Camdonbury paid me handsomely to ensure that all the loose ends were tied. Far more than the ten thousand pounds you accrued on Thorne's behalf," Lord Whitelock replied. *"Did you really think he was going to let you go unpunished after the scandal you caused?"*

Frances felt weak. She'd been wrong. Lucan hadn't gambled away the money. He'd taken on her father's debt. She'd been a fool to allow Whitelock to persuade her to ignore what she already knew in her heart...that Lucan was the noblest man she'd ever met.

"So my father sold you the land that was once my mother's." Lucan's voice sounded strained and distant. "Then why did you wait three years for your *fait accompli?* Why not kill me in a duel, arrange a carriage accident, or have me hanged earlier?"

"It takes time to ensure all the pieces are in play. You should know that better than anyone. One cannot rush the downfall of a reputation, after all. It raises too many questions if it happens overnight."

"Ah yes, all the pieces. When did one of those include your new shop in London, Tuttle's Registry? My guess is that it was shortly after you met Miss Thorne."

Again, Frances smothered a gasp. Lord Whitelock owned *Tuttle's,* the very registry that helped to force Mrs. Hunter's hand?

"*You are well informed,*" Whitelock snarled.

"*Yet instead of rescuing her from dire circumstances, like you do with the others, you created the events that led Miss Thorne directly to your door.*"

The viscount issued a low, sinister chuckle. "They're all so grateful to me. I'm their savior, you know. I've snatched them away from certain death or other cruelties of life. You won't find a single one who would speak out against me."

"What about the women you've sullied?"

"How can I help it if some choose to…give of themselves to the one man who has provided them a means for a better life? None of them has been forced. In fact, they are grateful afterward that they were of service to a man such as myself."

"I think Henny Momper would disagree. It is a pity that her death prevents her from doing so."

This time, Nannette also gasped. Unfortunately, she didn't cover the sound. Frances rushed back to the servants' stairway door and urged Nannette inside. She closed the door behind them. It wouldn't do either of them any good to be caught here, and it was entirely likely that there were some in Whitelock's employ who knew of his nefarious acts and sought to protect him. Frances did not want her friend to suffer.

Complete shock showed on Nannette's face, and Frances's own illusions were shattered as well. Whitelock only possessed the appearance of goodness. She should have trusted her instincts. She should have trusted Lucan. Would he ever forgive her?

Nannette shook her head. "Whitelock was so convincing."

"He was. But now we know differently. Go," Frances whispered to her. "Sneak back down the stairs. When the others return from church, tell Bess and Penny what you've learned, but be wary of trusting anyone else. There are likely a few who must already know of his baser actions and have helped him in the past."

Nannette began her descent, and Frances followed but slipped out at the next floor, hoping to catch up with Lucan before he was escorted out. She needed him to know that she'd heard everything. She needed to beg his forgiveness. And most of all, she simply needed him.

CHAPTER TWENTY-ONE

The servants' stairway door on the first floor opened to a wide landing decorated with potted trees in urns and sculpted busts on marble pedestals. From behind one of the trees, Frances listened carefully in order to find Lucan *and* Whitelock. She was fully prepared to confront the viscount and tell him that he could no longer keep his secrets.

"It takes three of you to do his evil deeds!" Lucan shouted from below.

She could hear him, but she couldn't see him from this vantage point. Then she looked toward the wide staircase, leading to the main hall, and stepped out into the open. While standing near the railing, she saw a scuffle in the corner of the main hall. Sampson and Hershell had Lucan by the arms and were dragging him toward the door. They weren't getting far. Lucan fought them every step, tripping them, punching when he could get his arm free. But then Mr. Greggs grabbed a letter knife from a table. "Lucan, behind you!" Frances shouted.

The men stopped, surprise showing on their faces when they looked up to see her. It gave Lucan enough time to get in a few more punches and earn his freedom for a moment. Then he looked up at her, his expression twisted in a grimace as Sampson kicked him, low in the back.

But Lucan pointed to her. "Frances, look out," he groaned.

The warning came too late. Before she could turn, she was grabbed from behind.

"It is a pity that you are sneaking around instead of sitting in church this morning," Whitelock hissed in her ear.

She struggled against him, remembering her training. But he had her arms pinned to her sides, and she couldn't claw, scratch, or hit. He dragged her to the wall, pushing her face up against it, forcing her to turn her head or else smash her nose. She tried to lift her leg to stomp down on his foot, but his legs bracketed her. How could a man as old as her father be so strong?

"Unhand me. I heard everything. I know what you've done. I know about the opium in your wife's tea. I know about my mother…"

He laughed, a low sinister sound. His lips grazed her ear. "You are so like her. So independent. Such a fiery temper. But ineffective in the end."

"You cannot claim my spirit or any part of me. I know your evil deeds, and I despise you."

He pressed against her, forcing her harder against the wall. "That's what makes you perfect. I no longer have to pretend with you."

"You sent my father to prison." Frantically, she took in her surroundings. There was nothing within her reach—no table, no fan, no fire poker. Below, she could hear more grunts, only some of them Lucan's, and she hoped he was winning his battle.

"And he will hang if you don't cooperate. Now, be still. I will keep him alive for you. All you have to do is come with me to my hunting box in Wales. As long as you are good to me, I'll be good to you and to your father. You'll never want for money. Never be hungry. Never live in squalor."

She refused to give him any of her tears, but she knew there was only one chance for her now. Frances went still.

"There now," he said, his breath coating her cheek. It smelled musty and old, as if he was rotting from the inside. His mouth opened over her neck. He ground his hips against her buttocks, pressing his erection into her soft flesh through her skirts. "I would take you now, here, with Montwood to witness, but the other servants will be back soon. I want you in my bed. All day. Willing. That will be your first payment of our bargain. Once I am satisfied of your cooperation, I'll have your father removed from Fleet and set up in a comfortable house."

He shifted slightly. His hand splayed over her abdomen and slid upward toward her breast.

Now that he was distracted, Frances jerked her head back hard against his face. She heard the crack of bone, followed by his shocked, pained gasp. He reared back. Frances twisted away and sprinted toward the stairs, dodging statues along the way.

Whitelock bellowed, close behind.

Rage coiled tightly inside Lucan.

At first, it frightened him. He didn't want to be the same man his father was. He didn't want Frances to witness the violence he needed to unleash.

But when she appeared, he suddenly knew that he still had control of himself. There was no monster within him. Only a man willing to do whatever it took to save Frances.

Lucan slammed a fist into Hershell's gut, sending him to the floor on a wordless groan. Greggs was in bad shape, down on all fours, spitting blood. Sampson was the only one left.

Lucan pummeled him. Sampson held strong, giving back blow for blow. A movement from upstairs drew his attention. He saw Frances running toward the stairs and Whitelock holding a hand to his bloody nose, murder in his eyes.

Having no more time to subdue Sampson, Lucan rushed across the hall. He was not going to stand by and watch his worst nightmare unfold. He was not going to lose another woman he loved to violence.

Horror filled him as Whitelock caught up with her. Reaching out, he pulled Frances's hair, jerking her to a stop. She cried out.

Sampson tackled Lucan, taking him down to the floor, punching him in full view of what was transpiring upstairs. With desperation driving him, Lucan blocked Sampson's next blow. Then with one uppercut, he sent the footman sprawling to the floor.

Frances grabbed hold of the railing while Whitelock took hold of her arm and twisted it behind her back. Crying out, she let go of the railing, and they both staggered.

Whitelock rammed into one of his pedestals, a bust of King George. It wobbled, clacking audibly on its marble base. The bust teetered, toppling forward, and Whitelock suddenly moved to save it. Apparently, he didn't realize how heavy the head of a king could be. He staggered again. Before he could gain his footing, he crashed against the rail. He lurched backward over the edge—

On a sharp gasp, the room fell silent. Then it filled with Whitelock's abrupt shout as he fell to the tile floor below. A sickening *crack-thump* echoed in the hall.

Focused on Frances, Lucan rushed up the stairs. Frances descended, tears streaming down her face, as she fell into his arms.

"I never should have doubted your honor," she said on a sob.

He shook his head, crushing her to him. "No, you were right. I should have told you everything from the beginning."

A low, warbling groan came from main hall. Lucan looked over the edge of the stairs to see Whitelock move his head back and forth on the floor. The bust of King George lay in pieces, scattered all around him. The viscount's legs looked to be in similar shape but twisted at odd angles. And his hips were turned unnaturally as well. It was obvious his back was broken. While he might live, there would be no full recovery for him. He would likely spend the rest of his days confined to bed, with only a nurse to watch over him.

"My legs…" the viscount croaked.

Mr. Greggs took one look at his lord and master lying crippled on the floor, turned on his heel, and walked out the front door. Sampson was still out cold. Hershell was just starting to stand up when the other servants came in from the back entrance.

There was a collective gasp at the scene. A maid with ebony hair looked up at Frances. "I told them everything. Mrs. Riley just…walked away. Burt is in the stables, comforting poor little Arthur."

"Are you all right, child?" an older woman asked Frances.

"I am now." Frances wrapped her arms around Lucan's waist and rested her cheek against his shoulder. "I imagine the magistrate will be on the way soon."

"Don't you worry about that," the woman said with a flit of her fingers. "We'll see to everything."

"Thank you, Mrs. Darby," Frances said before she lifted her gaze. "Take me home, Lucan."

On top of Quicksilver, they were both quiet on the ride to Fallow Hall. Frances leaned back against Lucan, taking pleasure in the steady strength of his embrace. She always felt safe with him, even when she had battled her better sense. Yet somewhere deep inside, she must have recognized his noble character. He was a good man. To have her faith restored, she'd needed only to open her eyes and trust what her heart had told her.

"I lied to you last night in the gallery," she admitted. "I never stopped loving you."

Lucan pressed a kiss to her head. "I don't suppose you'd allow me one confession as well?"

She lifted her head from his shoulder. "You can tell me anything, Lucan. I will trust whatever you tell me. Or at least, give you the benefit of the doubt."

"So then, if I were to tell you that I love you beyond reason, you would take the matter under consideration?"

Her breath left her lungs in one soft whoosh. Her heart felt light as vapor once again. "Well…it would have to be said in a convincing manner."

He grinned, flashing a dimple. "Would it be convincing enough if I said the words over a blacksmith's anvil in Gretna Green?"

He didn't allow her to answer. Instead, he kissed her, tender and poignant at first, and then with a promise of passion.

In the end, she was thoroughly convinced.

EPILOGUE

Ten years later. . .

"**A** game of hide-and-seek was a brilliant suggestion," Lucan rasped as Frances clung to him, urging him back against the music room door. It clicked into place as his mouth descended on hers. Eager, they reached for the key at the same time.

She smiled against his lips, nipping him lightly. Over the rims of her spectacles, her smoky gaze heated. "My husband tells me that I have a clever mind."

"And clever hands as well." Those hands slipped beneath his coat and skimmed down his torso to the fall of his trousers. He was thick and ready...*always*. In the ten years of their marriage, his passion for her had never waned. In fact, he wanted her—*he loved her*—more and more each day.

"*Mmm*...do you think we have time before—"

The brass door handle turned suddenly, in rapid back-and-forth movements. Lucan and Frances went still. They held their breath. Their hearts pounded hard against each other's chests. With a look between them, they shared a hope that they would be left alone for just a few more minutes…

"Mum, Da, I know you're in there."

Damn. Lucan let out a breath.

"Later," he whispered against his wife's luscious mouth before he pulled away. Then, stalling for a moment to adjust his clothing and until the telltale sign of what he and Frances were doing—or were *about* to do—subsided, he spoke to the child on the other side of the door. "How did you find us so quickly?"

"You always hide in the music room," the small, feminine voice answered on a sigh. She sounded far too exasperated for an eight-year-old. "If you ever expect to win, you should find a better place."

Frances stifled a giggle and smoothed her hands over her dress, her figure slightly fuller now and even more enticing. "An excellent observation, Margaret. Your father and I will take that under consideration next time."

Next time… Yet his body said, *Now, please now.* Lucan's passion flared once more and he took a step toward his wife. She answered with a saucy grin. Then the door handle rattled.

"Why did you lock the door? That's rather unfair."

It was no use. Their daughter was a determined creature. In fact, all four of their children shared that trait, which made Lucan love them all the more.

"It must have been a breeze that closed the door and jostled the key in the lock…" Frances said as she turned the key.

In the same instant, their daughter blew in like a force of nature, her dark bronze hair wispy around her face. Behind her RJ loped in, his muzzle more silver than gray, his stride a bit slower, but his eagerness for a good scratch never abated. He nudged Frances first before moving on to Lucan and then stayed close to Margaret.

Margaret's amber eyes took in the room at a glance. "The windows aren't open. Why are your spectacles foggy, Mum?"

"Margaret Elise, you are too perceptive by half." Frances laughed, tucking a lock of hair behind her ear.

Lucan cleared his throat to hide his amusement. "Well, she is named after your mother."

"And yours," Frances answered fondly, cleaning her spectacles. She moved to stand by his side and then stopped abruptly, staring at Margaret. Or more aptly, staring at what Margaret held behind her back. "What do you have there?"

It was a rather familiar-looking booklet, though slightly aged from when Lucan had last seen it.

"I don't know," Margaret answered, bringing the object around for further study. "I found it in your keepsake box with violet petals pressed inside. I thought it must be important, but it's just a bunch of sketches."

Lucan couldn't believe Frances had kept it all this time. Not to mention the violets he'd given her as well. Still, he couldn't resist teasing his wife when the opportunity arose. He tsked and addressed their daughter. "At one time, your mother entertained the idea of becoming a tailor. Quite scandalous."

Frances bent down and placed a kiss to Margaret's head before she took the booklet and slyly slipped it up the sleeve of her own dress.

Margaret's brow furrowed. "Why should it be scandalous? I believe a woman ought to be allowed to do whatever she wants with her life."

"*Woman.* Bah." A laugh came from the doorway as nine-year-old Theodore Lucan swaggered into the room. He was the very picture of Lucan, only with Frances's eyes.

A year younger, but with a much more mature soul, Margaret ignored the taunt. At first. "Grandfather says I have a head for figures, *unlike* Theo." This earned her an eye-roll from Theo, to which she responded by surreptitiously sticking out her tongue at him. "Perhaps I'll run a shop. Or I could teach *Artful Defense* like Mum does when she visits Aunt Kaye and Uncle Burt's registry in London."

"Run a shop?" Theo snorted. "You can't have a *business*. You're—"

"And why not?" Margaret interrupted, her eyes flashing as she set her fists on her hips. "Mum and Da are always telling us to find ways to practice good deeds."

Theo looked at his parents and shook his head as if to say, *You've created a monster.* But to his sister, he said, "You can't run a shop because you're the daughter of the Marquess of Camdonbury."

Lucan stiffened at the reminder. He'd never wanted the title. His elder brother, Victor, however, had been desperate for it. So desperate in fact that he'd poisoned their father. Unfortunately for Victor, he did not have a friend like Clivedale to cover up the murder. The garish evidence left behind on their father's corpse had sent his brother to the hangman.

Sadly, this happened the day before Whitelock's infamous ruin. If Victor had only waited, then their father would have gone to the hangman for treason, and the heir would have inherited the title.

Aunt Theodosia had been right. Clivedale had played right into her hand. When confronted about conspiring with Whitelock to keep the viscountess drugged on opium, he'd confessed that the viscount had been blackmailing him. Then, in order to worm his way into a prison cell instead of at the wrong end of a rope, Clivedale had sold out the Marquess of Camdonbury as well. Shortly afterward, the true evidence against the marquess, in addition to the false evidence against Thorne, had been found in a wall safe behind a lurid painting in Whitelock's bedchamber. To this day, the viscount had not regained the use of his legs.

Thankfully, after paying his debts, Hugh Thorne was released from gaol. He was living at Fernwood Glade as a reformed man and overindulgent grandfather. He'd even taken Arthur Momper under his wing and trained him. Now, at twenty years, Arthur was steward of Fernwood Glade.

"Title or not, you are children of a noble, generous man," Frances said from beside him, drawing Lucan away from the past and reminding him of the blessings in his life. "You ought to live by his example."

Unwilling to control the impulse, he slipped his arm around her waist, pulled her up to her toes, and kissed her, full on the mouth. "I love you beyond reason," he whispered and set her back down.

Leaning against him for a moment, she let out a slow breath and then adjusted her spectacles. Margaret smiled and rocked on her feet, her skirts swishing to and fro, and her anger at her brother temporarily forgotten. Theo was not impressed by the show of affection and issued a sound of disgust as he wandered back toward the door.

"When do you think they'll arrive?" he asked, peering down the hall, referring to Everhart's and Danvers's broods. "I left George and Marcus as lookouts on the stairs."

Each summer and at Christmastime, they gathered at Fallow Hall with all their family members, parents, siblings and *their* spouses, and children, until this vast manor fairly bulged with occupants. When they weren't here, Everhart and Calliope divided their time between Briar Heath and London. And of course, Rafe and Hedley lived next door at Greyson Park, but they also kept a house in town.

In addition to Fernwood Glade and Camdonbury Place, Lucan and Frances were the caretakers of Fallow Hall. After their infamous bachelor's wager gained them far more than ten thousand pounds could ever buy, Everhart, Danvers, and he had purchased this estate and now, each owned a third.

"Your brothers are supposed to be taking their naps." Frances clucked her tongue at Theo, but there was no scorn in it. Her excitement to see her friends was clear as she addressed Lucan. "We'll soon have a house full of exhausted and overexcited children."

Lucan grinned. For him, it was heaven on earth. He loved having his family together. All of them. "Let's set up a picnic in the garden. When they arrive, we'll sit on the terrace and watch the children play together."

"I had Miss Culpepper prepare Delaney and Rafe's favorite biscuits, as well as the tarts that Calliope and Everhart favor," Frances said but then winced. "Mrs. Swan insisted on preparing the main dinner. I didn't have the heart to remind her that she is here as our guest and that she needn't work in the kitchens anymore."

Lucan's stomach rolled at the thought, but truly, he didn't mind. He owed Mrs. Swan a debt. Ten years ago, on the day of his wedding, he'd asked her to prepare a glazed bun for him. He saw it as one final battle to overcome. Surprisingly, the pastry had been edible. However, a glazed bun was nothing he cared to eat again.

"It will be fine. I'm sure Everhart and Danvers will welcome the familiar cuisine," he said with a laugh. He couldn't wait to see their faces.

Theo began to pace the room, absently rolling a coin over his fingers. "Will they *ever* arrive?"

He possessed the same restlessness that had driven Lucan to mischief and then eventually to the life of a gambler. Although nowadays, Lucan was more of an investor than a gambler. With Theodosia, they'd settled some money on a railway venture that was doing quite well.

Even though his aunt was immensely wealthy, she still preferred to run the Flame and Spit. It was—Lucan had discovered—the place where she'd been meeting Valentine for years. And while the butler of Fallow Hall had proposed to her time and again, Theodosia chose to continue their monogamous, scandalous affair without a formal ceremony.

Margaret sat at the piano, plunking away, with RJ's head in her lap. She'd inherited her mother's musical ability. "Will I have a chance to perform, Mum? The last time he was here, Sebastian said I played beautifully," she said referring to Everhart's nine-year-old son.

"*Sebastian*," Theo mocked, halting in the middle of the room to clutch his heart. "I think he would prefer for you to call him the *troll king*, as you used to. He doesn't want you mooning over him. After all, he's going to be a duke someday."

Margaret stopped playing and straightened her shoulders. "I don't care about that, Theo. Even if he were just a troll king, I would be his troll queen."

RJ lifted his head and added a *woof* to the conversation.

Lucan looked at Frances. Mischief flashed in her gaze as her hands skimmed up the lapels of his coat, and she rose up to press a kiss to his lips. "The matchmaker has spoken."

He pulled her closer. "Would you care to wager on that?"

ACKNOWLEDGMENTS

This series, like all of my books, started out with a "what if" idea that kept me company through many sips of tea, loads of laundry, errand running, and sleepless nights. Before this concept ever made it to a paper proposal, it ran by my sisters—my league of supporters, my toughest critics. The phone conversations trotted along the usual paths, with familiar murmurs—*"Uh-huh…uh-huh…hmm…"*—as they multitasked before they eventually stopped, adjusted the phone, and said, *"Oooh…I like that!"*

Deanna and Cyndi, thank you for being my sounding board, for picking up the phone even when caller ID tells you that I'm on the other end, for failing to murder me when I was younger, and for attempting to understand my particular brand of oddness.

This series happened because of an extraordinary editor who read the proposal and decided to give it a chance. Her comments in the margin inspired, tweaked, and molded the stories, smoothing out the rough edges. She offered her time and valuable resources in order to see these books shine.

Chelsey, thank you for all the hours you've put in, for all the comments that make me dig deeper, for all the smiley faces and hearts in the margins, and for the precious gift of believing in me.

This series had a spectacular team of people behind it: the Avon Art Department—the magicians who create the most swoon-worthy covers in the industry; the awesome marketing and publicity departments—the creative geniuses who spread the love; and the copyeditors—the grammar fixers who sweep in and clean up the dirty sentences left behind after a lengthy writing binge.

Most of all, I'm thankful to God, each and every day, for blessing this weird introvert with whispered stories and characters' voices in my head.

Don't miss Vivienne Lorret's first two books in the
Rakes of Fallow Hall Series

THE ELUSIVE LORD EVERHART

and

THE DEVILISH MR. DANVERS

Available now from Avon Impulse.

About the Author

USA Today best-selling author **VIVIENNE LORRET** loves romance novels, her pink laptop, her husband, and her two sons (not necessarily in that order...but there are days). Transforming copious amounts of tea into words, she is proud to be an Avon Impulse author of works including *Tempting Mr. Weatherstone*, the Wallflower Wedding series, and the Rakes of Fallow Hall series.

Discover great authors, exclusive offers, and more at hc.com.

Give in to your Impulses . . .
Continue reading for excerpts from
our newest Avon Impulse books.
Available now wherever e-books are sold.

CHASING JILLIAN
A Love and Football Novel
By Julie Brannagh

EASY TARGET
An Elite Ops Novel
By Kay Thomas

DIRTY THOUGHTS
A Mechanics of Love Novel
By Megan Erickson

LAST FIRST KISS
A Brightwater Novel
By Lia Riley

An Excerpt from

CHASING JILLIAN
A Love and Football Novel
by Julie Brannagh

The fifth novel in *USA Today* bestselling
author Julie Brannagh's Love and Football
series! Jillian Miller likes her job working in
the front office for the Seattle Sharks, but
lately she needs a change, which takes her into
foreign territory: the Sharks' workout facility
after hours. The last thing she expects is a hot,
grumbly god among men to be there as witness.

As Jillian discovers that the new her is about
so much more than she sees in the mirror,
can she discover that happiness and love
are oh-so-much better than perfect?

One dance with him and Jillian was pulling herself out of his arms and getting back into the car. She could dance with him and not get emotional about it. He was just another guy. She was not going to let herself get stupid over someone who was clearly only interested in her as a friend.

His hold on her was gentle. He smelled good. She saw the flash of his smile when she peeked up at him. She'd felt shy with Carlos because she didn't know him. She didn't have that problem with Seth. She wanted to move closer, but she shouldn't.

She tried to remind herself of the fact that Seth probably had more than a few friends with benefits, even if he was between girlfriends at the time. He was a guy. He probably wasn't celibate, and they weren't romantic with each other. There was also the tiny fact that anything that happened between them was not going to end well.

She was in more trouble than she knew how to get out of.

At first, Jillian rested her head against his cheek. A minute or so later, she laid her head on his chest. They swayed together, feet barely moving, and he realized his heart was pounding. He'd never experienced anything as romantic as dancing late at night in a deserted city park to a song playing on his car's sound system. The darkness wrapped them in the softest cocoon. He glanced down at her as he felt her slowly relaxing against him.

It's not the pale moon that excites me
That thrills and delights me
Oh, no
It's just the nearness of you

He took a deep breath of the vanilla scent he'd recognize anywhere as hers. His fingers stroked the small of her back, and he heard her sigh. Slow dancing was even better than he remembered. Then again, he wasn't in junior high anymore, and he held a woman in his arms, not a teenage girl. There was a lot to be said for delayed gratification. Dancing with Jillian was all about the smallest movements, and letting things build. He laid his cheek against hers.

"I shouldn't be doing this," she whispered.

"Why not?" he whispered back.

"It's not a good idea."

"We're just dancing, Jill."

And if things got any hotter between them, they'd be naked. She didn't try to step away from him. If she'd resisted him at all, if she'd shown reluctance or fear or hesitation, he would have let her go, and he would walk away. Her fingers tangled in his hair.

They were just friends. He didn't think he had those kinds of feelings for this woman: the sexual, amorous, bow-chicka-bow-bow feelings, despite the fact his pulse was racing, his fingers itched to touch her, and he knew he should let go of her. It didn't matter that he was still having hotter-than-the-invention-of-fire dreams about Jillian most nights, either. He wasn't going to consider what kind of tricks his subconscious played on him. Instead, he pulled her a fraction of an inch closer. He slid one hand up her back, feeling her long, silky-soft blonde hair cascading over his fingers, and she trembled. He cupped her cheek in his hand. He couldn't take his eyes off her mouth. Just a couple of inches more and he'd kiss her. He moved slowly, but purposefully.

He watched her eyelids flutter closed. He felt her quick intake of breath. He wondered how she tasted. He'd know in a few seconds.

"I want to kiss you," he breathed against her mouth.

The silence was broken by the screaming guitars of Guns n' Roses.

That would teach him to use the "shuffle" function.

An Excerpt from

EASY TARGET
An Elite Ops Novel
by Kay Thomas

Award-winning author Kay Thomas continues her thrilling Elite Ops series. Fighting to clear her brother of murder, freelance reporter Sassy Smith is suddenly kidnapped and thrown into a truck with other women who are about to be sold . . . or worse. When she sees an opportunity for escape Sassy takes it, but she may have just jumped from the frying pan into the fire.

"You're thinking too much." She felt his words vibrate against the inside of her thigh as he kissed her there before easing up beside her on the bed. "Stop that."

She smiled, not at all surprised that he seemed to read her mind. He sat up on the edge of the lower bunk next to her and took his own boots and socks off, then his shirt, jeans, and . . .

She closed her eyes.

He was going to be naked soon, and she had to say something first. He slid up beside her on the mattress and pulled her back to his front, with his back toward the wall. She felt the insistence of his erection against her bottom.

She started to turn in his arms, but he held onto her with an arm clamped around her waist. "Slow down. I just want to enjoy holding you a while. I've thought about this for a very long time."

Really? That came as a complete surprise. It was on the tip of her tongue to ask how long, but when he trailed his fingertips back and forth across her rib cage, she quit thinking. Instead, she sighed in relaxed contentment. "I didn't know it could be like that."

Why had she been nervous about this for so long? She could tell him now. It'd be okay.

He kissed the side of her neck and whispered in her ear, "Well, I promise we're just getting started."

She tensed, and he absolutely noticed but misunderstood the reason.

He gathered her more snugly against his chest. "Don't worry, we can take this as slow as you want."

"You'd do that?" The mixture of relief and disappointment she felt was . . . confusing.

"God, Sassy. What sort of men have you—"

The sound of screeching brakes interrupted whatever else he'd been about to say. Sassy felt the momentum shoving her backward into his chest.

"What's happening?" she gasped.

"I don't know." He tugged his arm from under her body to see his watch. "We're not scheduled to stop for several more hours." The stark change from relaxed lover to alert super soldier was dramatic. "Get dressed. Now."

Bryan hauled himself forward out of bed and started shoving clothes toward her while Sassy was still playing catch-up. Her panties were inside out, but she slid them on at his urging without fixing them.

"C'mon, Sassy."

The horrific screeching continued, intensifying as she pulled her jeans, sweater, socks, and boots on. She was lacing up as a rumbling shuddering started.

"Fuck," Bryan mumbled.

"What is it?" She finished with the boots and looked up from her crouched position as the screeching abruptly stopped.

"Hang on!" He grabbed for her.

The rail car shifted, and she felt like she was in a carnival house ride as the compartment swayed wildly from side to side. The car tilted, and the bed she was sitting on flew up in the air. She hit her head on the bunk above, and the world went black.

An Excerpt from

DIRTY THOUGHTS
A Mechanics of Love Novel
by Megan Erickson

Some things are sexier the second time around.

Cal Payton has gruff and grumbly down to an
art . . . all the better for keeping people away. And
it usually works. Until Jenna Macmillan—his
biggest mistake—walks into Payton and Sons
mechanic shop all grown up, looking like sunshine,
and inspiring more than a few dirty thoughts.

Okay, so admittedly Jenna had known this was a stupid idea. She'd tried to talk herself out of it the whole way, muttering to herself as she sat at a stop light. The elderly man in the car in the lane beside her had been staring at her like she was nuts.

And she was. Totally nuts.

It'd been almost a decade since she'd seen Cal Payton and yet one look at those silvery blue eyes and she was shoved right back to the head-over-heels *in love* eighteen-year-old girl she'd been.

Cal had been hot in high school, but damn, had time been good to him. He'd always been a solid guy, never really hitting that awkward skinny stage some teenage boys went through after a growth spurt.

And now . . . well . . . Cal looked downright sinful standing there in the garage. He'd rolled down the top of his coveralls, revealing a white T-shirt that looked painted on, for God's sake. She could see the ridges of his abs, the outline of his pecs. A large smudge on the sleeve drew her attention to his bulging biceps and muscular, veined forearms. Did he lift these damn cars all day? Thank God it was hot as Hades outside already so she could get by with flushed cheeks.

And he was staring at her, those eyes which hadn't changed one bit. Cal never cared much for social mores. He looked people in the eye and he held it long past comfort. Cal had always needed that, to be able to measure up who he was dealing with before he ever uttered a word.

She wondered how she measured up. It'd been a long time since he'd laid eyes on her, and the last time he had, he'd been furious.

Well, she was the one that came here. She was the one that needed something. She might as well speak up, even though what she needed right now was a drink. A stiff one. "Hi, Cal." She went with a smile that surely looked a little strained.

He stood with his booted feet shoulder-width apart, and at the sound of her voice, he started a bit. He finally stopped doing that staring thing as his gaze shifted to the car by her side, then back to her. "Jenna."

His voice. Well, crap, how could she have forgotten about his voice? It was low and silky with a spicy edge, like Mexican chocolate. It warmed her belly and raised goose bumps on her skin.

She cleared her throat as he began walking toward her, his gaze teetering between her and the car. Brent was off to the side, watching them with his arms crossed over his chest. He winked at her. She hid her grin with pursed lips and rolled her eyes. He was a good-looking bastard, but irritating as hell. Nice to see *some* things never changed. "Hey, Brent."

"Hey there, Jenna. Looking good."

Cal whipped his head toward his brother. "Get back to work."

Brent gave him a sloppy salute and then shot her another

knowing smirk before turning around and retreating back into the garage bay.

When she faced Cal again, she jolted, because he was close now, almost in her personal space. His eyes bored into her. "What're ya doing here, Jenna?"

His question wasn't accusatory. It was conversational, but the intent was in his tone, laying latent until she gave him reason to really put the screws to her. She didn't know if he meant what was she doing here, at his garage, or what he was doing in town. But she went for the easy question first.

She gestured to the car. "I, uh, I think the bearings need to be replaced. I know that I could take it anywhere but . . ." She didn't want to tell him it was Dylan's car, and he was the one who let it go so long that she swore the front tires were going to fall off. As much as her brother loved his car, he was an idiot. An idiot who despised Cal, and she was pretty sure the feeling was vice versa. "I wanted to make sure the job was done right and everyone knows you do the best job here." That part was true. The Paytons had a great reputation in Tory.

But Cal never let anything go. He narrowed his eyes and propped his hands on his hips, drawing attention to the muscles in his arms. "How do you know we still do the best job here if you haven't been back in ten years?"

Well then. Couldn't he just nod and take her keys? She held them in her hand, gripping them so tightly that the edge was digging into her palm. She loosened her grip. "Because when I did live here, your father was the best, and I know *you* don't do anything unless you do it the best." Her voice faded off. Even though the last time she'd seen Cal, his eyes had been snapping in anger, at least they'd been showing some sort of emotion. This steady blank gaze was killing her. Not when she knew how his eyes looked when he smiled, as the skin at the corners crinkled and the silver of his irises flashed.

She thought now that this had been a mistake. She'd offered to get the car fixed for her brother while he was out of town. And while she knew Cal worked with his dad now, she'd still expected to run into Jack. And even though he was a total jerk face, she would have rather dealt with him than endure this uncomfortable situation with Cal right now. "You know, it's fine. Don't worry about it, I'll just—"

He snatched the keys out of her hand. Right. Out. Of. Her. Hand.

"Hey!" She propped a hand on her hip, but he wasn't even looking at her, instead fingering the key ring. "Do you always steal keys from your customers?"

He cocked his head and raised an eyebrow at her. There was the smallest hint of a smile, just a tug at the corner of his lips. "I don't make that a habit, no."

"So I'm special then?" She was flirting. Was this flirting? Oh God, it was. She was flirting with her high school boyfriend, the guy who'd taken her virginity, and the guy whose heart she'd broken when she had to make one of the most difficult decisions of her life.

She'd broken her own heart in the process.

His gaze dropped, just for a second, then snapped back to her face. "Yeah, you're special."

He turned around, checking out the car, while she stood gaping at his back. He'd . . . he'd flirted back, right? Cal wasn't really a flirting kind of guy. He said what he wanted and followed through. But flirting Cal?

She shook her head. It'd been over ten years. Surely he'd lived a lot of life during that time she'd been away, going to college, then grad school, then working in New York. She didn't want to think about what that flirting might mean, now that she was back in Tory for good. Except he didn't know that.

An Excerpt from

LAST FIRST KISS
A Brightwater Novel
by Lia Riley

A kiss is just the beginning . . .

Pinterest Perfect. Or so Annie Carson's life
appears on her popular blog. Reality is . . . messier.
Especially when it lands her back in one-cow
town, Brightwater, California, and back in the
path of the gorgeous six-foot-four reason she left.

"Sawyer?" All she could do was gape, wide-eyed and breathless—too breathless. Could he tell? Hard to say as he maintained his customary faraway expression, the one that made it look as if he'd stepped out of a black and white photograph.

"Annie."

She jumped. Hearing her name on his tongue plucked something deep in her belly, a sweet aching string, the hint of a chord she only ever found in the dark with her own hand. It was impossible not to stare, and suddenly the long years disappeared, until she was that curious seventeen-year-old girl again, seeing a gorgeous boy watching her from the riverbanks, and wondering if the Earth's magnetic poles had quietly flipped.

Stop. Just say no to unwelcome physical reactions. Her body might turn traitor, but her mind wouldn't let her down. She'd fallen for this guy's good looks before, believed they mirrored a goodness inside—a mistake she wouldn't make twice. No man would ever be allowed to stand by and watch her crash again.

Never would she cry in the shower so no one could hear.

Never would she wait for her child to fall asleep so she could fall apart.

Never would she jump and blindly fall.

Sawyer removed his worn tan Stetson and stood. Treacherous hyperawareness raced along her spine and radiated through her hips in a slow, hot electric pulse. He clocked in over six-feet, with steadfast sagebrush green eyes that gave little away. Flecks of ginger gleamed from the scruff roughing his strong jaw and lightened the dark chestnut of his short-cropped hair.

"Hey." Her cheeks warmed as any better words scampered out of reach. The mile-long "to do" list taped to the fridge didn't include squirming in front of the guy she'd nurtured a secret crush on during her teenage years. A guy who, at the sole party Annie attended in high school, abandoned her in a hallway closet during "Seven Minutes in Heaven" to mothballed jackets, old leather shoes, ruthless taunts, and everlasting shame.

He reset his hat. "Did I wake you?" His voice had always appealed to her, but the subtle rough deepening was something else, as if every syllable dragged over a gravel road.

She checked her robe's tie. "Hammering at sunrise kind of has that effect on people."

He gave her a long look. His steadfast perusal didn't waver an inch below her neck, but still, as he lazily scanned each feature, she felt undressed to bare skin. Guess his old confidence hadn't faded, not a cocky manufactured arrogance, but a guy completely comfortable in his own skin.

And what ruggedly handsome, sun-bronzed skin it was, covering all sorts of interesting new muscles he hadn't sported in high school.

"Heard Grandma paid you a visit," he said at last.

Annie doused the unwelcome glow kindling in her chest with a bucket of ice-cold realism. He wasn't here to see her, merely deal with a mess. *Hear that, hormones? Don't be stupid.* She set a hand on her hip, summoning as much dignity as she could muster with a serious case of bedhead. "Visit? Your grandma killed one of our chickens and baked it in a pie. Not exactly the welcome wagon. More like a medieval, craz—"

"Subtlety isn't one of her strong points. We had words last night. It won't happen again." He dusted his hands on his narrow, denim-clad hips and bent down.

Unf.

The hard-working folks at Wrangler deserved a medal for their service. Nothing—NOTHING—else made a male ass look so fine. "Found this, too." He lifted her forgotten bottle of scotch.

"Oh, weird." She plucked it from his grasp. "Wonder how that got out here?" Crap, too saccharine a tone, sweet but clearly false.

He raised his brows as his hooded gaze dropped a fraction. Not enough to be a leer, but definitely a look.

Her threadbare terrycloth hit mid-thigh. Here stood the hottest guy west of the Mississippi and she hadn't shaved since who-the-hell knows and sported a lop-sided bruise on her knee from yesterday's unfortunate encounter with a gopher hole.

Maybe she failed at keeping up appearances, but God as her witness, she'd maintain her posture. "About your Grandma, I was two seconds from calling the cops on her last night."

"That a fact?" The corner of his wide mouth twitched. "Next time, that's exactly what you should do."

"Next time?" She sputtered, waving the bottle for emphasis. "There sure as heck better not be a next time!"

That little burst of sass earned the full-force of his smile. Laugh lines crinkled at the corners of deep-set eyes that belonged nowhere but the bedroom. As a boy, he was a sight, as a man, he'd become a vision. "Why are you back? I mean, after all this time?"